CHAOS THEORY

TWIN RIVER HIGH SERIES

CHAOS THEORY

TWIN RIVER HIGH SERIES

NYT & USA TODAY BESTSELLING AUTHORS
RUSH & BLOUNT

This book is a work of fiction. Names, characters, places, and incidents are the product of the author's imagination or are used fictitiously. Any resemblance to actual events, locales, or persons, living or dead, is coincidental.

Copyright © 2021 by Lynn Rush and Kelly Anne Blount. All rights reserved, including the right to reproduce, distribute, or transmit in any form or by any means. For information regarding subsidiary rights, please contact the Publisher.

Entangled Publishing, LLC
644 Shrewsbury Commons Ave
STE 181
Shrewsbury, PA 17361
rights@entangledpublishing.com

Crush is an imprint of Entangled Publishing, LLC.

Edited by Lydia Sharp, Stacy Abrams, and Liz Pelletier
Cover illustrated by LJ Anderson/Mayhem Cover Creations
Cover art by CreativeDesignArt/Getty Images
Den.the.Grate@gmail.com/Deposit Photos

Manufactured in the United States of America

First Edition May 2021

To God, from whom all blessings flow. ~Lynn

"Want to hear a joke? Sleep. I know, I don't get it either."
~Kelly Anne
(Author of original quote unknown.)

Content Warning

This book contains the following elements discussed on the page—cancer, death from cancer, death of a parent, drunk driving, and car accidents. These elements are not depicted or detailed in the story, only talked about, but readers who may be sensitive to these, please take note.

Chapter One

Victoria

"This"—my boyfriend, Todd, pointed from me to him and back to me—"isn't working for me anymore."

The hard plastic tray in my hands trembled as his harsh tone rippled through my body. He did *not* just break up with me in front of everyone like this.

Seriously. My boyfriend of almost two years was breaking up with me?

In the *cafeteria*?

Everyone around us morphed into nothing more than fuzzy images that *somewhat* resembled humans. Static sounded in my ears and my heart thudded painfully against my chest.

The room fell eerily silent. "Excuse me?" My voice cracked as all the moisture in my mouth evaporated. Heat clawed its way up my neck.

Todd's normally soothing blue eyes were cold. "I said, we're over. Done. Through."

"Oh my gosh," someone whispered from behind me. "Todd just dumped Victoria!"

Heat scoured my cheeks and my stomach clenched. This wasn't really happening, was it? I had to be in a nightmare or something. Any second I'd wake up.

"I tried to tell you after school yesterday." Todd shrugged, then stole a glance at his friend, Matthew Halliday, who gave him a nod of encouragement as he held up his phone. That prick was recording this.

Oh, hell no. If Todd wanted this to be public to humiliate me, he had another thing coming. I tossed my tray onto the closest table, rage bubbling to life in my stomach. "So you were *trying* to tell me you wanted to dump me, huh? Was that in between shoving your tongue down my throat and trying to feel me up?"

"You wish," Todd said, redness pooling at the apples of his cheeks.

"Ohhh..." Gretchen Mead, queen bee of Twin River said from nearby. I didn't bother to look, but I recognized her voice.

"I wish?" I huffed. "Is this because I wouldn't have sex with you?"

Gasps erupted around me.

I didn't wait for him to respond. "You're an asshat, Todd."

"Whatever, Victoria. I'm done with you." He and Matthew turned around and left me standing in the middle of the cafeteria, surrounded by tables filled with people laughing and pointing at me.

My best friend, Mia, hadn't made it to the table yet, and my other friends that were standing by were also friends with Todd, so I stood there alone, and now that the heat of the moment was gone, I was totally embarrassed.

How could he do this to me in front of everyone like that? And to claim he tried to tell me yesterday? Flat-out lie. This didn't make any sense.

"What's going on?" Mia's voice called out behind me.

I whirled around but then moved right past her, my blood thrumming and my eyes stinging. I'd been embarrassed enough already; I wasn't about to let myself cry in front of everyone, too. I planted my sweaty palms on the cold cafeteria door and pushed it open, then sprinted down the hallway until I hit the junior wing.

A sharp left then right turn and I barged into the bathroom farthest away from the lunchroom. Farthest away from Todd. From the laughter. Tears streamed down my cheeks as the reality of what had just happened slapped me across the face.

Todd had totally dumped me in front of everyone, two weeks before the school's biggest dance of the year, the Ice Ball, and Twin River's Ice Festival. Last year we'd gone to the dance together *and* we'd attended all of the town events together. Now I'd be alone—

The door behind me slammed shut and I whipped around. Mia crept in, her eyes wide and her jaw tense. She showed me her palms like she was approaching a wild animal.

And I felt like one inside. A wild, wounded animal forced into fight-or-flight. I'd lost it on Todd in the lunchroom, but he had absolutely crushed me. Out of nowhere. He deserved it!

"What happened?" Mia asked, stopping a foot or two from me.

A sob caught in my chest as I sagged against the closest wall. The stalls were to my left and the sinks to my right, and Mia stood in front of me, watching me as she chewed her bottom lip. I let out a long breath, trying to calm myself as I slid down the wall until my butt hit the floor.

I didn't even care how nasty it was right now.

"Oh my gosh, Vic! Talk to me. What happened?" She crouched in front of me.

"T-T-T-Todd broke up with me." My breaths came out hitched and ragged. "In front of everyone in the cafeteria *and* Matthew recorded the whole thing! Gretchen probably did, too. I heard her there."

A mixture of pain and anger clawed at my chest. Mia fell to her knees beside me, then pulled me in for a hug.

Resting my head on her shoulder, I said, "He didn't say anything about it yesterday. I went to his house after school and we kissed for like three hours."

"Asshole." She stroked my hair. "I'm so sorry, Victoria."

"It doesn't make sense. I—we—I thought we were happy."

Mia didn't say anything, but I felt her arms tighten and then release.

"Wait..." Gently easing back, I narrowed my eyes at her. "Did you know about this?"

Her mouth opened but nothing came out.

"What did you know, Mia?"

"Nothing," she said. "Well, mostly nothing."

"What do you mean mostly nothing?"

"Yesterday, I overheard Piper say something, but I figured it was gossip. Especially since you and Todd hung out after school. I didn't want to worry you over some made-up bullshit, you know? Piper's always spreading rumors."

Shivers raced down my spine. "What did you hear?"

Mia sighed. "Nina told Piper that she overheard Matthew and Todd talking after school the other day. You know how she's like the assistant to the athletic trainer or whatever. Anyways, she was walking by them on her way to the field and she heard Todd tell Matthew that some girl from East River Prep has been texting Todd. *Allegedly,* he asked her to the Ice Ball last night. She said she wouldn't go with him until he broke up with you."

Fresh tears cascaded down my face. He'd been texting another girl? While we were dating?

"Why didn't you tell me?"

"I thought it was just gossip. I swear!"

I dropped my head into my hands. Things had been going so well with us, with me. I'd been worried when we moved to Twin River, worried I wouldn't make any friends, that I'd be too different—an L.A. girl living in the Midwest. That's like trying to stuff a shark into a goldfish bowl. I was convinced I wouldn't fit. But I'd met Mia right away, started dating Todd a couple months later. It had finally felt like I belonged.

Until about five minutes ago.

"How did I not see this coming?"

"Because he was hiding it," Mia said quietly as she rubbed my back. "I thought Todd was one of the good ones, too."

"I wasted almost two years of my life with that jerk." I

sniffled and swiped at my nose. "I even told him that I loved him. I've never said that to a guy before."

"Todd sucks. You're amazing. Forget him. You can do nine thousand times better, when you're ready. Until then, we're going to hang out, eat a lot of ice cream, and I'll even go to one of those live poetry nights that you like."

Mia hugged me again and I buried my face in her hair. "Thanks, Mia. For everything."

"Of course. You're my bestie." She eased back and looked down at me with her pretty, light brown eyes. On the friend scale, she was a ten out of ten. I was lucky to have her.

Her phone dinged in her pocket. She reached for it, but then stopped. "Sorry."

"No. Check it, it's fine." I worked my way to my feet. The world tilted slightly, so I palmed the wall and drew in a deep breath. Smoothing my hand down the front of my shirt and brushing off a piece of lint from my jeans, I stepped toward the sinks. A disheveled, puffy-eyed girl stared back at me from the mirror.

Freaking Todd Miller. I wiped the tears from under my eyes. When I'd gotten here two years ago, he'd swept me off my feet, and we'd started dating a couple months after I'd arrived. He'd been great to me. Sweet. Thoughtful. Everything.

This came out of nowhere. It didn't make any sense.

Screw him!

I caught Mia shaking her head in the reflection of the mirror and I turned around. My phone buzzed in my back pocket.

I slid it out and unlocked the screen.

There was a notification on Instagram. Wait, there were

three, no, five notifications. The first one was a tag.

Oh shit…

I tapped on the screen and gasped. Pain ricocheted through my chest and a fresh wave of tears stung the corners of my eyes.

The video of Todd dumping me in the cafeteria played on a loop on Matthew's Instagram account. Me standing there, holding that stupid lunch tray, my mouth hanging open.

Everything blurred and the phone fell out of my hand. The sound echoed off the tiled bathroom walls surrounding us.

"Shit," Mia said. She tapped on the screen a few times. "I can't untag you from my account. But I reported it."

Of course he'd posted it.

Me standing there, shock twisting across my face. Todd looking smug.

I crouched and picked up my phone. But before the video could play again, another flurry of notifications flooded my screen. Including the same video, but from a different angle, Gretchen Mead's angle. She'd tagged me in it, too, like Matthew had. Her caption was a single hashtag, #LunchDump.

"No!" I shrieked. "This can't be happening!"

People were already commenting. They were mostly using the "laughing so hard they're crying" emoji. Worst of all, there were a few names I recognized, but a bunch I didn't. Which meant I was on track for going viral.

I'm the star of a viral video capturing the worst moment of my life… Fan-freaking-tastic!

I closed the video on my phone, but it started buzzing

over and over again.

I tapped on the hashtag. The video had been reposted to at least thirty other accounts. My humiliation was on display for the world to see. I furiously started untagging myself and blocking the accounts that shared the video. Then I went to my settings and tapped on the screen. Now, no one could tag me in anything.

"I can't believe they did that!" Mia said, coming up beside me.

"I can. Gretchen is a miserable, mean bitch and Matthew is an absolute pig."

"You know what," I said, drying my face, "*screw* Todd Miller. I'm going to find the hottest date and bring him to every Ice Festival event and to the Ice Ball."

"Yes!" Mia said brightly, then her face fell. "But how? It's only a couple of weeks away."

"You'll see." I shot her a wicked grin, as if my plan was already clear in my head. Because I actually had no freaking clue.

Chapter Two

COREY

Chaos wasn't only my last name—it was my *life*.

I sagged against my dressing room chair and closed my eyes, trying to quiet my mind. I'd spent the last hour under bright, hot, uncomfortable lights, recording my third talk show appearance this week. I just needed five min—

"Yo, Corey!"

The door to my dressing room burst open and the stage manager stormed in. He looked like a forest ranger with all the gear strapped to him and cargo pants pockets filled to the brim. "What's up, *Ranger* Rodrigo?"

"Jerk," he said, playfully smacking my shoulder. "I don't know how you got so popular online with your sucky attitude."

I shrugged. "It's what they love. Well, that and the covers I did of old rap and hip-hop songs."

Rodrigo smirked. "Yeah, well, if the zombies ever come calling, it's my *ranger*-type preparedness that everyone will love." He motioned to his oversized pockets. "I could survive for at least a month out in the woods with the stuff I've got on me right now."

I drew in a deep breath and closed my eyes again. While I loved being a YouTube and Instagram "sensation," it got tiring. I could never get five seconds to myself. Not even when my door was closed with a Do Not Disturb sign on the handle and the lights dimmed.

Everyone thought they owned a piece of me. Too bad that popularity didn't allow me to play my own songs. The ones *I'd* written.

"So...what do you think?"

I sat up, fully looking at Rodrigo now. "Sorry, man. I missed what you said."

He shook his head and the black hair sticking out from beneath his baseball cap flopped against his broad shoulders. "Come shoot this one part again," he said.

I nodded, not moving from my comfy chair. "Give me a sec."

He held up his huge hand, splaying his fingers. "Five minutes, man. Ricki Meredith doesn't like to be kept waiting."

I waved him off with my middle finger and chuckled. "I hear ya."

Ranger Rodrigo shuffled out of the room and I leaned forward in my chair, resting my elbows on my knees. My agent, Jethro, who was a pretty cool guy, had set this up for me. We'd raised fifty thousand dollars on my latest Instagram campaign, so Ricki from *The Ricki Meredith*

Daily Show wanted me to come on as a guest, play some songs, and chat it up.

My phone chimed and I picked it up from the vanity counter in front of me. I caught my reflection in the mirror and shook my head. I didn't even look like me with all this makeup. Faces were meant to shine. Sweat was meant to show.

Then again, I was sporting a massive zit on my cheek, so that was covered. But with all this crap on my face, I looked…fake.

And maybe I was. All I did was cover other peoples' songs.

I checked my phone and saw it was Rita, my tutor, who had texted me.

RITA: Paper on George Washington!

ME: I'm on it.

RITA: That's what you always say.

RITA: Can't pass you without it, Corey!

It was the first week back to school after winter break; how could she be talking about failing already? Then again, I had barely squeaked out a C in algebra two last semester.

I wasn't so sure about this virtual school and tutor thing. Might be nice to just go back to my normal high school here in L.A. If that was even an option anymore. My chest tightened at the thought of my old friends from school. Damn, I missed some of those guys.

Bitching about homework while we hung out at the beach.

Playing pickup ball at the gym, even though we totally sucked.

Dating...

Sure, I dated, but it was different. It didn't last. I hadn't found a girl actually interested in *me*. They were usually more interested in getting seen in my Instagram lives or getting their picture with me and posting it.

I pulled up my assignment on my phone, then tapped open the paper that I'd started. I had to get this—

"Hey!" A tiny blond girl burst through my closed door and I jumped out of my chair, almost dropping my phone. "Corey Chaos! OMIGOSH! Corey—"

Ranger Rodrigo barged into the room after the girl and then darted in front of her, his hands up. "Back off, miss."

My heart shot into my throat and my hair stood on end. Nothing like a screeching fan barging in to rip you out of your thoughts.

The girl leaned around Rodrigo, reaching for me, her fingers wiggling. "Corey!" Her voice was high-pitched and her eyes wide. For such a small girl, she carried around a pretty massive wave of wild energy.

Rodrigo shifted more in front of me as I stepped back. I bumped against my chair, which rammed into the vanity. The glass of water I'd set there tipped over and I jumped to the side to avoid getting wet. My hand darted out and I grabbed the chair, barely managing to stay upright.

Shit, this girl was intense.

"I'm going to have to restrain you, miss, if you don't back away from Mr. Chaos."

Mr. Chaos. Man, did that sound weird. I was only seventeen...

The girl backed up, wriggled out of Rodrigo's arms, then tried to dodge him, but he intercepted her, this time curling his arm around her waist and physically keeping her from me. She squealed, still reaching for me.

"Sorry, Mr. Chaos," Rodrigo said, his dark eyes wide and apologetic. He always tried to avoid physically touching someone, but sometimes he had to in order to keep me safe.

"It's okay." I smiled and waved to the girl. "Bye."

She all but melted into Rodrigo's arms with a big sigh and held up her phone. I heard the camera click and hopefully I didn't look too annoyed.

I used to think it was cute in the beginning when people recognized me on the street and stuff, but now…it was different.

My phone dinged and then a split second later it rang.

"Jeez!" I yelled and checked the caller ID.

Jethro's name and picture filled the screen and my temper doused a few notches. He was probably checking to see how the taping went. I slid my finger across the screen to answer.

"Hey kid!" Jethro said.

I should probably tell him to not call me that, but it actually felt pretty nice. My dad had passed away five years ago, and not that my agent was my dad, but sometimes, when he called me that, it reminded me of my old man, so I went with it.

"Hey Jethro. What's up?"

"How'd the show go?"

"Still going. Have to redo one segment, I guess." I stepped toward the door, just as the makeup artist scooted in with her powder brush at the ready. Even though I was already caked up with makeup, she added another layer.

I stopped, closed my eyes, and the synthetic bristles brushed against my nose with a couple of swift motions. Heaven forbid any shine peek through.

"Oh, okay. Well, how's it going?" Jethro asked.

"Fine. Pretty much the same as every show." I tried not to move too much. I'd been scolded by makeup artists enough to know better.

Sure, I didn't want my zit showing up on the taping, but *jeez*, enough with the makeup.

"Well, next up we have— Oh, just a minute."

In the background I heard a girl's voice. Must be Victoria, his seventeen-year-old daughter, who I'd met a few times before they moved out of L.A. She was funny, sweet, and seemed like a completely normal high schooler, at least according to her Instagram feed. And normal was good. I *wanted* more normal in my life.

"Yeah, sure, Pumpkin Nose," Jethro said, "that's fine."

"Don't call me that!" she said in the background.

They were close, and it was nice to see, but it also made me miss my dad that much more. We'd been close, too. Shared our love of music.

Things had heated up so much this past year that I hadn't even gotten to write any new songs lately. I didn't have any time anymore.

More bristles dusted over my cheeks and forehead. "Okay, Mr. Chaos, you're good."

I opened my eyes and gave her a nod, then followed her out the door.

"Sorry about that," Jethro said.

"That's okay, how's the fam?" *How's Victoria?*

"Good. Some drama going on, from what I hear from the next room, so I'll figure that out in a second." Jethro chuckled. "Let's see what I've got lined up for you next."

"About the schedule. Any chance we can clear out some time soon? Like...just have *nothing* scheduled? I need to get my homework done, man. I've got a killer semester ahead," I said as I pulled my dressing room door shut behind me and stepped into the hallway. "It's only the first week of school and I'm already getting chewed out by Rita."

"Want me to talk to her?"

"No. I want you to get me five freaking minutes to myself so I can get stuff done." I cringed at how loud my voice ricocheted off the walls. "Sorry. I—"

"You sure you're okay?"

"Yeah." I let out a breath and headed toward the set but then paused, leaning against the wall as I looked over the staging area. There were people crisscrossing, talking into their headsets, checking their phones, and drinking coffee or eating food.

Multitasking at its finest.

Hustle.

Hustle.

Hustle.

"Can you do it?" I asked. "Even if it's a half day so I can sleep in for once and—"

"I'm on it," Jethro said. "I'll get it worked out."

"Thanks, man." Maybe I'd even have some time to write down a few notes to some lyrics that'd been rattling around in my head the last couple weeks.

"Text me when you're done there and onto the next one."

"Will do and thanks."

"I got your back," he said, then hung up.

"Chaos!" someone yelled from the set. "You're on!"

I jumped at the sudden bellow, then put my phone on do not disturb and clicked the screen to black.

Time to face the chaos.

Chapter Three

Victoria

The gymnasium vibrated as the juniors and seniors stomped their feet and pounded their hands against the bleachers.

Ignoring the knot in my stomach, I zeroed in on the massive fish painted on the opposite wall. *The Fighting Pike, what a strange freaking mascot...* Focusing on that image was the only thing that kept me from stealing glances at Todd. He was all smiles, sitting next to Matthew, joking around, like nothing in his life had changed. Asshole.

Me, on the other hand, I'd been rehashing every detail of our relationship since he unceremoniously dumped me at lunch yesterday. Over the last few months, he'd brushed me off at least three or four times to hang with his family. I hadn't questioned it; I'd assumed he'd been telling the truth. Same with the unanswered texts last weekend. He said he'd fallen asleep early. *Yeah right...* He was probably with that other girl.

Stop thinking about him!

I shook my head and put my focus back on our aquatic mascot, trying to push the image of Todd's face out of my mind. And the way he smelled, and the way his arms felt around me—

Mr. Navarro, the head principal, cleared his throat and waited for everyone to quiet down. "Our final nominees for prince and princess of the Ice Ball are…"

I dug my nails into my jeans. All of the other nominees had been announced. I'd kept my fingers crossed, silently willing Mr. Navarro not to say my name. Twenty-four hours ago, it had been my dream for Todd and me to be nominated for the Ice Court. Couples rarely made it on together, but every now and then it happened. After yesterday, though, hearing my name paired with his would be nothing but a freaking nightmare.

"Juniors Victoria Knight and Todd Miller!"

And, cue the nightmare.

The crowd fell silent. Everyone had obviously watched Todd dump me in the cafeteria yesterday or they'd seen it on Instagram… It was like we were the stars of a reality show I'd never agreed to be on, but here I was, facing the next challenge. If only there were a fifty-thousand-dollar prize at the end of this, it might all be worth it. Maybe.

Mia looked at me, a sad wrinkle forming between her bunched brows and her mouth on the verge of pout. "Want me to walk down with you?"

"No. I'm good." I drew in a deep breath. "I will *not* let that asshat own me *or* my emotions."

Normally, I didn't care about popularity contests like

this, but making the Ice Ball royal court was a huge honor. Too bad it meant nothing now.

I stood up, fully intending to walk down the steps of the bleachers, but my legs refused to budge. My heart slammed so hard my breath caught in my chest.

"You got this, Vic," Mia said, nudging me forward.

I took my first step, legs shaking, and navigated my way down the creaking bleachers. We were only about ten rows up from the gym floor, but it felt like a mile away. Almost like one of those nightmares where the hallway keeps getting longer and longer as you run forward, trying to escape. It never ends.

The crowd was banging against the wooden stands and their loud cheering echoed throughout the gymnasium, drowning out the sound of my thumping heart. But I still felt it pulsing in my temples.

Just yesterday they were laughing because of what Todd had done. Then again, all this cheering was probably for the entire court, not me specifically.

As my feet hit the gym floor, Todd was almost already to the center, where the rest of the group was standing. He hadn't even waited for me or anything. *Dick*.

My stomach clenched and for a second I thought I might puke.

The rest of the nominees were standing in front of us, grinning at everyone in the bleachers. As Todd and I took our spots at the end of the line, he stood behind me. Distant and cold. Damn, things had changed, hadn't they?

From kind to asshat with a flick of a switch. We'd been together almost two years and he'd become my rock. He was kind, everyone loved him, and he wasn't reckless or a troublemaker. Not like my previous choice of guys in L.A.

Todd was exactly the kind of person I needed in my life. But right now, it was like he was a totally different person.

"Please give a round of applause for this year's Ice Ball royal court!" Principal Navarro said into the mic. He held the microphone in his left hand and a clipboard in his right. His hands were massive, making anything he held seem unnaturally small. He was nearly seven feet tall and had played professional football for five years before blowing out his knee in the early 2000s.

The junior and senior classes of Twin River High let out a deafening roar. I hadn't heard it this loud in the gym since we'd beaten Woodhaven last year, securing a spot in the first round of the state basketball tournament.

"Voting for the prince, princess, king, and queen will open on Monday," Principal Navarro said. "It is open only to juniors and seniors and you'll need your student ID. You can vote in any of the principals' offices, including mine. You have twelve days to cast your ballot."

"Hops, Hops, Hops," a bunch of basketball players chanted for their star point guard, Tony Mathison.

Principal Navarro held up his hand to silence Tony's teammates.

"Now, the Twin River Ice Festival starts on Saturday. The Annual Food Pantry Drive will kick off in three days. The school that gathers the most food wins the Ice Festival trophy. As you know, we've won the past two years."

Everyone on the royal court and in the stands clapped and whistled.

The Ice Festival always took place in January. The city had been celebrating it forever. At first I thought it was ridiculous to have a huge festival in the middle of winter in Wisconsin. But between the canoe races on the frozen river, a massive town-wide snowball fight, and a bunch of activities indoors at the civic center, it was pretty epic.

Principal Navarro smiled broadly. "In order to make it a hat trick, our PTA has thrown in a major incentive. The student who turns in the most food, as in, the number of items, not weight, will win..." He paused and looked down at a note card in his hand. "A party for themselves and nineteen of their friends at Adventure Zone with unlimited pizza and soda afterward at Giuseppe's Pizzeria."

"Yeah!" Tony punched his fist into the air.

The crowd cheered loudly. The Twin River Pantry was something I really cared about. Any time they had food drives or fundraisers, I did my best to get involved.

Principal Navarro waited for the cheers to quiet down before lifting his microphone. "And before we dismiss, a quick reminder. Any suspensions or detentions over the next two weeks will automatically disqualify you from attending the Ice Ball."

Several people booed.

"Ahem," Principal Navarro said into the mic, "that brings our pep rally to an end. Please make your way to your eighth-hour class in an orderly fashion."

Everyone thundered down the bleachers. I rolled my eyes. No one ever listened to that "orderly fashion" stuff.

I peeked over my shoulder to see Todd rushing away. Snickers drifted to my ears as Matthew strode past me. It took everything I had inside me to not lay into him or even lay him out. Neither he nor Todd deserved my time.

I'd been the perfect girlfriend since day one. I'd had to

be. I'd had to show everyone, including myself, that I could walk the straight and narrow here and not march down the street of mistakes and regret like I did in L.A.

One, two, three...

No. I'd come a long way since then, but maybe not far enough to deal with my boyfriend's—*er*...ex-boyfriend's crap.

Four, five, six, seven, eight, nine, ten. I let out a deep breath.

"Congratulations!" Mia wrapped her arms around me from behind. "I knew you were going to make it!"

My heart was still racing, but not from the thrill of being nominated.

"Todd's an ass. You don't need him," Tony said as he strode up to us.

He was six-foot-four and had sky-blue eyes that held a depth of something super intellectual, but sweet. The guy was an amazing basketball player but not conceited like most people would be with his talent.

"Thanks, Tony. Oh, and thanks for the text last night." I nudged his ribs with my shoulder. He was a good friend. Cute, too, just not my type.

"Anytime. I almost punched the guy this morning," he said, shaking his head.

And that was saying something. Tony wasn't violent at all. Pretty passive, actually, except on the basketball court.

Mia pulled out her phone from her back pocket. "And he will not ruin this moment. Lean in, I want a picture of you two!"

Tony draped his arm over my shoulders and I spread the biggest smile I could muster. Todd would not steal this joy from me. I'd find the best-looking date and take him to everything. I'd show Todd what was what.

"Okay. Let's bolt. Only one more class of the day!" Mia sang out as she took off.

"Hang in there, Victoria," Tony said, nudging my shoulder right before he hustled after his basketball buddies.

I nodded. Even though it was more like hanging by a thread.

...

Buzz. Buzz.

Pretending to get something out of my backpack, I leaned to the side and slid my phone out of my back pocket to see who or what had pinged me. I shouldn't have checked my phone during class, but I could hardly pay attention anyway, with Todd still wreaking havoc in my head. Just as long as this wasn't another embarrassing video of me…

I propped my phone behind the guy sitting in front of me, out of view of my AP U.S. history teacher, and checked my notifications.

A picture of a couch in the middle of a set, surrounded by cameras and a sound boom filled my screen.

NOMIE: Just another day in paradise.

NOMIE: Miss it?

Nomie was an up-and-coming actress I used to hang out with in L.A. But when we started to get into trouble and the whole Grayson Stryker situation went down, my parents decided the family needed to move back to Wisconsin, where they grew up.

Being ripped away from my friends freshman year sucked. Up until twenty-four hours ago, the best part of moving to Twin River was meeting Todd and Mia.

Well. At least I still had my best friend.

ME: I miss poke burritos on the beach.

I sent a drooling emoji.

Sure, Twin River had sushi, but nothing beat the poke burritos from the Hokey Pokey food truck at the pier.

NOMIE: How are you doing?

ME: I got nominated to the Ice Ball court…

NOMIE: Congrats!

ME: Yeah… Not so much.

ME: I'm on the court with Todd…

NOMIE: NO!

ME: Yup…

NOMIE: I wish I was there so I could punch Todd right in the face!

NOMIE: And give you a hug.

ME: Thanks, Nom.

NOMIE: You should totally come out here for spring break.

ME: Yes!

NOMIE: Remember when we got lit and snuck onto the ninth hole of the golf course at the Royal Oaks Country Club?

ME: The sand trap!

ME: My parents were so pissed when they found the hot tub full of sand the next day!

Nomie sent me a string of laughing with tears emojis, shocked face emojis, and beach with palm tree emojis. It felt so good to think about something other than Todd and his weasel-ass for a minute.

NOMIE: Damn girl, I miss you!

ME: I miss you, too.

NOMIE: Boo! The tutor is here.

NOMIE: I gotta go.

ME: Love you!

NOMIE: Love you, too!

NOMIE: XOXO

I flipped over from text messages to Instagram, and a picture of Corey Chaos with a beautiful girl popped up on the screen. I rolled my eyes and kept scrolling.

People were so obsessed with him. Fans swarmed him wherever he went.

I'd met Corey a few times. He was nice enough and a great musician, but I was just one of his eleven million followers. I was *just* "the agent's daughter." He probably didn't even remember my name.

None of that mattered anyway. *Focus, Victoria.*

It was time to find the hottest, most delectable date for the Ice Ball. There was no way I was going to let freaking Todd show me up!

Chapter Four

Corey

I jolted awake to a sharp stabbing pain in my neck.

Darkness surrounded me. Where was I? What the—

My back tensed and my neck pulsed with pain again. I grabbed it and squeezed the knot as my surroundings fell into place. I was at my desk in the far corner of my living room.

I was home.

I'd fallen asleep.

Shit. I let go of my neck and let out a breath. My laptop was open in front of me, taunting me with the unfinished history paper I'd started... I checked my phone. 2:00 glowed so brightly it burned my eyes.

Two o'clock.

In the freaking morning.

The TV flickered behind me, sending a wicked shadow dancing across the wall in front of me. The sound was muted so I could concentrate on my paper, but that hadn't helped much. Thirty minutes into writing it, I'd zonked out.

I switched my phone to selfie mode to see if I had a keyboard imprint in my forehead.

Sure as shit, I did. The rounded corner of my MacBook Air indented my forehead. I snapped a picture, chuckling. That might make for a funny post later.

I rubbed my head and sat back in the leather desk chair. If I didn't finish this paper by morning—well, later this morning—Rita would have my balls on a chopping board.

I checked my computer screen to see how much more I needed to write.

I only have one page done? It felt more like ten.

Okay. I could do this. I shook out my hands and tilted my head side to side, cracking my neck. This should be easy, right? I mean, I was used to writing lyrics to songs. Lots of them.

Then again, I hadn't written anything new in months. My chaotic schedule had sucked my creativity dry.

Had sucked *me* dry.

I pushed my computer away and snagged my phone again. Maybe I'd find some inspiration on Instagram…for a paper on George Washington. *Right.*

By inspiration I meant procrastination.

I tapped the app open and went to my notifications. Reading comments from fans was fun, sometimes overwhelming, but fun. I skimmed through a few and replied, then tapped over to my feed. A post from Victoria was at the very top, but it wasn't new. It had a lot of comments, though. More comments than likes—

I sucked in a breath. Something bad had happened.

The last comment made was simply the hashtag

#LunchDump. What the hell?

With a sinking feeling in my gut, I tapped the hashtag.

More than two hundred posts filled the #LunchDump stream. All of them showed Victoria standing in a school cafeteria, while a guy—wait a second, wasn't that her *boyfriend*?—loomed over her with a smug look on his face. I'd seen them together in her other posts. She always seemed happy with him, but now...

I turned up the volume and held my breath.

"I said, we're over," the guy said.

My teeth ground together at his cold, harsh voice. But what slashed my heart was Victoria's wide eyes filled with hurt.

That asshole dumped her in front of a crowd. What could she have possibly done to deserve that?

A *Bomb Drop* notification suddenly popped up on my screen, smack in the middle, blocking the Instagram video.

Teen Influencer, Corey Chaos, outed as bastard son of Hollywood playboy, Brenden Kennedy...

"What the *hell*?" I pushed hard out of my chair, knocking it over.

A sour taste filled my mouth as I skimmed the news blast. No, that was bile. I was going to puke in a second.

Bastard son? What kind of sick son of a—

ROBERTS: Don't overreact.

Of course my publicist would text me the link, too, even in the middle of the freaking night.

ME: How can I not overreact?!?

ME: My dad died of cancer!

ME: This is bullshit.

ROBERTS: I know.

ME: Can you fix this?

Normally, I wouldn't care what magazine or who was harassing me with another fake story, but this one crossed the line. They attacked my *dead father*.

I paced the hardwood floor in front of the fireplace, squeezing my hair. My phone rang; it was Roberts, but I silenced it. My chest heaved as I struggled for air. My hands went sweaty and my stomach churned. I really might puke.

How could this be happening? I looked at the headline again and the stomach churning intensified into a cramp. This was too much. I *needed* a break.

I flopped onto my couch, my thumb brushed over my screen, and the video of Victoria's humiliation popped up again. Anger surged through me, both at the news flash *and* at her video.

She must be so upset.

"Fuck this," I said and dialed Jethro's phone number. "I'm done."

I needed help. This *Bomb Drop* wouldn't be the last gossip rag to write a shit article about me. He'd know what to do. I trusted him more than Roberts. And I could maybe ask him about Victoria. See how she was doing with what happened to her—

No. I shouldn't call him. It was four in the morning there. And I couldn't ask him about his daughter. Hell, he might not even know about the video.

I should hang up—

"Hello?" Jethro's voice cracked, sounding more like gravel crunching than a voice. Like he just woke up. "Corey?"

"Um...yeah." I should have hung up.

"You okay?" His voice sounded clearer now. "No, honey, it's fine, just Corey on the phone," he whispered.

Shit. I'd woken up his wife. I shouldn't have called.

"Corey?"

"Um...hi. I'm sorry. I—" I hopped back onto my feet, fighting the burn in my eyes. "I just... There's been another story... It's the worst one yet and...I don't know what to do."

And I want to know how Victoria is doing, too. She'd kind of had a *Bomb Drop* of her own.

"Hold on..." Jethro coughed a couple times, then I heard some shuffling in the background and my stomach fell to my feet.

"I'm sorry, Jethro. It's early. I shouldn't have called."

"It's okay. I'm logging into my laptop..." There was a brief pause and the sound of a clicking keyboard. "Wow, that's low. I'm sorry. Does Roberts know?"

"Yeah, he's on it." I jammed my hand in my hair. "This is bullsh—crap. Bullcrap. You know that, right?"

"Of course I do. I'm sorry," he repeated.

"I can't do this anymore, Jethro. The press, the schedule. I have to stay up until three o'clock in the morning to get my schoolwork done." I shook my head and stopped before the fireplace. A picture of Dad and me, playing our guitars, back when I was seven, was on the mantel. The sting in my eyes worsened. He'd been gone for five years now and I needed him here with me, now more than ever.

"A lot has been thrown at you," Jethro said. "I get that."

I turned away from the picture on the mantel. "It's too

much."

"You have every right to be pissed." He let out a long breath. "Look. You're getting overwhelmed. Things are a little hot right now."

"And I'm tired."

"And..."

"And I'm about to fail some classes," I said. "I need a break from everything. Oh, and did I say I'm tired?"

"I do have an idea," Jethro said. "You might not like it, though."

"Well, now I have to know what it is or I'll die of curiosity. And it'll be all over the news."

"All right..." He paused to let out a sigh, and I opened my mouth to tell him to forget it, but then he blurted, "Come here for a month."

I froze and it felt like all the air had been sucked from my lungs.

"Corey?"

"Um...here. You wanna run that by me again?" I made my way to the couch and sat down.

"Look, I know Twin River isn't as hopping as L.A., but it might be a nice break for you."

"You want me to go to Wisconsin. Like...actual *Wisconsin*. Is that even possible?"

"I'll make it possible. We need you at your best and right now you're not. You need a break."

The idea of having a whole month off. The songs I could write. The schoolwork I could finish. The sleep I could get.

"Yes!" I shouted into the phone. "I'll do it!"

Twin River, here I come.

Chapter Five

VICTORIA

TERRELL: Sorry can't.

TERRELL: I'm seeing someone.

Heat flooded my cheeks as I sat in my car, reading the text message. Terrell and I had met at Sushi Palace last summer and he'd found me on Instagram later that night. He'd messaged me and told me that if I ever dumped Todd, I should call him.

His Instagram account was mostly pictures of him and his friends playing football, swimming at Bear Lake, stuff like that. No evidence of a girlfriend, which was why I'd added him to my list of last-minute options to come with me to the Ice Ball. I couldn't show up to the dance alone; that would be one more embarrassment added to the pile. Crap,

I'd already hit my humiliation quota for the year and it was only January.

ME: Oh, sorry.

ME: Um. Thanks.

ME: Talk to you later.

ME: Or not.

ME: I mean, since you have a girlfriend.

I sounded ridiculous.

ME: Bye.

He didn't respond.

This is pointless.

Looking down at the list of seven names on my note app, I put an *X* in front of Terrell. He'd been the last one. It had taken me all day today to come up with these options. Guys who were so gorgeous, charming, and magnetic that they'd make everyone forget about #LunchDump. Or at least I hoped they would.

But, like the true crapstorm that my love life had become, the guys on my list were either already going to the dance with someone else or they were in a relationship.

Maybe I should text Nomie? Maybe I could convince her to fly out here and be my date?

I rubbed my face with my hands and let out a sigh as I killed the engine of my RAV4. I'd been sitting in my driveway, reading through the messages that'd come in on my drive home from school. The light snow falling had left a layer of white over my entire windshield blocking out the rest of the world.

I shoved the door open, grabbed my bag from the passenger seat, then trudged through the snow toward the front door. Usually snow made me smile because it felt like everything was fresh and clean, but today...nothing felt right.

At school, people were either pointing and laughing or, even worse, it got painfully quiet, like people were holding their breath, until I passed by.

Scratch that, I needed some pool-house time to chill out a second. I bolted around the side of the house, then through the gate that led to the backyard. I threw a glance toward the windows that showed the kitchen area. Dad hunched over the stove, wearing his WORLD'S BEST CHEF apron, and I couldn't help but smile.

Breakfast for dinner...I loved Friday nights. But if I was going to withstand the happiness in there, I needed to chill a few more minutes and calm down.

I shot a text off to Dad that I was home and gonna chill in the pool house for a few minutes, then tapped the Do Not Disturb on my phone and dumped it into my back pocket.

Coming out here, relaxing, writing some poetry; that always seemed to work. Granted, I hadn't been writing as much lately, but still. Everything that'd happened yesterday and today merited some *me*-time for sure.

With a quick motion, I pulled open the door. A wave of warmth enveloped me and I drew in a deep breath. *Weird, wonder if Dad was out here today and left the heat on by accident?* I let the door shut behind me, then stepped to my right toward the fireplace. With a flick of the switch beside the stone face, I turned on the flame.

I loved sinking into the leather couch, watching the fire. It was mesmerizing.

Something to my left moved. The hairs on my neck shot up. It was big.

A person? But Dad was in the kitchen...

Spinning to my right, I snatched the decorative fire poker and took a swing.

"Whoa!" The person ducked, then grabbed my hand, and the next thing I knew I was on the couch.

I screamed, squeezing my eyes shut, hoping Dad could hear me. We were being robbed. Someone had broken into our place.

Oh hell no. Not after the day I had.

I shot my eyes open, fixing to kick this intruder in the balls. He'd regret coming—

Wait a second. I recognized those dark brown eyes. And that wispy brown hair flipped over his ears.

"Corey?" I said with a gasp. "Corey Chaos?"

"I'm going to let you go. Okay? Nice and slow." His tenor voice was gentle, soothing. "Just don't take batting practice with my skull. That thing you're holding looks pretty lethal."

He released his grip on me and stepped back, then I hopped to my feet, nearly tripping in the process.

"What the *hell* are you doing in my pool house?"

A subtle smirk curved the corner of his mouth and he said, "I'm living here for the next month."

• • •

Eleven blueberry pancakes and three strips of bacon later,

Corey rubbed his stomach and leaned back in his chair. "That was *the* best meal I've ever had."

"You're lucky to be alive to have eaten it," I said, shaking my head. "I can't believe I almost bashed you with the fire poker."

"You got a mean swing." He winked at me.

"That'll teach you to send a text then put on your Do Not Disturb, huh, Pumpkin Nose?" Dad said, holding back a laugh.

After I'd calmed down I'd checked my phone and saw a text from Dad telling me not to go into the pool house. A lot of good that did, *after* the fact.

"Seriously. You're staying here? As in here." I shook my head. "You'll be bored in two days."

"Perfect." Corey flipped some of the hair that'd dropped over his forehead.

"You came here to get bored." I took a sip of my orange juice. "That makes total sense."

"You've been here only a few hours and already *bored* looks good on you," Dad said.

I wondered what Mia would do in this situation, being less than three feet away from Corey Chaos. She'd probably pass out. A small smile crossed my lips as I thought about what she'd say when I told her. Then again, maybe I shouldn't. He and my dad might want to keep it a secret. Maybe he planned on wearing a disguise when he went out? Like a ski mask and sunglasses. The smile playing on my lips got bigger as I pictured Corey walking in downtown Twin River, completely unrecognizable.

Corey caught my expression and lifted an eyebrow. "Admit it. You're impressed with my pancake consumption."

"I don't know how you haven't puked yet," I joked.

My dad placed his fork and knife on his plate. "Before I head off to get some work done, I trust both of you to make good choices while Corey is here, understood?"

We both nodded. I was sure Corey didn't want to hear the "good choices" lecture any more than I did.

Dad removed his WORLD'S BEST CHEF red-checkered apron, hung it on a hook next to the refrigerator, and then went up to his office. Leaving me alone with Corey and a million thoughts, just staring at him and wondering what we do from here. For a whole month. Corey closed his eyes, letting out a long, relaxed sigh, and leaned back in his chair.

It'd been six months since I'd last seen him and it was only a quick hello at one of Dad's functions. Normally we'd hang out a little more when I was in L.A. with Dad, but once Corey got popular, he usually didn't have time.

"So. You needed a break, huh?" I asked, totally curious as to what led him here.

Corey let out another deep breath, but he didn't say anything, so I took it he wasn't ready to elaborate on things yet.

"I'm assuming I shouldn't tell anyone you're here, then?"

"We're still working out all the details. It happened really fast." Corey closed his eyes, letting out a long, relaxed sigh, and leaned back in his chair.

That's when a wild idea hit me, and screw it, I dove into it headfirst.

The perfect way to get back at Todd.

"Hey, Corey?"

"Yeah?" His eyes were still closed.

"Want to be my fake boyfriend?"

Chapter Six

COREY

"*Wait,* what"—the front legs of my chair slapped down against the hardwood floor and I grabbed the table to balance myself—"did you just say?"

Victoria's cheeks were instantly red. "Okay, so…I have an idea. It might sound a little bit ludicrous, but hear me out."

Or maybe a lot ludicrous. Fake boyfriend? I came here to get away from drama, not step into the middle of it. But I was curious to hear her explanation, at least. I leaned forward, resting my elbows on the wooden tabletop. "All right, I'm listening."

Her brown eyes lit up. They went from pure embarrassment to calculated and energized. This was gonna be good—so good that some of my fatigue from traveling all day vaporized.

Maybe it was from being near her. She was real,

authentic; it radiated from her with every smile, every laugh, every movement. I didn't see much of that...ever. It was refreshing.

"It's just, there was, well, *is*, this video, and—"

She hesitated for a beat, then launched into the story of the #LunchDump video.

My stomach sank. I should have known this was about her ex. Should I tell her I'd already seen it?

No, that might make her feel worse.

"So this asshole broke up with you in the lunchroom. In front of everyone." Now that I had the full story, I was even more pissed off at this guy. Talk about a total dick thing, to do that to a girl. To Victoria.

"And you dated him for almost two years?" I shook my head and leaned back. "That's a freaking lifetime."

She huffed and went to get up from her chair. "You know what? Never mind. I just thought—"

"No, wait. I'm sorry." I leaned forward and lightly slapped the table in front of me. "Sit. Please. I want to hear this out, hear *you* out. "

The more I thought about it, the more intrigued I was by her idea. It might be fun to hang out with her without any expectations or hidden agendas, since we'd both know it was fake from the start. We'd know right where we stood from day one. I wouldn't have to find out three weeks into a relationship that it was totally fake.

Like I had the past four I'd been in.

"I'm sorry. I didn't mean to get upset there. It's just that you're right. We were together a long time. I can't believe he was cheating on me. He was—"

"*Is* a dick. A jerk. He's a complete asshole for doing that."

"Are you seriously considering helping me?"

"Sure." I shrugged, hoping to throw off the attitude of indifference. But she'd been publicly humiliated. How could I say no? "Okay," I said. "Spill."

"Seriously?" She clapped her hands together and squirmed in her seat. "You're for real right now?"

I nodded and picked up the last bit of bacon she'd not finished from her plate. Couldn't let this awesome food go to waste.

"So, there are two things. The first is the Ice Festival."

"Whoa, hold up." I held up my hand in a "stop" motion. "Is this Ice Festival by any chance indoors?"

"Very funny."

"I wasn't kidding. It's *freezing* outside."

"And if it wasn't, the ice would melt. Not much of an Ice Festival without ice."

"Yeah...true." I sighed. *What did I just get myself into?* "Sorry. Go on."

"So anyway," Victoria said, smiling—and it was that smile that reminded me why I was doing this. If it made her keep smiling like that, totally worth it. "The Twin River Ice Festival. It's this big thing that goes on for two whole weeks. Everyone in town gets involved. There's all of these events and really good food, and... Todd and I went to everything last year, together." Her shoulders slumped. "It's always a big thing for couples."

Her smile disappeared completely. I needed to keep her mind off that jerk. "Okay, so what's the second thing?" I asked.

"The Ice Ball. Not to be confused with the Ice Festival, the ball is a big dance at school. I'm on the royal court with

Todd. I can't show up alone. It would be humiliating."

I dipped my head, listening as she vented.

"I mean, normally, it wouldn't be a huge deal. People break up, it happens, but the way he did it. It was literally the worst. It was recorded and posted online. It's everywhere and if I show up to everything alone, on top of all that, I'm socially screwed, with a capital *S*. *Forever*." Her chest heaved.

Yeah, that video *was* messed up. I shook my head, my blood starting to boil. Some people sucked. Jethro, his family, they were legit nice people. Victoria shouldn't be treated like this.

Then again, if I did start hanging with her around town I'd be out in the public. Someone would notice, then Victoria would be dragged into my shit. And then there was Jethro…

"What about your dad?" I asked.

"He can't ever find out about this, not *any* of it." She shook her head. "Actually, maybe we shouldn't do this. I shouldn't have brought it up."

"What? No. I mean, we could probably keep things low-key so he wouldn't find out, right?"

She gulped, as in audibly *gulped*. I wanted to do this for her. This asshole, Todd, couldn't get away with what he'd done. Victoria was too nice. Too sweet.

"I guess, maybe, if you don't post pics of couple-like things on your social media and we're careful, we can just pull off that we're friends when we're around my parents." Energy flashed through her eyes.

"One question," I asked, smiling. "What's in it for me?"

"Um…" Her jaw dropped slightly and her cheeks reddened. "What…do you want?"

"Normalcy," I said.

She quirked up her eyebrow, but then settled into her chair more. "Explain."

"I used to be in high school before. You know. Like, even ran track." I picked at a random stray piece of thread on the placemat. "Used to write songs, listen to music, things like that."

"But not anymore, I bet," she said, her voice calm and quiet.

"Not even close. Now my schedule is always booked solid, I get barely any sleep, constantly running around... and just generally *stressed*."

"I get it." She shifted in her seat. "Twin River is small compared to L.A., but it's not a tiny town in the middle of nowhere. People out here know who you are; they'll recognize you."

"They might." I wasn't sure how this would work, but I still wanted to try.

"And I'd be using you to get back at Todd. That's not cool. I'm sorry I brought this up." She shook her head. "I wasn't thinking. I was—"

"I'm in."

"For real?" A grin cracked through the seriousness that had hardened her jaw.

"We should totally do it."

"You'll be my fake boyfriend?"

"Yup." I sat up straighter. It wasn't just for her benefit, either. It did sound like fun. Dating. Hanging out. Pissing off this jerk who broke her heart. I couldn't wait to start messing with him. "When do we start?"

Victoria smiled. "Tomorrow night."

Chapter Seven

Victoria

Standing face-to-face with a half-naked, perfectly tanned Corey Freaking Chaos with bedhead hair was not anything I'd ever imagined I'd see. It actually wasn't fair how great he looked right out of bed like that. My face instantly heated and, to no one's surprise, my mouth took over before I could stop it.

"Did you just wake up? It's *noon*—"

"Get inside before I freeze my nuts off."

My eyes darted downward and back up, but if he noticed, he didn't show it.

I moved past him, into the pool house, which must have been close to eighty degrees. That would explain why Corey was wearing board shorts and...nothing else. And if it was eighty degrees in here, then my cheeks were at least a hundred. "You do realize you're not in California anymore, right? Around here, we usually wear pants and socks once it's below forty."

Corey rolled his eyes, but with a smile. "Thanks for the tip."

He closed the door behind him and shivered, then turned and stood there looking at me instead of putting on a shirt. The guy could totally own a board shorts TV commercial with those six-pack abs, his smooth, flawless skin, and the slight sprinkling of hair just above the tie strings…

Focus, Victoria.

"Here." I handed him the papers I was holding. "I—I was wondering if you might want to go over this together and then, um…we could sign it."

His eyes skimmed the front page. "A fake relationship contract?"

"Yeah." Heat crept up my neck again and spilled out into the apples of my cheeks. Oh, who was I kidding—it never left since he opened that door. "I thought it could, ah, help us keep some"—my eyes darted downward again and thank goodness he was still focused on the paper—"clear boundaries."

Looking completely comfortable and at home here already, he meandered over to the couch and sat down beside his guitar.

It was out of its case, lying on the cushion, and there were some papers strewn about next to it and on the coffee table. Some were crumpled, some had scribbles on them, but one stood out that had a big black *X* through the entire page.

"Have a seat," he said, still reading what I'd handed him.

I sat gingerly on the arm of the couch, unable to relax. What if he thought this whole thing was ridiculous now? What if he'd changed his mind overnight?

I snagged his guitar and slipped the strap over my head.

"Hey, careful with that," Corey said, eyeing me with a flare of concern.

"I won't hurt it. I promise." I held the instrument close to my chest. I'd never been super musical, actually, I was pretty tone deaf, but he didn't need to know that.

"Both parties must agree to the five following rules. Rule One: do not tell anyone about the fake relationship." Corey read aloud.

"Not even your best friend," I clarified. Keeping this from Mia would be a challenge, but as much as I loved her, I knew she would leak this on day one. Not intentionally, of course, but that wouldn't matter once the truth was out.

"Easy. The only friend I have out here is you." He winked at me, tickling my insides and forcing me to hold back a giggle—a *giggle*—then he focused on the paper again.

Damn. Who knew a wink could be so powerful?

"Rule Two: fill out the attached questionnaire, then memorize the other person's answers." He arched an eyebrow. "What questionnaire?"

"Next page there," I said.

He flipped to that part and read silently for a minute. "You think someone is going to call us out if you don't say my favorite food is taquitos. I've eaten them on my Instagram stories practically every week."

Duh. People at school already knew more about him than they did me. He was famous. I shrugged, suddenly regretting the idea of it.

"I'm teasing," he said. "It's fine."

"Thanks. I already did mine." I pulled out the folded paper from my back pocket and set it on the coffee table.

"Rule Three," he continued, "you agree to go on at least seven public dates over the next two weeks. What kind of dates?"

"Mainly Ice Festival stuff. It sounds kinda corny, but I promise, it's actually pretty fun."

"And Todd will be at them, too?"

I nodded, grinding my molars. *Freaking Todd.*

I strummed Corey's guitar and he flinched. "Um...you better hand her over." He reached for his guitar. "Todd seems to trigger violence on your part."

He wasn't wrong. I handed him the instrument and he wove the strap over his head, then focused on the contract again.

The guitar looked like an extension of Corey. Like it was a part of him.

"Rule Four: attend the Ice Ball together. Does that count as one of the seven dates?"

"No," I said automatically, but I wasn't sure why. He didn't seem to care, so I let it go.

Then I held my breath. The next one was the most important one of all.

"Rule Five: engage in limited PDAs such as hand-holding and kisses on the cheek. Such behavior will only occur while in public, as part of the ruse. No kissing on the lips or anything." He glanced at his guitar and the scattered papers filled with musical notes, random words, and *X*s, but then he nodded. "Okay. That's fair."

Even just hearing him say those things—*kissing,*

touching—had my nerves doing somersaults. Which was all kinds of wrong. A few days ago I was doing those things and feeling that excitement with Todd. Now I was going as far as having a fake boyfriend to make him feel like shit because he'd made me feel like shit. What the hell was my life right now?

"Question," Corey said, jolting me out of my thoughts. "What about Jethro? I mean, your dad." He let the paper hang in front of him as he looked up at me. "He's gonna be ticked when he finds out I'm holding your hand and kissing you on the cheek."

"He won't."

Corey tipped his head down and gave me a look of doubt.

"Okay. So. He might." I rubbed my hands over my thighs as I riffled through ideas of how to keep this from Dad. With Corey's massive online following, the first time we showed up at an event together would be chronicled by the hour.

"We should tell him, Vic—"

"No!" I jumped off the couch and paced between the TV and the couch. "But if and when he finds out, sees a picture or something, we can say that we're just friends. I mean, Tony has kissed me on the cheek before, but only *as friends*. So, I'll just tell Dad you're being sweet and I'm being protective with his star client. He'll totally buy that I'm just showing you around town and hanging out with friends."

"Like normal high schoolers," he said and I didn't miss the hint of wistfulness coating his words. He probably didn't have a very normal anything since he hit a million followers on Instagram.

"We'll have to be extra aware of who's around us and what they're doing. Try our hardest to not get caught on camera kissing."

Kissing Corey Chaos… No, stop thinking like that. This was 100 percent fake. Not the time to catch feelings!

"Right. We can, you know, tell him the press are throwing whatever spin they want on this." Corey paused. "But you'll be in the spotlight. You okay with that?"

My stomach dropped. I'd been on the sidelines of the spotlight before, when I lived in L.A. and was getting into a little bit of trouble. Well, if I was being honest, it was more like a medium-high amount of trouble. I shook off the fear, though. That was all hidden, thanks to my dad and his PR team. Plus, I was a different person now. I wouldn't make bad decisions like I'd done before.

And Corey was a nice guy. I couldn't even imagine what kind of trouble I could get into with him, especially here.

"I'll be fine. They'll be more focused on you, anyway, being in Twin River, Wisconsin." I chuckled. "Even *I* can't believe you're here."

His lips twitched into a smile, but it didn't light up his eyes like usual.

"Last one," he said. "Rule Six: keep things platonic. No falling for each other." He paused. "Wow. You really put a lot of time and effort into this."

I stopped pacing and faced him. "Do you think it's silly?"

"No, not at all." He sat up straight and caught my gaze. "It's smart and everything makes sense. It's good to have the lines drawn clearly. It should help shove it in Todd's face and hopefully help me land that spot on *What's Your Note?* I might want to negotiate a couple of these, though."

He winked at me again, and *again* my body reacted on instinct. Heart racing, shallow breathing, and a touch of lightheadedness.

"Like, this questionnaire, I'm thinking I want to get to know you the old-fashioned way, you know?"

"Meaning..."

"On our dates." He grinned. "We could just talk, let our relationship happen naturally."

My eyes widened.

"For the contract," he said. "For the sake of it looking real, I mean."

"Oh, right. Yeah. For the contract."

"And it's not like we can show up somewhere together already holding hands, playing kissy face right after you and Todd broke up."

"That's true." Okay, he was getting into this and making good points. It might actually work. "We're really going to do this, aren't we?"

"Yep." He disconnected with his guitar, then stood up from the couch. Threading his arms through his shirt sleeves and sliding it on, he said, "But I'm not signing it."

"Wait, what?" My stomach bottomed out. "I thought—"

"No. I agree with what's in it. And I'll do it." He smoothed his hand down the front of his shirt. "It'll be fun. But me signing something...if that ever got out, even if it's not an official contract, it'd be a PR nightmare."

"Ahhh. I get it." I knew what I'd drawn up wasn't legal and binding, but yeah, I understood where he was coming from.

"But I'm in, okay?" He flipped the hair off his forehead and unleashed a smile that had my body quivering. "When's our first event?"

I stood there, gaping at him in his bare feet, shorts, and T-shirt. *Damn.*

I shook my head and said, "It's tonight and it's outdoors, so we're going to have to find you some winter clothes."

Shaking out his hair, he grinned. "That asshat Todd isn't going to know what hit him."

Chapter Eight

Corey

"You're going to freeze your ears off if you don't wear a proper hat." Victoria pulled a stocking cap out of her glove compartment and handed it to me.

"It's pink!" I held it up.

She huffed, then pushed open her door and hopped out. "I think I have a black one in the back. One of Dad's."

She slammed the door shut, rocking the entire vehicle.

I shifted, pulling the thick jacket down a little more. Jethro had given it to me, and he wore a larger size. It was moving around all over the place, rubbing my chin. But, I didn't even own a winter jacket, so I couldn't complain.

And this was kind of fun. Totally new experience and exactly what I wanted. What I needed.

The rear passenger door opened and Victoria leaned in. "I think it's back here…"

"We're going to go shopping tomorrow. I need a whole new wardrobe."

"I can't believe you've only ever seen snow, like, three times before this."

"And I've *never* gone to a party *on* a lake." I shook my head, then looked out my window. "We're seriously going *out* on the lake. As in...out there where we could crack through and freeze to death?"

She giggled as she dug around in the backseat pockets. "You're such a California boy."

She wasn't wrong.

"Aha!" She held up a black knit hat, then tossed it to me. "Put that on."

I shoved it down over my mop of hair as she hurried back around and hopped into the car again. She cranked up the heat and let out a shiver. "Damn it's cold out there."

It was pitch-black outside, except a faint glow of lights a ways up from us. Music thumped through the air and from here, the stars in the sky flickered brighter than I'd ever seen.

"Is a little chill in the air going to scare Corey Chaos out of our first non-contract contractual event?" She puckered out her bottom lip, teasing me.

"Hardly." I pulled on the thick mittens Jethro had given me. Actually, now that I thought about it, people might not even recognize me beneath all this cover. That might be nice for once. Not that I was recognized *everywhere* I went all the time, but it happened a lot.

Victoria pulled out her phone. "It's Mia."

"The best friend, right?" I asked. "I remember her picture on your Insta feed."

She sat up straight and nailed me with a wide-eyed look. "My Insta?"

"Oh, yeah. Um…" Heat crawled up my neck. She didn't need to know I'd watched her account and stuff since I'd first met her. "Just…checked it out. You know. To see what you're into."

"For the non-contract. Good idea." She held up her phone. "Mia's meeting us near the Kettle Corn stand."

I blew out a breath, relieved by the change of topic. "I love that stuff, but I haven't had any in forever. I'mma eat a five pound bag."

She flashed a smile then drew in a deep breath. "Okay, Chaos. Ready to face the music?"

"Pun intended?"

"Totally." She pushed open her door.

"Then yes. I'm ready to whip a snowball right at Todd's face." I hopped out of the car and an arctic blast slapped me across the face. I had a scarf around my neck, a huge, thick jacket on, and a warm hat pulled down over my ears, but still, the icy air sliced through me.

"How do you live in this?" I slammed the door shut and took a step. My foot slipped right out from beneath me and I landed on my ass.

Graceful, Chaos, graceful.

"Corey!" Victoria rushed over to me, panting, her breath creating little puffs of mist. She offered me her hand and helped me up. "Are you okay?"

"Yeah." I brushed the snow off my butt and a dull ache bloomed to life in my right cheek. Maybe this wasn't such a good idea. I had no clue how to behave in ice and snow.

Victoria snorted through the mitten over her mouth.

"Sure. Laugh at the L.A. beach bum." It was kind of funny, though, even if I was going to have a bruise on my ass tomorrow.

We made our way through the parking lot, and once we broke through the last row of cars, all I saw was people. Beyond the crowd was a huge stage with lights flashing every color of the rainbow.

"Cool, huh?"

I glanced at her and she was watching me, a smile filling her face as we walked onto the lake.

"Very." I still couldn't believe we were walking on a frozen lake toward a festival.

On a freaking lake!

Victoria smiled. "Twin River is pretty nice. It's like a medium-sized city, well, compared to L.A., but it has small town feels. That's one of the main reasons why I like it here so much."

I nodded, but had trouble paying attention to what she was saying. I looked down at my feet. "You sure this ice is thick enough?" I asked.

"We're good. There's an official ice depth checker for the Ice Festival."

"And they're sure it's safe?"

"Sure. Otherwise, there'd be headlines like, 'Entire town turns into human Popsicles after plunging through the icy waters during the Ice Festival.'"

"Victoria!" someone shouted. A girl hustled toward us from beside a little rolling cart stand. She had a nose ring and long, blond hair spilled out from beneath her black beanie. "Is this him?" she whispered, but it wasn't too quiet, and she didn't sound too impressed.

"Shhh!" Victoria tugged her close. "Corey, this is Mia. My best friend. Mia, this is Corey."

"Hey." I smiled at her, and instead of smiling back, her eyes narrowed. What the hell was that all about?

A high-pitched screech tore through the air, a sound I knew too well. Feedback from speakers. Everyone groaned.

"Hello? Is this thing on?" A man's voice tumbled over me like a freight train. Damn that was loud.

Mia gave me one last look, then sidled up next to Victoria. A wave of anxiety flushed through me at her scrutiny. I wasn't used to such a cold response when people met me.

"Let's kick off the ninety-fifth Twin River Ice Festival!" A stream of fireworks shot up into the air, blasting blue and white lights. The crowd oohed and aahed as if it were totally normal to be standing on frozen water in the middle of winter, watching fireworks.

"Hey, Victoria," a guy said, coming up beside me. "Mia, what's up?"

"Hey!" She grinned.

The guy looked down at me, then smiled. "Hey. I'm Tony."

"What's up?" I knuckle-bumped him with my mittened fist.

"Wait a second..." Tony leaned forward.

"Hey, Tony," Victoria said, stepping closer to me. "Um...this is Corey. Corey, this is Tony Mathison."

"But everyone calls him Hops," Mia said.

"Corey as in...Corey Chaos?" Tony's big blue eyes widened.

"Keep it low-key, Hops," Victoria said. "Okay?"

"Whoa. Wait a second. I—"

A series of wicked-loud fireworks blasted through the night air, thankfully interrupting Tony. I kind of wanted to stay hidden a little longer. Once everyone found out who I was, trying to be a normal teenager would get a whole lot harder.

After the fireworks ended, everyone cheered and clapped.

"Come on." Victoria grabbed my hand and Mia's, then started pulling us back toward the shore. "Snowball fight time!"

Tony followed behind us. I might have seen him in some of Victoria's Instagram posts, but I couldn't be sure, because it was pretty dark out here and he was decked out in a massive stocking cap and jacket.

The speaker crackled and the same voice we'd heard before boomed out over the crowd. "Those of you who would like to participate in the annual snowball fight, please make your way to Twin River Park."

"A snowball fight? Like an official one? I thought you were joking." Sweet. I'd never been in a snowball fight before. I tugged on my hat as we approached a well-lit open space that, beneath all this snow, was probably an open field of some sort.

Her eyes flashed with excitement. "I would *never* joke about a snowball fight."

"How do we know what side we're on?" I asked.

"Everyone who lives in the upper part of the Y takes the south side of the field and everyone who lives outside the Y takes the north side," she explained.

"What Y? What are you talking about?"

As we got to our side of the field, Victoria drew a capital Y in the snow. "The Y is the river. See this area"—she pointed to the *V*-shaped space between the upper branches of the letter—"this is the Twin River High School district. Downtown is here," she said, pointing to the bottom point of the *V*.

"Oh, right."

"Ten, nine, eight," the speaker-voice called out.

"Get ready." Victoria crouched down and her hands hovered just above the snow.

Wow, she was really taking this seriously.

"Seven, six, five, four, three, two, one!" A whistle cut through the crisp, cool air.

Victoria, Mia, and a ton of other people who had joined us on the field furiously started balling up snow.

Before I could even bend over, someone to our left launched the first one into the air. It flew at least twenty feet high and landed square in the middle of the other side, hitting a tall guy with red curly hair smack dab in the chest.

He dramatically fell to the ground like he'd been shot or something. I couldn't help but crack up. Everyone in this town was getting into this, huh?

Suddenly, snowballs filled the air. One landed at my feet. Victoria screamed as she dove to the side, evading getting hit by one. Another ball was headed right toward me. I spun and ducked, grabbing a handful of snow. I tossed it and I didn't even care if I hit anyone. It was awesome whipping it into the air.

Talk about freedom.

And being hidden beneath all this winter garb, even more freeing.

Snowballs crashed down all around us. Laughter and screams of pure joy broke out from both sides.

I grabbed another clump of snow. After packing it into a ball, I launched it into the air and watched it arc before it plummeted down and landed on the head of a short girl wearing glasses.

For a second there, a flash of worry froze my lungs more than the cold air, but then the girl fell down laughing.

And then ice-cold powder slapped me right in the cheek. My face stung for a few seconds before it went numb. I spun around as I wiped the freezing snow from my face.

Victoria nudged me with her hip. Wait a second. "Did you throw that?"

She innocently batted her eyes.

"You're so getting it." I gathered more snow in my hands and she squealed.

"Wait. We're on the same team." She playfully shoved me. "You still glad you came to Twin River?"

"Totally! And you were right, this is pretty epic." I formed another snowball and threw it.

Several minutes later, the whistle blew for the second time and the sky cleared.

Everyone turned toward a man in a bright orange jacket. He tipped his head to the left and then to the right. Before pointing toward our side of the field.

Victoria and Mia let out excited shrieks and jumped into the air. Tony high-fived me and then threw another snowball at my chest.

"We won!" Victoria snatched my hand. "Hell yeah this is epic!"

I was actually thinking *she* was pretty epic...

"Now let's go find Todd and shove some snow down the front of his shirt."

Chapter Nine

Victoria

"Two minutes!" the emcee yelled into his microphone.

I rested my hands slightly above the foot-deep snow next to Corey. His cheeks were rosy and his brown eyes looked like acorns clinging to an oak tree in this bright sunlight. Last night, at the snowball fight, he'd gotten his first taste of the festival and it looked like he was enjoying it so far.

The snowman-making event was one of my favorites. Out here in the open fields behind the convention center was a sea of smooth, white snow. And it was perfect for packing.

Beside us were Tony and Mia and next to them, Landon and Hope.

McKenna and Jace were getting ready on the other side of me. Jace suddenly frowned, his dark eyebrows pulling together. I followed his line of sight and saw why.

Todd.

And a girl.

She was nearly as tall as Todd with long blond hair spilling out from a pink Twin River Prep stocking cap. Her sea green eyes zeroed in on me.

"Hey Victoria," Todd said as he strode by, holding the Prep girl's hand.

I gulped, suddenly breathless. I hadn't seen him at the festival event last night. At first I was disappointed. I'd wanted to show him that I'd already moved on, but at the same time I was glad, and this was why. He'd rendered me speechless. Unable to form even a simple response. I looked ridiculous!

Every memory of us together flashed before my eyes on fast-forward. The kisses. The flirting. The fun.

And it stung.

"You must be Todd," Corey said, sliding up beside me.

Todd put his arm around his new girlfriend and pulled her close. "Yeah. Who the hell are you?"

Todd's girlfriend elbowed him. "That's Corey Chaos."

I did my best not to laugh.

"I just go by Corey." He held out his first to bump knuckles, but Todd raised his chin and let out a sarcastic huff.

"It's super nice to meet you," Todd's girlfriend said.

The annoyance on my ex's face was worth its weight in gold.

"Yo, Todd!" Matthew play-tackled him. They stumbled down a few spaces and camped out to do their snowman.

I let out a long exhale.

"You good?" Corey asked.

"At first, that sucked as hard as I thought it would, but

you totally saved the day."

"I got your back." Corey handed me a snowball. "Here. Have at it. His head is big enough to see from the space station."

The weight and size was perfect for pelting someone in the head with...but, I wasn't going to stoop to his level.

"Ooh! Nice, Chaos!" Jace grabbed the snowball and chucked it at Todd.

It burst into white powder as it pelted Todd in the middle of his back.

My ex whipped around, but Jace had already play-tackled McKenna into the snow and laid a kiss on her.

Corey and I both burst out laughing, which earned us a glare from Todd and his new girlfriend.

"All right snow architects. It's time to display your skills! The snowman building contest will begin in ten, nine, eight, seven, six, five, four, three, two, one, and *go*!" the emcee yelled into a megaphone.

Corey jumped into making the snowman's head. He balled up snow, but it was anything but round. "How the hell do you do this?"

I started digging around the snow, packing it together. "Follow my lead!"

He piled snow on top of the mound I'd started. Then we packed it down and rolled it into a ball.

"Come on, Chaos. Focus!" I yelled at him. "I wanna win."

"I didn't think there were prizes." He glanced at me, then went back to focusing on his work, tongue sticking out. He almost looked as if he was working some kind of mathematical equation for how intense he was.

"There's always one for the snowman-building event. Annie from Annie's Coffee Shop usually hands out a gift card to the team who makes her favorite snowman."

"Coffee? *I'm in.*" He started packing the snow even faster.

"Screw that. I'm winning Annie's coffee card this year!" Tony yelled from beside us. He and Mia were nearly done rolling the base of their snowman.

Something thudded against my shoulder. A splat of snow slid off my jacket. Corey pointed at me.

"You did not just throw a snowball at me," I said.

"Kinda did." He dove to the side and started packing more snow on the base of our snowman.

"Help me." I dug under the mound. "Let's push it a couple times to build it up."

He flopped next to me and followed my lead. Two revolutions later, the base was quite a bit bigger. "Okay, do that again, then start another ball, and I will, too. Yours will be the middle one."

"Ma'am, yes ma'am." He gave a fake salute and winked at me.

"Hey, I'm the snow pro here, you're just a thin-skinned boy from California who can't handle the cold."

"Ohhh!" Tony pointed at Corey. "She's calling you out, man!"

A couple people came up to our area and stood off to the side, watching. I didn't know them, but I figured they might recognize my snowman-making partner in crime.

I'd kind of expected a lot of double takes and people recognizing Corey at last night's event, but nobody did. Well, other than Tony, but he kept it quiet. It was probably because Corey was so bundled up and it was super dark last night that no one recognized him. But today, it was bright outside and not as cold, so Corey wasn't hidden behind as many layers of winter wear.

He'd mentioned media swarms didn't always happen. He wasn't *that* kind of famous. It was mostly teenagers who'd recognize him. And it would take a day or two before the paparazzi found out. Corey said unless it was a specific event his publicity team had planned out and hyped up, the chances of them flying out to Twin River were low.

Dad and Corey's publicist said they'd play up any questions or inquiries as a vacation, time off. No appearances or anything scheduled for a month or so.

He worked on the midsection, eyes focused and a smile filling his face. His floppy hair swayed in the frigid wind tearing through the open field, but he didn't seem to mind. Last night when he'd wiped out on the ice, I thought for sure he'd bail on this arctic land living.

My first winter here was pretty rough. I wore my big black puffy coat until the end of April. On the same day, Mia showed up in a T-shirt and I was wearing my coat plus three layers underneath.

A smile crossed my face as I crawled over the snow, rolling my snowball to make it a little bigger. Corey was coming toward me on his final run of packing his.

"Mine's bigger than yours," he sang out.

"That's what *she* said," Xavier yelled from beside us.

Landon laughed. Hope chucked a handful of snow at her boyfriend, then tackled him into the snow. He hugged her close and kissed her smack on the mouth.

A pang of jealousy shifted through me at the sight. Todd

and I had flirted and played around like that last year. He'd chased the cold away from me better than the steaming hot cocoa.

"Victoria?" Corey asked, pausing at the base of our snowman. "You good?"

"Oh. Yeah. Yes." We met back at our base with our snowman body parts. "Nice! Let's get these on here."

He kneeled down and dug his hands beneath the huge snowball and pushed it onto the base. I guided it and then we did the same with mine, lifting it together.

"Holy shit. That *is* a snowman." Corey pulled out his phone.

"First time building one?" Tony came up beside him.

"Hell yeah, it's pretty awesome!" Corey said, looking up at the six-foot-four basketball star.

Tony shoved Corey like they were old friends or something and rejoined Mia beside their half-finished snowman.

"Okay, I like that guy." Corey came in beside me, helping me pack snow between the head and torso so they stayed affixed.

"Tony's a good guy. He wears his heart on his sleeve."

We continued to mold the snowman. My hands were getting chilly even with thick gloves on. Corey was probably freezing!

"I take it that she's the resident brainiac?" Corey said, then glanced over his shoulder in Hope's direction. "I'm pretty sure I just heard her say that identical snowflakes are possible and that someone found two matching snowflakes here in Wisconsin like thirty years ago…"

I laughed out loud. "Yeah, that's Hope and her boyfriend

Landon. She's wicked smart. Landon is a good guy, too. He's really into soccer."

"Got it. Tony, Landon, Hope. I'll get these names down eventually."

I grinned. "You've only been here for two days. You're doing great!"

Corey shivered.

"Cold?" I smashed a handful of snow against his cheek. "I need to toughen you up, Beach Bum."

"I can't believe you just did that." He wiped it off his face, but at least he was smiling. He was a good sport. Laid back. Calm. Easy to be around. Todd probably would have gotten annoyed if I'd done that to him.

"You got me earlier," I said, shaking Todd out of my memory.

"Not in the face, though." He held up a handful of snow, like he was going to smash it against me.

"No!" I grabbed his wrist. He wrenched away, but fell to the side and, since I was hanging on to him, I went down, too. I rolled away, laughing, and shoveled some snow at him.

"It went down my jacket!" he yelled as he hopped to his feet and charged me.

I bolted around our snowman and screamed. His arm snaked around my waist and we spun. The soft snow broke our fall as we both landed on our sides. My cheeks ached from smiling so hard and laughing.

Man it felt good to laugh.

"Oops." I rolled onto my back, sucking in the cold air. My cheeks felt so hot that I was sure snow would instantly turn to steam if it touched my skin.

Corey stood before me, hand out for me to take as he

stifled a laugh. "Quit messing around. We have a snowman to finish."

"Yeah, yeah."

To think, only four days ago, I'd been humiliated by Todd in front of the entire lunchroom at school, and now...I was laughing and goofing around with Corey Chaos.

I was happy and actually having fun.

Corey started packing snow, a smile still on his face. Maybe this was as good for him as it was for me. We were both sad, overwhelmed with our lives, but in this moment... not so much. He was easy to be around. Didn't say a lot, but watched everything, taking it all in.

Then again, this was all new for him. The snow, the cold, the small town, well, small compared to L.A.

"So what's after this?" Corey asked.

"Mexican food, totally delicious, followed by a trip to the Vanilla Ice Cream Parlour with the fam."

He quirked an eyebrow at me. "Vanilla Ice," he paused, "Cream Parlour."

"Yup, it's iconic, not only for its name, but the ice cream is a taste sensation."

"That's awesome." Corey laughed.

"So, yeah, Dad, Mom, me, and you, if you want. I mean, you don't have to come. It's just...well, there aren't any Ice Festival events tonight and, going to El Ranchos every Sunday night, followed up by ice cream, is kind of a family tradition."

"Count me in. I'm down for some Mexican food. Not sure about the whole ice cream thing in January, though."

"It's really authentic. The owners are from Xalapa. They've got a daughter who goes to our school. She's a sophomore, I think her name is Julissa. And yes, you're getting ice cream."

"Sounds awesome. There's this little food truck near me, back in Cali, and they serve the *best* horchata you've ever had. I get it at least three times a week."

"Is it called Elana's Elotes?" I asked. "My best friend Nomie and I always went there. I love their breakfast tacos."

"No. Mine's called The Tamale Truck. Best. Ever!" He winked, sending a shiver down my spine. And no, it wasn't from the cold.

It was from him, my *fake* boyfriend.

Chapter Ten

Corey

"So does this count as one of our seven dates?" I jabbed Victoria with my elbow as we followed her parents into the Vanilla Ice Cream Parlour.

"Hardly." She rolled her eyes. "It's not an Ice Festival event, silly."

She had a hint of playfulness in her eyes sometimes, one that looked like she purposely suppressed it. Being so organized with the contract was fine, but the way she plopped onto the arm of the couch and snatched up my guitar while we were talking about it…it looked good on her. When I'd looked at her, holding it, for just a second, she froze, her eyes laser focused on me as if she'd done something wrong. It was adorable. Like her little eye roll now.

And then, earlier today, at the snowman making event, her eyes lit up with energy and excitement, even after that asshat, Todd, had tried to douse it.

I held the door for her. I scanned the dark street behind me. Sure wasn't a lot of lighting around here. In Los Angeles, it never seemed like night, since there were so many lights and people always wandering around.

Right now, I counted about ten people on both sides of the road. The stores were dark across the way and the two that flanked the Vanilla Ice Cream Parlour were dark, too.

"Does this town always close down at eight thirty on a Sunday night?" I let the door shut behind me and I pulled my cap down more to shadow my face. A few people had given me strange looks at the snowman making event today, but no one had outright called me out. It was weird. I was sure it wouldn't last much longer, but I'd take the time I got. Plus, hanging out with Victoria and her parents was like the first normal thing I'd done in years, and it was really fun.

Kids our age normally didn't like their parents, but Victoria seemed to enjoy hanging around hers. They were cool and actually seemed to like each other. I didn't mind either. Back when my dad was alive, my mom, he, and I would hang out and do fun things on the weekends all the time. Then again, that was before I was a teenager.

Wonder what we'd all be like now if he were still alive and my mom wasn't lost in her own private world of overworking, grief, and the multitude of boyfriends.

My stomach lurched at the images of Dad suddenly bombarding my mind. What would he think of all this? Of my covers? Of me being here, hanging with Victoria?

What would he think of *her*?

The door dinged as it shut behind us. The scent of sugar and chocolate chip cookies baking in the oven swirled around me and I drew it in. Reminded me of Mom, back when she used to bake for Dad and me.

Ice cream would be perfect after that wicked-hot Mexican food we'd just eaten.

A few people looked up and in our direction, but no one seemed to react. Then again, most of the people sitting down looked like they were in their fifties or older.

I turned my attention back to the counter. Victoria had challenged me to shoving all the bubblegum pieces of this place's famous bubblegum ice cream into my mouth, so I ordered a triple scoop.

She was so cute. Her dark blond hair was natural, unlike most of the girls in L.A. Her brown eyes were pretty, too. Not a super deep brown, but more subtle with flecks of amber mixed in there. Along with that smile. It was like she was hiding a secret or something the way the corner of her mouth would tilt up into a half smile. She really was beautiful. Not like the fake-boobed, collagen-lipped girls I'd been hanging around lately. Well, more *they* were hanging around me. And it wasn't like I was against people getting plastic surgery done or whatever, but when it was paired with a fake personality, it was a major turn off.

The ever-present hundred-pound weight on my shoulders lessened a little as I settled into the stress-free calm of the moment. Hanging out, getting some ice cream… normalcy.

"When we lived in L.A., I felt like it was daytime all day because of the lights," Victoria said.

"I was just thinking that!" I stepped up to the counter beside her dad. "So, Jethro, you've been back here in BFN for a couple of years now, right?"

"You did *not* just call Twin River bum fricking nowhere!" Victoria playfully punched my arm.

I leaned over and whispered into her ear, "Be nice or I'll break our contract."

Her eyes went wide.

"I'm kidding. I'm kidding," I whispered before turning back to her dad. "You glad you moved?"

"Best move ever," he said. "And yes, it's been about two years now."

"I can't believe how fast it went by," Mrs. Knight said, leaning into Jethro.

It was cool seeing a married couple together and actually seeming to still like each other. Jethro was tall and lanky with thinning brown hair, but Victoria's mom was more of an older version of Victoria. Same dark blond hair and feisty brown eyes.

It was nice here. The town wasn't super small, yet small enough to not feel so big-city-like. There weren't any skyscrapers but, according to Victoria, there was a decent downtown, at least. And people here moved slower. Said hi to you. Held the door open for you. And apologized for everything. Victoria said it was a Midwestern thing to constantly say, "Sorry." Everyone was so damn polite. I'd found myself imagining, more than a few times since I'd landed, what it would have been like to grow up here.

A few minutes later, we got our ice cream treats and started walking out of the store.

"We're not sitting?" I asked Victoria. It was freezing out. Surely they didn't think we were going for a stroll.

Her gaze fell to the bench a few feet away. "It is pretty nice out." She licked her cone and took a step to the bench.

"Nice? Um...it's snowing and *freezing*." I hugged the oversized jacket of Jethro's I was wearing.

"Aw, is the Cali boy cold?" Victoria teased.

Jethro and his wife looked over their shoulder as they meandered down the sidewalk.

"If you've lived here long enough, you'll realize this *is* nice weather." Victoria grinned. "I mean, look how pretty it is." She lifted her free hand, palm up, and huge snowflakes gently landed.

I drew in a deep breath and slowly let it out as I looked around. There was something peaceful about the snow fluttering around us. Quiet and calm. Centering.

And she was right. It was pretty. Even more, *she* was pretty. A snowflake landed on her cheek and she brushed it away before it had a chance to melt. "See, it's not so cold when you realize how beautiful it is."

I nodded and licked my cone. The snow wasn't the only beautiful thing around here... But ice cream? In the cold? It seemed so ironic that we were walking out in the snow, eating frozen food. I kind of pictured us maybe carrying hot cocoa or something instead.

Then again, what'd I know?

"Remember to save the gumballs."

Her mom and dad walked ahead of us, holding hands and chatting. I tugged at Victoria's elbow to hold her back a few steps.

"What's up?" she asked.

"Nothing. So. Um...you're an only child?"

"I am. They tried. Guess I wasn't supposed to have a brother or sister. You have siblings?"

"I figured you'd know if I did or not."

"Well, we *did* decide to trash the questionnaire..." She beamed up at me.

Yep. She sure would fit nicely beside me if I draped my arm around her right now. It was a surprising thought, but one that didn't suck. I'd be proud to have her by my side. She was sweet, cute, and funny.

But it broke one of our rules. No PDAs near the rents. Everything about this fake dating thing happened so quickly, and we'd jumped right into Ice Festival events, we hadn't had much time to actually talk yet.

"A questionnaire like that kinda takes the fun out of our dates, though, right? I mean, what are we gonna talk about if you know everything about me from reading that? Then again, most everything is out there on the web..."

"Yeah. Pretty much. But I'll get the deeper scoop, right?"

My hackles went up at the mention of deeper scoop as if she was doing this just to get the dirt on me and then use it. She wouldn't do that, would she? I mean, she was my agent's daughter.

Crap. And now there was a contract out there? Sure, I hadn't signed it but still. What if Victoria published that? Or if her dad found it. It could be used against me.

That was all I needed was someone all up in my—

"You okay?" Victoria asked.

I hadn't realized that I'd stopped walking and my cone was dripping over my gloves.

"You look kinda sick. It's okay if you don't want to save the gumballs. I thought it'd be fun. I—"

"No." I shook my head and then licked the dribbles off my gloves.

She stepped toward me, her big eyes wide with concern. "For real, do you have jet lag or something?"

"It's only two hours difference. To me it's like six p.m., so no, it's all good."

"Was the food at El Ranchos too spicy for you?"

"Dude. It's so not that." I walked by her. "Hurry up, waiting on you now."

She hustled after me. Jethro peered over his shoulder at me and I raised my cone in cheers. I'd lucked out finding him as an agent. He always had my back. A lot of people in my position would have ditched their agents if they moved out of L.A., but not me. Jethro was the real deal and he flew out to L.A. at least once a month, if not more. He was at all of my big gigs and kept me busier than I thought was humanly possible.

Victoria caught up to me and tugged on my elbow. "You got all weird about something I said, didn't you?"

"I did *not* get weird."

"You so did." She took a bite of her ice cream.

"You're supposed to lick the ice cream. What are you, a cannibal?" I slid my tongue over mine slowly and purposefully so she got the hint. Her eyes went wide and then her cheeks turned red. "At the rate you're chowing down that ice cream, it's not going to melt into the cone and make it all soft."

"You're weird." She mimicked licking her cone as I just demonstrated.

Holy tongue action. The sight of her doing that triggered a flash of heat storming down my spine. Images of me kissing her, right here, right now, blindsided me and my chest tightened.

Where the hell had that come from?

"What?" she asked.

"Nothing. Um. Are there any other Knight family traditions I should know about?"

"Breakfast for dinner every Friday night, El Ranchos and Vanilla Ice Cream Parlour on Sunday nights, and we usually have homemade pizzas at least once a week, too."

I gently elbowed her side. "That's cool." I shivered again as the heat of my thoughts of kissing her simmered down. "Oh, and I need to *for sure* hit a store tomorrow after school to get some cold weather gear that fits a little bit better than your dad's stuff. You in?"

"Sure! You do look kind of ridiculous in that old jacket."

"Hey, I make this coat look hot." I brushed my hand down the front of it. "I own this thing."

"Sure you do." She laughed.

Damn, I could get used to hearing that laugh.

We were approaching a corner and the street light turned red. Her parents were already on the other side, so they stopped and waited for us. I pressed the walk button and turned to face her.

"It's cool, you know, the whole family dinner and ice cream thing. You're lucky."

She looked up at me with big eyes. She must have been about five-foot-four if I was measuring against my five-foot-ten height. She was wearing a thick jacket, stocking cap, and massive mittens. I caught a scent of her lilac perfume above the sugary cone she was munching on. It was a nice combination. Sweet, with a hint of sexy.

"You sure you're okay?" Victoria asked.

"Yeah. But I had a thought." I drew in a quick breath,

hoping to calm my heart down. "Where's that printed copy of that non-contract?"

She smiled. "In the pool house, I think. Why?"

"Got a shredder?" I peeped at her to gauge her response. Her eyebrows drew together as she licked her cone, almost as if she were trying to decipher what I was asking.

"Oh...yeah. PR nightmare." She slouched. "We should shred the unsigned non-contract and questionnaire."

"It's not that I don't trust you, but my publicist would kill me if that got out, you know?"

"Totally get it."

"Besides. We don't need them. I told you I'm in on our agreement and I'm having fun at family night with the Knights, getting to know you. *Without* a questionnaire."

"Like it matters. Wisconsin-me is utterly boring."

"No you're not."

What did she mean by *Wisconsin-me*? I'd known her in L.A., seen her on Instagram, and there wasn't much drama in her life until recently.

"Compared to the girls you—"

"Stop right there. I'm adding a rule to this here fake relationship. No comparisons."

She smiled up at me, her face beaming beneath the dim lights lining the sidewalk we were strolling down.

I nudged her with my elbow as I bit into my ice cream cone.

"Hey, you said no biting the ice cream."

"Well, there were some gumballs, I had to." I shifted the two gumballs into my cheek. "How am I supposed to not chew these things? I'm gonna look like a chipmunk soon."

"You're such a goof!" Her dad looked over his shoulder

and she yelled up to him, "I don't think he's ever gone out for gumball ice cream before!"

I reached out and tickled her waist and her giggle ricocheted off the surrounding buildings. It sounded like music. Legit laughter. Nothing fake about it. Relaxed, honest fun. I'd almost forgotten what that was like.

I pulled out my phone and leaned in next to her. "Smile!"

As I tapped the camera button she shoved her finger into my cheek. The picture captured the most ridiculous face I'd ever made.

Ridiculously *happy* face.

"Come on." I nudged her and she leaned in.

I tapped the camera again and it turned out perfectly.

"You're not gonna post that, are you?" she asked.

"Maybe. If you're okay with that?" I asked.

Victoria met my gaze. "I don't mind, but this will definitely let everyone know that you're here. Are you okay with that?"

"I think some people saw me at this weekend's events, so...it'll be fine. Plus, it was going to come out at some point that I'm here... But I might keep this one just for me." I slid my phone into my back pocket. I didn't want to think of security or anything else. Just wanted to be here and in the moment with Victoria and her family. I could practically hear Ranger Rodrigo telling me to hurry up and that I had only five minutes until the next photo shoot. "So, what'd you have in mind for the next date in our fake relationship?"

"Ah, one sec. Our car's parked up there." She glanced around, then looked up ahead where her folks were. "Hey, Dad. We're gonna sit here a second, k?"

"Sounds good." Jethro brushed the snow off a bench

up ahead, then he and his wife sat down. They didn't look to be in any kind of rush. That wasn't something I got to experience much lately. It seemed like I was always hurrying around from one event to another. I kind of like this kicked-back lifestyle.

Victoria steered us off the sidewalk a few feet to a bench. It overlooked a dark area that might have been a park. It was dim enough that I couldn't see it very well.

"What's up?" I asked.

"Date. You know...like when and stuff. Mom and Dad are a ways ahead of us, but I don't want them to accidentally overhear."

I leaned in as I bit into my cone. "So, how am I supposed to eat the cone without it getting all mixed up with my gumballs?"

"You spit them into a napkin until you're ready." She held hers up.

"You're a sneak. I didn't even notice you were doing that! And that's gross. I'm chewing them now." I chomped into a few of them and bursts of cherry and blueberry and grape exploded in my mouth. "Oh man. That's good."

"Told you so." She chuckled. "Okay. Focus. How 'bout tomorrow? First day back at school after the world's most embarrassing breakup. You could...I don't know, pick me up from school?"

I nodded.

"That'd be great." She chewed on a gumball. "That rental Jeep Dad got you looks awesome. I so want a ride in it."

"I can do one better." I leaned closer to her.

She pulled in a sharp breath and then she held it. "What?

What are you doing?"

"Relax. Just whispering." I winked at her.

She sat still, her eyes wide, but her focus shifted slightly. Might have been to my lips, I couldn't be sure, but it was hot. She might not have realized it, but she licked her lips right then and there.

Wow.

Focus.

"Um…tomorrow," I said and I swear my voice cracked.

"You're going to pick me up?" Her voice was quiet, a little raspy, and some of her hair fluttered in her face from the breeze, but she didn't move to fix it. "Um…from school?"

"How 'bout this." I brushed my napkin along the ice cream melting over her mittens. "I'll drive you to school *and* home."

"To school? I figured you'd be sleeping in. You're on vacation."

I grinned, then blew a bubble with my ice cream gum. "Oh. I didn't tell you? I'm going to Twin River High, too."

Chapter Eleven

Victoria

"I still can't believe you *want* to go to high school." I shook my head as I pulled out my strawberry lip gloss from my purse. "I kinda wish I could snap my fingers and make time fast-forward through high school right now."

Corey steered the Jeep into a spot near the last row in the junior parking section. "Well, I'm not going full-time. But study sessions and catching up on everything I owe my tutor will take up more than most of my day."

"Right. My friend Nomie, who's back in L.A., has a private tutor now. She said it's rough, but it's the only way she can audition and actually get parts." I put on a fresh coat of lip gloss and smacked my lips together. "Todd is going to have an absolute meltdown when he sees us walking into school together."

As soon as I said the words, I felt less sure about

everything. What if Todd, or anyone for that matter, saw through my fake relationship with Corey? I'd be an even bigger laughingstock than the moment the #LunchDump video went viral.

"Everything okay?" Corey reached over and squeezed my hand.

The simple touch of his hand on mine chased away the doubt.

"Yeah. I think everything is going to be fine, now that you're here." I gave him a small smile and thought about the look on Todd's face as he saw me and Corey walking down the hall together.

"Before we head in, let's review," Corey said.

I sat back in the leather seat. "Go."

"Gretchen Mead, tall blonde, totally bleached hair but says it's not, and I need to steer clear of her."

"She always has perfect makeup, no matter what, and she's always got something nasty to say about somebody else, usually behind their back. You can't miss her."

"Tony, the basketball player everyone calls Hops. He's cool. I remember him from the snowman building contest. Then, there's Hope and Landon. Hope's super smart and Landon plays soccer."

"Perfect." I gave him a nod of approval.

"And then there's McKenna, but I can't remember her last name."

"Storm." I was seriously impressed at how much he'd remembered so far. "Dating Jace."

"The writer! Got it." He shook his head as he turned off the car. "I remember a few more names... Trinity and Ernie. We didn't meet them, but they got third place in the snowman building contest on Saturday, right?"

"Yup, after our impressive, but underrated, second-place finish." Tony and Mia had totally annihilated the competition with their snowman.

"It *was* awesome," Corey said.

"You know, you're good at remembering so many people."

He shrugged, then reached for his phone from the cup holder between our seats. This Jeep was pretty decked out. Rollbar and everything. But what I liked the most was the woodsy scent that somehow carried a hint of mango to it.

"Mia is your best friend. We met her that first night but got the chill factor big-time."

"Yeah, I texted her asking how she was doing to see if she was okay. She's not normally like that."

"Best friends…just being protective, right?" He winked at me. "She was the first person you talked to when you moved to Twin River and you two have been friends ever since."

"Yeah." I slouched in my seat. "I told her we'd met up in Annie's Coffee Shop and that's how we ended up going to the Ice Festival that first night. Wasn't sure I should say much else."

"Good call. It'll be fine. That will be an easy story to keep straight and that way no one will know that your dad is my agent. Which isn't a big deal to me, but I know you don't want to get hounded."

"Yeah, thank you." The fewer people who knew my dad was his agent, the better. Even though it was highly unlikely, if someone like Gretchen really dug into my past, they might be able to connect my dad with Grayson, since he was one of

Dad's clients. She'd spread that kind of gossip around faster than I could say queen bee. No way. I especially didn't want Corey finding out. I didn't want him worrying that I'd mess up his career like I did Grayson's. I wasn't that girl anymore.

"Okay," he said. "That's enough review. Just say their names a lot when we're talking to them and I'll run with it."

"Sounds like a plan."

Corey pushed open his door. "Lead the way."

We got out of the Jeep and the chilly morning air bit at my cheeks. The clouds muted out the sun, giving everything the dreary Monday morning blahs. I didn't care, though. Todd was going to be so jealous.

Corey looked over at me and smiled, then gently put his arm around me for a brief second in a reassuring hug. The grin on his face told me that he was at ease, but my heart was beating a million times a minute.

He could do that with one look. I wondered if he knew of his superpower. Because he needed to rein that thing in a little or the whole junior class was going to melt when they saw him walk through the halls of Twin River High.

As we approached the main doors to the school a blond girl with purple highlights let out a loud shriek. "Oh my gosh!"

Her friend craned her neck, trying to get a better look at Corey and me. "Is that who I think it is?"

Kyle Walker pointed at us. "Dude! That's Corey Chaos! Wait, what's he doing with Victoria?"

What is he doing with me?

Fake dating me, that's what!

I leaned into Corey and said, "That's Kyle Walker, football star. Complete asshole."

"Yeah, he's an ass for that comment about what I'm doing with you," Corey said as he tossed a glare in Kyle's direction. "Didn't see him at the festivities this weekend."

"He thinks he's way too cool for the Ice Festival. He and Todd sometimes hang out in the same circle. Matthew Halliday, too."

By the time Corey went home today, no one would even remember that Todd dumped me in front of everyone.

Kyle and Matthew would forget, too. It might take a while, per the disbelief that dripped off Kyle's voice when he said my name. Like it was so hard to believe Corey was here with me? Okay, I could hardly believe it, so I had to give him a break, but still. That hurt a little.

People stared in awe or shock—I couldn't be sure which—as we made our way into the building. They literally stopped what they were doing and went wide-eyed. It was almost like we were walking through a wax museum. No one moved.

Surely people had seen the photos people posted when they saw him at the Ice Festival events this past weekend. Then again, they probably hadn't suspected he'd attend classes here.

Even I was surprised when he told me last night.

We stopped in front of the main office. Corey held the door open for me again.

"Why, thank you." So far, everything was going perfectly. I was actually surprised nobody rushed him. Dad had worked on that marketing and security side of things pretty well, it seemed.

"Hi, Mrs. Rupert. This is Corey. He's supposed to check in this morning."

The portly woman behind the desk shuffled through a stack of paperwork. "Corey, last name?"

"Chaos," Corey responded.

"What an unusual name," she said with a smile. "I like it."

"Thank you, ma'am," he said, flashing her one of his million-dollar smiles.

I remember the first time I saw that smile when I'd caught his video upload on Instagram. I'd shown it to Dad, and he was all over that, especially when Adam Keefe from the Beastie Boys commented on how great Corey's cover of "Sabotage" was.

She got up from behind her desk and shuffled to the counter, paperwork in hand. "Here you are, dear. I see you'll be with us part time for about a month?"

"Yes ma'am." Corey accepted the paperwork.

"Well, we're glad to have you here. Welcome to Twin River High."

"Thank you," he said.

Mrs. Rupert smiled at me. "It looks like you already have someone to show you around."

"I do." Corey gave me a quick wink. It sent another flutter ricocheting through my stomach. I needed to get that under control. He was here for a month and this flirty-dating thing was fake.

Fake, Victoria!

"If you have any questions, please let me know." She smiled and pushed her floral print glasses back up her nose.

"Thank you." Corey flashed her one more smile before we exited the main office.

A small crowd of students had gathered in the hallway.

"Hey, Victoria!" Sophia and Bailey pushed through the crowd, eying me for a second, then focusing on Corey. "What's up?"

"Hey, guys," I said. "This is—"

"Corey Chaos," Sophia said. "We saw you at the snowman event yesterday. What are you doing here? I mean, it's cool you're here, but—"

"Corey, this is Bailey and Sophia," I said, trying not to crack up at their hyper-ness.

"And I'm Noah," Noah said, coming up behind Bailey and grabbing her sides to tickle her. "But everyone calls me Pitch."

"*Noah!*" Bailey shoved him. "Jeez, what'd you do, bathe in your grandpa's Old Spice this morning?"

Corey laughed beside me, then high-fived Noah. "Classic scent, bro."

"It is *not* Old Spice." He tossed a glare at Bailey and her cheeks reddened. Those two were always bantering back and forth. How they'd never hooked up was beyond me.

"Come on, Corey," I said.

As we made our way through the crowd, I heard someone whisper, "Todd dumped her on Wednesday, then Saturday she shows up with Corey Chaos at the festival and now…she comes to school in his car?"

"Todd's going to feel *so* stupid," someone else responded.

Perfect.

With a huge grin on my face, I headed to my locker.

"That went surprisingly well," Corey said.

"I'd say." I spun the combination dial on my locker to get it open and throw my bag inside.

"Hey, Corey." Gretchen Mead eased in beside him,

resting her hand on his shoulder. "I'm Gretchen and I loved your last cover."

"Thanks." He stood straight and his jaw tensed.

"I never thought you'd be the special guest coming to Twin River." Gretchen giggled.

"Huh?" I asked.

"Principal Navarro sent out a text to everyone this morning. He said there was a special guest coming to Twin River High for the next month and that we needed to be on our best behavior. No mobbing him, begging for autographs, recording him without his permission, stuff like that. If people break the rules, no Ice Ball."

So that's why people were remaining somewhat calm.

I pulled out my phone from the side pocket of my bag, then shoved it into the locker. I tapped the screen, wondering why I hadn't gotten the text.

Sure enough, there it was. Must not have felt it vibrate.

Gretchen cast a look at me and her fake smile faltered for a second. "If you ever need someone interesting to interview..." She shifted her focus to Corey again. "I'm your girl."

And then she sauntered away, a little extra sway in her step.

What the hell?

"Dude," Corey said inching closer to me. "You weren't wrong about her."

I shook my head. "Watch out for her."

"Noted." He let out a huff then faced me.

"What class do you have first?" I asked.

"Homeroom with Mrs. Watson, room C25."

"Ah, my dad must have worked his magic. That's my

first class, too." I grabbed my chem book from the locker, then shut it. "After that independent study?"

"Yup! I should be able to get most of my school stuff from Rita done while I'm here. Maybe even get ahead." Corey leaned against the locker near mine. He stood so close to me, I caught a whiff of his woodsy cologne.

"Oh emmmm geeeeee," someone squealed from behind us. "Corey Chaos and Victoria Knight! Are you two like *together*?"

Corey turned around and winked at the sophomore who'd thrown the question at us. "Wouldn't you like to know?"

Chapter Twelve

Corey

"Can I walk you to lunch, Miss Knight?" I came in beside Victoria and leaned against the locker next to hers.

"Oh!" She jumped and whipped around.

"Sorry, didn't mean to scare you," I said, holding back a laugh.

I shouldn't have enjoyed that so much, but it was fun. I'd gotten through my assignments during independent study and felt like sticking around today. Our first day at school together as a fake couple.

Her long, dark blond hair had a hint of curl to it, cascading over her shoulders. She was sporting a long-sleeved, fitted navy sweater and jeans that hugged her curves perfectly.

"You're here?" she asked as she shut the locker door. "I thought you were heading home after your first two classes today."

"Decided to hang around and thought I'd go with you to lunch." I leaned in and whispered, "I know it's not on the non-contract, but it's okay, right?"

She shivered and her eyes shot wide. "Um...yeah. Perfect."

I actually wanted to see Victoria's ex, AKA The Ultimate Asshat, in the place that he'd so epically dumped Victoria. I'd seen him at the snowman making event yesterday but the interaction wasn't long enough for me to really see who I was dealing with.

Two girls waved as they walked by, then huddled in to each other as they continued on their way.

There'd been a lot of that so far today, but it wasn't as bad as I thought it would be. And I was totally okay with that. A wave of contentment washed over me like warm water. Reminded me of how I felt back when I was actually enrolled in regular high school. Hanging out at the lockers between classes, talking to girls, flirting...

"You sure you want cafeteria food?" Victoria said.

"As long as there's pizza, it's golden. Plus, I wouldn't want you facing The Ultimate Asshat in the cafeteria on your own today."

Victoria froze, her wide brown eyes fixed on me. A subtle blush darkened her fair skin and she bit at her bottom lip. "Thanks, Corey."

I grinned, happy to help, then nodded to her to start walking with me. The few hours I'd been here today, I was noticing that if I stayed still too long in one place, people tended to gather.

It hadn't been super weird, so far. Sure, people knew who I was, but not everyone. And other than a few of the younger freshmen, nobody really approached me. Mostly it was disbelief that it was actually me here at the high school. But, per the text from the principal, no one asked me for an autograph. It was nice!

A girl approached us, going against the tide of students heading to lunch. She had blond, shoulder-length hair, bright blue eyes, and a silver nose ring in her left nostril. She wore a V neck T-shirt and torn jeans.

"Oh, that's...Mia," I said, barely recognizing her without all the heavy winter gear on.

"We always eat together," Victoria said, leaning toward me. "Is that okay?"

"Count me in."

Once again, Mia scanned me from head to toe with narrowed eyes.

"Yikes, she's really anti-Chaos," I whispered to Victoria.

She giggled and elbowed my ribs, then hiked her bag up over her shoulder. "No. She's...well, maybe not believing this whole hanging out with me thing."

"Hey," Mia said as she joined our little group by walking beside Victoria.

The halls were filled with kids, some chatting, but most were staring. Guess it'd take a while to get used to me being around. It was like this at my other school when I'd first gotten discovered, before I'd started the virtual school thing.

Being back in school again was actually really nice. It reminded me of my music teacher, Miss Murphy. She had always encouraged my love of the guitar. I still missed her.

Signs hung on the walls, announcing the Ice Ball in just under two weeks, school clubs, and all that fun high school stuff. I'd overheard some students talking about the dance on my way to independent study and it sounded like the perfect thing to do with Victoria. I hadn't been to one in over two years.

"So...Corey," Mia said. "You're here? At Twin River?"

"Yeah, only half days, though. Homeroom and independent study."

"If you're only here for half the day, why are you at lunch?" Mia's sharp tone cut through the air.

"Mia." Victoria nudged her with her elbow.

"Is there a reason I shouldn't stay for lunch?" I followed them around the corner. "Is the food *that* bad?" I teased.

My phone buzzed in my back pocket and I pulled it out. More Instagram notifications and a text. I tapped that open and saw it was from Roberts. I cleared it and shoved the phone back in my pocket. No time to deal with publicity stuff. Right now, I was a normal high school student about to sit with his girl at lunch.

Er...sit with *Victoria* at lunch.

"This isn't the five-star dining you're probably used to. You sure you're going to be cool with it?" Mia asked with a smirk.

Victoria poked her friend in the shoulder. *"Rude."*

"As long as they have pizza and I can eat, like, six pieces, I'm good," I said. "I'm starving."

Mia bantered. "Typical boy. So...what's up with you two? Victoria hasn't told me crap other than she met you in Annie's."

Okay, that surprised me. Victoria really was serious about not telling anyone about our deal, including her BFF.

Time to get into my role, which wasn't hard.

"Just here, taking a break." I shrugged. "Relax a little."

"And you come to Wisconsin in January?" Her dark eyebrows scrunched. "And high school?"

"Please excuse my best friend's attitude." Victoria looked at Mia and frowned.

"I've only seen snow a handful of times, so what better place to come than Twin River, the town that, in 1805, had the worst ice and snow storm in the history of Wisconsin?"

Mia's jaw dropped and Victoria stutter-stepped to the side, watching me. We hadn't specifically discussed what I'd tell people other than it was a vacation time for me, so I had to have a little fun with it.

"You sound like a textbook," Mia said, but finally she was smiling.

"I'll take that as a compliment." I grinned.

Victoria burst out laughing and leaned in to me. Mia giggled, too, but straightened her face as quickly as she'd smiled. It was like she was forcing herself to be pissed at me.

"Seriously, though, I came because I needed a little break, and my agent thought I'd get a kick out of this town, so he set me up. But school doesn't go away. As much as I wished it would..."

"So where are you staying?"

"Nowhere special." I winked.

"Oh, can't tell...got it." Mia nodded. "Afraid the girls will tear down the front door to your hotel and accost you?"

"Yeah, well, it wouldn't be the first time." I rolled my eyes.

Mia squished up her face in response.

"Joking. Just joking."

Her face relaxed, but she didn't smile.

"So how'd you connect with my girl, then?" Mia asked.

"I mean, come on...seriously?"

We rounded the corner into a hallway filled with tons of students, marching forward slowly. Clanking silverware and loud voices filtered out from the propped-open doors.

This must be the cafeteria. The sounds and the smells felt familiar.

"The truth," Mia said.

I looked at Victoria and she grinned, then looked at Mia. "Annie's Coffee Shop. Like I told you. Come on, quit giving him a hard time."

"What, you don't believe her?" I asked. "I got a chai latte and she got a caramel macchiato."

"And you fell for her just like that?"

"Yup!" I threw my arm around Victoria.

We strolled through the open doors, into the chaos of the high school cafeteria. Scents of salt and sugar assaulted me and my mouth started watering as my stomach growled louder than a lion.

"So, what classes do you have this afternoon, Victoria?" I asked as we got into the hot food line.

"Calc test, sixth period."

"Ugh, I'm so not ready for that." Mia grabbed trays for us and I stepped in behind the girls. "Mr. Vermeer is the worst, throwing a test at us so early in the semester."

"Right?" Victoria said.

"Have you seen Todd yet today?" Mia asked as she reached for some pizza. "I haven't, but I bet he's up in arms about your latest snag."

"Snag?" Victoria said.

"Yeah. Corey. The festival, arriving in his decked-out Jeep this morning. Lunch. Doting on you and all," she said, glancing over her shoulder. "I mean, you're totally crushing on my girl here, aren't you?"

"Maybe," I said as I piled six slices of pizza onto my tray.

"I can't believe how much you eat!"

"Growing boy."

"Yo. Corey Chaos," someone shouted from behind me. "I can't believe it."

Tony, the six-foot-four giant, lumbered toward me. A broad smile filled his face. He had light brown hair, broad shoulders, and wore a T-shirt with Twin River High Basketball printed on it and jogging pants.

He offered me his knuckles to bump and I did. "Hops, your wingspan is massive!"

"You thaw out from making your first snowman?" He slapped me on my back.

"That'd be a no," I said. "I still can't feel my toes. How do you guys do it?"

"You grow up in it *and* you don't know any better." He laughed as he patted his chest. "Makes you tough, surfer dude."

"Hey now, be nice." I inched to the side, following Victoria toward the end of the food line.

"What are you doing *here*, man?" Tony asked as he butted in line and snagged a bunch of pizza. "Figured you'd get the golden ticket out of school."

"I wish," I said, following the girls. Evidently Tony was joining us for lunch, too. Which was fine by me. He was cool.

We found a table off to the side. It was round and sat six people, but it was only us four, so we spread out, except I picked the chair directly beside Victoria and pulled it close to her. I caught Mia looking at me, but this time her eyes weren't narrowed.

She was definitely the protective type of friend from the kind of looks she was throwing around. Worried I'd hurt Victoria, maybe.

That was cool. I'd had a good friend at my school, Jason, who was protective like Mia. We hadn't stayed in touch much after the Chaos thing took off, though.

"Hey, Victoria," someone said from behind me.

Mia's eyes practically launched grenades as she looked over my shoulder.

Victoria tensed beside me. "Todd," she whispered.

I turned around and there stood a spectacularly average-looking guy. Average height. Average eyes. Average size. *This* was the guy Victoria hung out with for almost two years? In the pictures she'd posted on Instagram, he looked like more of a specimen. But now? He seemed positively boring right down to the tan boat shoes he wore.

"So, you're the asshat who dumped Victoria in front of the entire lunchroom."

His jaw dropped.

I stood up and pulled out my phone, then leaned into him. "Smile."

I snapped a selfie with him before he even realized what'd happened based on how stupefied he looked.

Tony and Mia were laughing. A smile filled Victoria's face, but she seemed to be holding in her laughter as she hunched over her tray.

"Keep walking, buddy," I said as I sat back down next to Victoria and edged my chair even closer.

Without a word, he slouched away beneath heavy stares and snickers.

"Holy hell," Victoria said. "That was absolutely perfect."

I nudged her with my shoulder as I reached for some pizza. "I got your back."

Oh yeah. I was *so* going to enjoy my time at Twin River High. Especially making Victoria smile!

Chapter Thirteen

Victoria

"You look like a chipmunk." I broke out laughing as Corey squished up his nose and faced me with a mouthful of gumballs.

He started chewing. "Mmmmm hmmmm phhhh mmmm mmmmm."

Mia, Tony, Landon, Hope, Alice, and I all lost it to the point we were snorting. We all crammed into the booth at the Vanilla Ice Cream Parlour after skating at the pond event at the Ice Festival.

We'd had our fill of hot cocoa and Corey pleaded with the group to go out for gumball ice cream. Funny thing, he didn't even ask if this was one of our non-contract contractual dates. It looked like he was having fun, too, and that made me smile.

I was just glad Mia had softened up toward Corey a little

more. I hated not telling her everything, especially my past connection to Corey, but I had to keep it from her. I didn't want it getting out that Dad was his agent, because things would change for me here in Twin River if that happened.

Back in L.A., people used people for connections. My dad was a talent agent, so I'd been used for sure. I didn't want that to start happening here.

And I couldn't let it get out that Corey and I were in a *fake* relationship.

Corey slid his phone from his back pocket and started a live video on Instagram.

"Hmmm, mmmmm mmmm gggggghhh bhhhhhh." He turned his phone toward me.

"Oh, uh, hi." I gave an awkward wave, heat instantly flaming my cheeks. How the heck did he turn it on like that? He seemed so natural and confident in front of his bazillion fans. As I saw the number of people watching the live reach the low thousands within about ten seconds, I choked. My mind went blank. But he just kept it up.

Corey leaned over until he was in the frame and a gumball popped out of his mouth and landed on the table.

We all started laughing so hard, it echoed through the empty shop. Evidently nobody else wanted ice cream this late on a Thursday night. Hope swiped her hand beneath her eyes as she leaned in to Landon.

They looked so happy together and jealousy sliced through my stomach like a bunch of razors. I used to have a flirty, cuddly boyfriend. While I didn't miss Todd, I missed the having a boyfriend part. Corey was a nice substitution for the real thing, but we had only a month together, so I couldn't get too used to it.

"And that's how they do it here in Wisconsin." He pointed at the screen. "This place rocks, and I'm living it up with my new friends, Victoria, Mia, Landon, Hope, and Hops!"

He leaned toward them, keeping the camera close.

"This guy." He pointed at Tony. "He's like seventeen feet tall. Legit, I could practically limbo under his legs."

Tony slapped Corey on the shoulder, laughing. "Dude. We so need to try that!"

"Oh, it's on!" Corey stood up, pulling Tony with him. "It's so on...stay tuned!"

Ending the live, Corey turned toward us and gave us two big thumbs up.

My phone vibrated in my back pocket, so I pulled it out.

"Aw, it's my friend Nomie from L.A." I smiled.

NOMIE: Um.

NOMIE: Excuse me!

NOMIE: Why is Corey Chaos in Wisconsin?

NOMIE: And why are you hanging out with him?

ME: Long story.

ME: It's just temporary.

NOMIE: Did your dad bring him out?

ME: Yeah, but we are keeping that low-key!

NOMIE: My lips are sealed.

ME: Talk more later!

NOMIE: We better!

I locked the screen and slipped my phone back into my pocket.

"That was epic," Tony said. "Are we seriously going to try that limbo?"

"I don't know, maybe?" Corey high-fived him, then sat down again on the booth next to me. "We could set it up to raise some money for a charity or something cool."

"Definitely," Tony said. "Covenant House. Or maybe the Twin River Pantry?"

"Yes!" Mia said. "That would help us *crush* Twin River Prep."

"Yeah, they almost beat us last year." Tony shook his head. "Can't have that again this year."

"Food Pantry?" Corey asked, settling back in the booth beside me.

"It's part of the Ice Festival. One of the events is a fundraiser. All four high schools here in Twin River compete against one another to raise the most food for the pantry. The school that donates the highest number of items wins a trophy and bragging rights."

"Very cool."

"I still can't believe you're actually *choosing* to hang out in Twin River," Mia said. Her tone had a bit of a bite to it, but she had a small smile on her face. I knew she was just being protective, but I wish she'd let up a little.

"Trust me," Corey said. "It's amazing. Clean air. Lots of trees. Nice people. And bubblegum ice cream!"

"But L.A... I would give a kidney to have a place out there on the beach."

"It's great, don't get me wrong." Corey spit out the half-chewed gumballs into a napkin. "But it's so busy. I'm so busy. There's no way I could just go out and get ice cream with friends like this."

"I guess that makes sense." Mia pushed up and out of the booth. "I'll be right back."

She made her way toward the restrooms. I turned to Corey and said, "I better go check on her."

"Want me to come?" Hope and Alice asked at the same time, which caused them both to start laughing.

"It's okay. I'll be quick." I pointed to Corey and Tony as I shuffled out of the booth. "You guys keep these two outta trouble."

I pushed open the restroom door and stepped into a world of old-fashioned checkered tile floors and walls.

Mia stood, leaning against the white sinks, her arms crossed over her chest.

"You feeling okay?"

She let out a breath. "What's going on here, Victoria? You and Todd break up, then within two days you show up at the Ice Festival with Corey Chaos. You two have been glued at the hip since then. Legit, what's going on? How is this happening right now? What's seriously going on?"

She wasn't wrong. We'd been together constantly since he'd come here, but mostly we were working out the details of our fake relationship. We'd even planned our, "We are better off as friends than as a couple," statement along with multiple pictures that he would continue to share once he went back to L.A.

I hated that I couldn't let Mia in on our fake relationship details. Admittedly, I hadn't thought about the fact that

I had to keep such a big secret from her when Corey and I initially agreed to do this. I trusted her, but what if she accidentally let something slip? However, at the same time, she was almost as pissed off at Todd as I was. She'd understand.

"Seriously, you met at Annie's?" Mia asked. "And now you can't get enough of each other?"

"No. No. It's not like that." I let out a breath and stepped toward the sinks.

I checked my reflection in the mirror and fixed some loose strands of hair flopping around as I focused on my breathing. In and out. What should I tell her? What could I tell her? It was only fair... She was my best friend.

Facing her, I leaned against the sink and said, "I'm going to tell you something, but you have to promise not to tell anyone else. Okay?"

"Okay," she said slowly, turning to face me.

"I'm serious, Mia. Like, you cannot tell *anyone*."

She made a cross over her chest. "I promise."

I gulped before admitting, "My dad is Corey's agent."

Her eyes popped wide open and she slapped the counter with her hand. "What?"

"Yeah...I don't talk about it with anyone. My dad dropped all of his clients except Corey when we moved out here. Just...downsizing, you know?" *Little white lies won't hurt, right?* "And we agreed that we wouldn't tell anyone. That way we don't end up with people flocking to our house, trying to find out Corey's business."

Mia took a step back, resting her hand against the tiled wall. Her bottom jaw dropped, then she quickly shut her mouth. "I—I—I'm shocked."

"Yeah, well, like I said, it's not something we share with anyone. I guess I've just gotten used to it," I explained.

"So you lied to me. About the whole meeting him at Annie's thing." Her jaw ticked and she crossed her arms again.

"I know, Mia. I'm sorry. It's…please don't be mad. We can't let it get out."

"And this whole flirting and hanging out thing…" Mia leaned toward me, narrowing her eyes as she looked at me. "He's a total player who dates models and actresses." Her tone had softened, *slightly*. "He's with a different girl like every other week."

Anger coiled in my core. Corey wasn't like that. The media painted ugly pictures of his dating life. Sure. He dated. And some of them were models, but…still. I hated what the media did to him. "It's not like that."

Her shoulders slumped. "I just don't want you to get hurt. You're my best friend."

Maybe I should tell her what was really going on. She could help. She'd be on board with the whole fake dating thing to get back at Todd. Then again, Corey needed discretion and so did I. My dad and his lawyers had worked too hard to cover up the results of my bad, scratch that, illegal behavior back in L.A. with his client, Grayson Stryker… If that got out, I'd be even more humiliated than when Todd broke up with me. Plus, if Corey ever found out…he wouldn't want anything to do with me.

No, even though it sucked, I couldn't tell Mia. She'd be one more person who knew, which meant one more opportunity for this scheme of ours to get out. No. I couldn't tell her. No matter how much I wanted to.

"Mia, I know it's weird, but trust me. It's all good."

She put her hands on my shoulders. "Todd hurt you so badly and I hate when you're sad. You promise you're okay in all this? Won't get hurt?"

"Promise." I yanked her into a tight hug. She was a great friend. Someday I'd tell her all about this. Hell, maybe someday I'd write some poetry about it. Maybe post it anonymously to that Scribbles site Jace was so popular on.

Mia hugged me back and said, "But I will say this, if he does hurt you, I will retaliate. It won't be pretty, either."

"I wouldn't expect anything else."

Thank goodness this thing with Corey wasn't a real relationship. Mia had mad skills when it came to online detective work. I was actually surprised she'd never dug up anything on my L.A. life. I'd told her some, but it must have been enough to keep her from digging around. As for Corey...she'd probably find every single girl he'd dated, get dirt from them, and post a tell-all on Instagram before I could even blink.

After releasing me, she started laughing.

"What's so funny?" I asked.

Her shoulders shook. "Todd's face was priceless tonight when you showed up to ice skate with Corey tonight."

"Right?" I did my best impersonation of Todd's shocked face.

"He's such a jerk," she said, shaking her head. "I can't believe I didn't see through it earlier."

I looked in the mirror and twisted my hair into a bun. As it fell, I muttered, "I wish I didn't have to stand on the stage with him at the Ice Ball."

"Ugh, I know." Mia put her hand on my back. "You

could always drop out."

"No way." I shook my head vehemently. "There's no way I'm going to give him that satisfaction!"

"Good. You showing up with Corey will be all that matters anyway."

"Exactly," I said, though part of me was starting to think there might be more to it than that.

Chapter Fourteen

Corey

"And, the Woodhaven High Wolverines take the lead, two-one."

"Ahhh, come on!" I shot up out of my seat and punched the air. "That was roughing! Get some glasses, ref!"

"Yeah! That's BS!" Tony yelled. "That ref sucks. He's freaking from Woodhaven!"

Tony was sitting in my row, a few people down from me. He was cool. Treated me like a normal person.

Then again, he knew what it was to be known for something other than yourself. He came from money, *lots* of it. And he was awesome at basketball. People hung around him because of those two things, at least that was what he said yesterday when we were hanging at lunch together.

"So, got a new bromance going on there with Tony? Should I be jealous?" Victoria poked my side and chuckled.

I sat back down, laughing. "Can I get in on some of that popcorn?"

Victoria tilted the bag toward me.

I stuck my hand into the salty goodness. "So what's your thing?"

"My thing?"

"You know, like, some have cheerleading, or debate club or whatever."

"Do I need a thing?" She leaned in to me. "Can't I be my amazing self without a thing?"

"Everyone's got a thing."

"Like your guitar and covers of old rap and hip-hop songs?" She tossed some Skittles into her mouth.

"Hey, where'd you get Skittles?"

She held the bag of candy out to the side, away from me. Mia was sitting beside her, and then two other girls, I think their names were Holly and Carlin if I remembered correctly. They looked at Victoria with wide eyes as she leaned toward them to get away from me.

"Come on, Tor, I need me some sugar." I tackled her and snagged the bag of treats. She'd stopped fighting me suddenly, and her smile faded somewhat, though it was still there.

It was a different smile, actually. Normally her smiles filled her face, little dimples forming around the corner of her eyes. I loved that. It was like she was super happy.

But now it was more subtle, like she was surprised.

"What's wrong?" I leaned in. Maybe Todd had shown up.

"You called me Tor."

"I did?" I sat up and popped a few candies into my

mouth. "Tor. I like it."

"Me too." She smiled a little more and her cheeks flushed.

I liked *her*, actually. It was Friday, which meant we'd been at this fake relationship for about a week. It was the most fun I'd had in a long time. Two trips to the ice cream shop, flirting, and hanging out. She was easy to be around. So were her friends and family.

"I didn't know you were such a hockey fan," she said, reaching for the candy.

I dumped a few into her palm. "These are mine now."

"Oh, so that's how it's going to be."

"So seriously, you don't have your own thing?" I asked again, totally wondering what her thing could be. She had to have one. Everyone did. It was what made us unique, driven.

Or maybe I was just a freak? I'd always had my music. It was something I had shared with Dad. He was an amazing musician.

She glanced around, then leaned in. Her lips brushed my ear and she cupped her hand near her face and whispered, "I like to write poetry."

"Really?"

"Shhh." She batted at me and whispered, "No one knows."

"Not even Mia? Why?"

"Mia knows a little bit. But it's...*my* thing. Don't want to share it with just anyone."

She'd told me, though. What did that mean? And why did it make me feel so good that she told me when she'd not told anyone else?

I looked down at her. Her hair was loose again tonight

and she was wearing eye makeup. I liked that it wasn't caked on, though. And she only took, like, fifteen minutes to get ready. That was so unlike my other girlfriends. They'd—

Oh crap. Did I just call her my girlfriend? As in...*my* girlfriend?

"That's wicked cool. About the poetry," I whispered back to her. "Seriously."

I popped some candy into my mouth and watched the star right winger, Matthew Halliday, break away and slap a goal into the net, tying up the game at two. "YES!"

I jumped up and the popcorn fell onto the ground, but I didn't care. We'd totally scored a goal. I high-fived Victoria and pointed at Tony. He nodded at me, then high-fived some tall dude next to him. I forgot his name, but he had to be on the basketball team, because he wasn't more than a few inches shorter than Tony.

Dang, I was starting to like this place, huh? Or maybe it had something to do with the beauty sitting beside me.

I sat back down beside Victoria. "I'll get us more popcorn in a sec. Sorry about that."

"It's okay. We have Skittles." She leaned in close.

I offered her a few more candies and she looked at me with bright eyes. She popped some candy into her mouth.

A goal buzzer sounded, but I'd missed it, staring at Victoria. She jumped up and so did I, screaming like everyone else around us.

Sweet. We were ahead now.

Suddenly Victoria's smile vanished.

Todd Miller, asshat extraordinaire, stepped onto the bleachers with a long-haired beauty in tow. He was holding her hand and nodding at a few people as he made his way to the stairs leading to where we were sitting.

Sweet. *Keep coming, buddy.* I was about to turn on the charm, big-time. Maybe I should start an Instagram live and stick it to him. No. That wouldn't be cool. No need to stoop to his level of assholery.

He turned and started up the steps closest to us. We were seven rows up but sitting on the end. He'd walk right by us.

"Shit," Victoria whispered.

The color drained from her face. She bit her bottom lip. I hated how much that jerk affected her. It felt like someone had thrown fifty darts at my chest and punctured my heart. She did not deserve that kind of crap.

That Gretchen Mead girl was a row in front of us and down about ten people, but as soon as she saw Todd, she whipped around and nailed Victoria with a glare. The two girls with her did the same, then snickered.

She really was a piece of work, wasn't she? A few more people around us glimpsed Victoria. They leaned in to one another, but I couldn't hear what they were saying.

"Do you trust me?" I asked Victoria.

"I do," she said, her big eyes focused on me.

"Then hold on." I bent down and wrapped my arms around her waist and hoisted her into my arms. She was a good six inches shorter than me, so I got her up into the air really well.

She squealed and wrapped one of her arms around my neck, then shot the other one up into the air and let out a cheer. The laughter flowing out of her made me smile. So did holding her close. She was a tiny thing and fit perfectly against me, like I knew she would. For a second there,

I kinda hated that this was all for show. I wouldn't mind holding her like this all the time.

Todd paused a step as his gaze raked over us. *Perfect.* I winked at him, then hugged Victoria close, burying my face in her neck.

He had no clue what he'd discarded when he'd dumped her so viciously. And that girl he was with, she must be the reason. She glared at me with her sea-green eyes. Hopefully this sent a nice, clear message that Todd wasn't missed. That he'd been thoroughly replaced. And that they should keep on moving.

Todd tugged the blonde close, then threaded his fingers through her hair to the nape of her neck as they walked by.

Weak attempt to counter what Victoria and I had just done.

She shifted in my grasp and I looked at her. She'd eased down in my arms enough that she was directly at eye level with me. This close, her sugar-laced breath mingled with mine. Her eyes, they were brown, yeah, but this close I could see the little slivers of amber in there, close to her pupils. Drawing in a breath, her lilac scent fused with me.

I could easily lean forward a few inches and I'd get to sample those shiny, strawberry lip-gloss-covered lips that were shimmering under the arena lights. What would she think, though? Would she be okay with it?

"Thanks," she whispered. "Perfect timing."

"I saw them coming up," I said, still not releasing her. I didn't want to. She felt absolutely perfect in my arms right now. "Hopefully this was okay; I kinda went with it."

Her cheeks flushed again and she bit her lip. Her gaze shifted down slightly and she pulled in a deep breath. That subtle action kicked my heart rate up a few beats. For a second, the cheering and crowd faded away into oblivion. It was just me and her.

Her and me.

Us two.

I couldn't help but look at her lips again. They were glistening, beckoning me to kiss them. It was only for show, right? To shove it in Todd's face.

Although he wasn't watching anymore. But that wasn't the point. I needed to kiss her. But did she want to—

"That was epic!" Tony reached past the people separating us and shoved me.

I was so into Victoria I didn't have time to get my balance, so I tipped to the side.

"Whoa!" Tony yelled as he reached for my arm.

Victoria planted her foot back and, with surprising strength, she kept us up, with Tony's help.

"Graceful, Chaos." Tony shook his head. "Graceful."

"You big oaf!" I punched his arm, then glanced at Victoria. She was staring at me with wide eyes and that smile of surprise again. Her chest was heaving and her cheeks were bright red.

I was treading dangerous ground with these not-so-fake feelings starting to simmer.

Chapter Fifteen

Victoria

"Which dress do you like best?" I asked.

Mia, Sophia, and Bailey all took a moment to inspect the four dresses that I had picked out for the Ice Ball.

"Do you want us to be honest?" Bailey asked.

I was actually surprised she'd asked first; she was pretty blunt and to the point. That was what I loved about my redheaded friend.

"Of course." I shifted my weight nervously. I'd never brought my friends dress shopping before, but the stakes had changed. I wanted to show Todd what he was missing.

"I don't think any of them are right." Bailey adjusted one of the pens holding her messy bun in place.

She usually had at least three pens shoved in her hair during her shifts at the Greasy Spoon and today was no exception.

"Agreed," Mia and Sophia said.

"What?" I looked at them. "Really?"

"I found this one hiding behind some other dresses." Sophia held up a backless black dress with a V neck. "I think you should try it on."

"Oh wow." My eyebrows shot up. "I don't think I can pull that off."

"Trust me, Victoria." Sophia thrust it toward me. "You will *own* this dress."

She did have an eye for fashion. She was always dressed perfectly. Her long black hair was healthy and shiny, and it always looked like she'd had a professional blowout. Her gold-and-umber eyes were bright and I never saw her without a smile.

"Okay, okay." I disappeared into the changing stall.

I slid out of the dress that was evidently not doing it for me, my heart thudding in my chest. I wasn't sure I had the body to pull off backless and such a deep V neck. Then again, what did I have to lose? I needed to take a risk if I wanted to make a statement.

And the statement I wanted to make was *Screw you, Todd!*

"Girl, you and Corey were looking awfully cozy yesterday at the hockey game," Bailey said. "You have got to spill on him."

"Nothing to spill," I said, tugging the dress down over my shoulders.

"Liar!" Sophia and Mia jokingly yelled, then fell into a fit of laughter.

"Jinx. You owe me a Coke!" they both said at the same time, which led to even more giggling.

"We're just..." I trailed off.

In a fake relationship.

"Just what?" Sophia asked.

"Hanging out."

Crap... Were we just hanging out, though? There had been some serious heat in his eyes when he was holding me last night at the hockey game. It might have started out as a *screw you* aimed directly at Todd, but for me, it felt like more.

I hugged my midsection, remembering the heat of his body so close to mine. I could almost feel it right now. And his scent. I could get lost in that.

But I shouldn't. No, I couldn't. First, this was all fake. I had to remind myself of that. Second, Corey's success was new, barely two years old. He was on his way to make a name for himself, even more than he already had. I didn't want to hold him back. Or worse, ruin it for him like I ruined Grayson's career.

Maybe I shouldn't have ever pulled Corey into this fake relationship. If anyone found out about Grayson, I'd be beyond screwed. It could ruin everything. Corey's future, my dad's career, and who knew what else...

I held the cool, silky dress to my half-bare body. *Okay, let's see if Sophia was right.*

As soon as I slid the dress over my head I knew it was the one. It hugged my waist and then flowed out into a beautiful skirt with multiple layers of tulle. I stared at my reflection in the mirror and it was almost like a stranger looked back at me.

No, a princess stared back at me.

"Does it fit?" Mia asked from outside the dressing room.

Exhaling, I opened the door and did a twirl.

"Ohmigosh, Victoria! It's perfect," Sophia gasped, then

rushed to me and pulled me out of the dressing room stall. "I knew it!"

"Corey is going to love it." Mia and Sophia guided me to the mirrors and had me step up on the platform so I could see the dress from all angles. "Seriously, that dress was made for you!"

I twirled around again. The material lifted up and flowed outward. I felt so beautiful.

It reminded me of a dress that I'd seen in a Valentino fashion show, but in the show, there was a line from Edgar Allen Poe's poem, *Romance*, written down the side.

Maybe I'd ask Mrs. Jacobson, our fashion design teacher, if she could show me how to use the sewing machines so I could add a line from one of my poems in the same spot? My body tensed at the thought. Up until a week ago, no one knew that I wrote poetry, not even Todd. I mean, I'd mentioned it to Mia a little, but never let her see any of it. Plus, I hadn't been writing much while dating Todd.

Then, I met Corey and I told him about it almost immediately.

He wasn't judgmental and it was like he stoked my creative fire.

Looking at myself in the mirror, I did one last spin.

A flutter of nerves stirred in my stomach at the thought of dancing with Corey all dressed up like this. Would he like it?

Not that he had to. Our relationship wasn't real. I kept telling myself that over and over, but it wasn't holding up as firmly as it was eight days ago.

"That dress is everything." Bailey beamed as she stood up from the dressing room chair and pulled her jacket on.

"Sorry to bug out early, but I've got to get to work. Text ya after my shift!"

An hour and a half later, Mia, Sophia, and I had new dresses and shoes. The excitement of the upcoming dance skittered along my arms like little electrical pulses.

We were heading out of the mall when we passed The Hot Dog Shack.

I gave a quick wave to McKenna Storm.

"I hear she and Jace are working on a sequel to Kingdom of Swords," Sophia said as she waved at McKenna.

"I can't wait!" Mia wove her arm through mine. "Jace and McKenna…their own love story."

"Kind of like you and Corey, huh, Victoria?" Sophia wiggled her eyebrows at me.

"Ha-ha…" I said, even though the idea of having a love story with Corey didn't sound horrible.

"Is he a good kisser?" Sophia said. "I'm dying to know. I mean, I can't even…"

"Sophia!" I slapped at her shoulder, but then she snatched up my hand and tugged me close.

When Corey and I hung out, everything felt so natural. He genuinely seemed to like me for me.

Maybe Corey and I have a real chance at making something work?

No, no! He's leaving in a few weeks.

This isn't real.

It's just two people pretending to like each other.

Pretending…

Luckily, the girls and I had plans to go get pizza from Giuseppe's. If anything could distract me from Corey Chaos and my pretend love life, it was the best pizza in town.

...

"Whoa," Sophia said as she set down her glass of soda. "Pitch and Gretchen broke up."

"Wait," I said. "I thought she was still seeing or whatevering with Kyle."

"Nope, they called it off last weekend. She and Pitch got together that night, allegedly. Check your phone." Sophia showed Mia her phone screen.

"Dang, that was fast," I said.

Sophia shook her head. "That guy never stays with anyone for more than two minutes."

"Same could be said about Gretchen." She was so hot and cold, I couldn't keep track of her moods. Plus, she was on my shit list right now for starting up that #LunchDump hashtag. I didn't get why she got off on being so mean.

"I wonder what happened?" Mia asked. "She and Kyle made it a whole three weeks. That has *got* to be some kind of record for him."

I rolled my eyes, smiling. It was surprising the normally packed restaurant was fairly empty. I didn't mind, though. We'd scored a great booth and I was glad to have girl time. Everything had happened so quickly with Todd, then Corey and the Ice Festival... I'd missed my girls.

"How could you breakup with someone on freaking Instagram?" Sophia muttered in disgust.

The memory of my breakup with Todd in the cafeteria flashed through my mind. My heart ticked a few rapid beats, but I pushed the thought out of my head. It was done. Over. He was nothing more than an asshat. I could do better.

"He did it on Instagram?" Mia screeched. "Dang. I used to think he was cute. Even thought about asking him out a while back."

"Stay away from that player," I said. "I wouldn't want him hurting you like that."

"Hey, Victoria, did... I mean, what happened with Todd?" Sophia asked. "What he did was shitty. I never thought you two would ever break up."

"You and me both." I shook my head and took a sip of my soda. "I had no clue. He had to have been cheating on me. I mean—never mind. I don't want to talk about him."

"Yeah and you have Corey now."

"I don't *have* Corey," I said, my cheeks heating. I was starting to kind of want him, though, but I knew I couldn't have him. "We're just hanging out a little while he's in town."

My stomach flip-flopped. *In a few weeks, when Corey is gone, are my friends going to think he screwed me over? Is our plan to say we want to remain friends really going to work?*

"How are you and Corey going to make it work once he goes back to L.A.?" Sophia asked, as if my thoughts were written all over my face.

"Oh, um." I needed to pick my words carefully. "Long distance isn't that bad with FaceTime. Plus, we're just talking... It's nothing serious."

Sophia gave me a sympathetic nod. "Right..."

Luckily, the conversation turned back to Pitch and Gretchen, leaving me to my thoughts about Corey. Not that they were awesome thoughts, actually, they were pretty sad, because even though we'd been hanging out for only a week or so, I liked him. What *would* happen when he left?

Chapter Sixteen

Corey

"Dude. We should *not* have chosen basketball." I wiped the sweat from my brow, then leaned over, resting my hands on my knees.

Tony glanced around the empty high school gym. "Yeah, well, I need the practice."

"I'm thinking you're doing *just* fine." I clapped my hands together and motioned for him to throw me the ball. "Okay. Let's try this again."

Tony zipped the ball to me, then took the guarding position, holding his massive arms out. It was like he was from planet giant or something. Like I, a five-foot-ten guy, could get by that.

I dribbled the ball to the right, then bounced it behind me and picked it up with my left hand and went left. He mirrored me, not giving me an inch to go around. I spun, taking the ball with me.

"I'll ignore that you just carried the ball," he said, cracking up.

"Yeah, yeah." I juked again and plowed into him with my shoulder. He let me go by him; that was the only reason I'd made it. Had to be. I dribbled the ball, then hustled in for the layup.

"Nice," Tony said, his hands up for me to throw the ball to him.

"You're going easy on me."

"Don't want to damage your ego or anything."

"Please. When it comes to basketball…it's okay. I know I suck."

Tony dribbled the ball but didn't really move anywhere. We stood there, near the hoop in the empty school gymnasium, hanging out. I couldn't remember the last time I'd done that with a friend.

"Now, get a guitar out…" I winked at him. "Then we're talking a totally different ball game."

"Yeah, I was meaning to ask you about that. How'd you get into music and doing covers?"

I motioned for him to throw me the ball. He did and I sunk a shot from two feet away. "I think we should play HORSE instead of one-on-one, dude. I'm dying here. And you're not even sweating. That's just not right, man."

"I'd be sweating if I had to play the guitar in front of thousands of people."

"Yeah, well, trust me. I sweat during that as well." I laughed.

"So…how'd you get into it?" Tony took my spot where I'd made my shot and sunk one.

"A little bit of an accident, a splash of luck, and a whole ton of Fate I think." I dribbled to the free-throw line. The clap of the ball hitting the slick floor echoed against the stone walls. The bleachers were still pushed in from gym glass yesterday.

It was Saturday afternoon and there wasn't anything going on in here until Monday. Some big gymnastics thing, but I couldn't remember. The emptiness and quiet, other than our dribbling sounds, was refreshing. Tony was cool and laid back, so I'd had no problem saying yes to him asking to meet up for some hoops. He called it an after official basketball practice cooldown.

I called it a workout. The guy was an amazing athlete.

"Victoria told me that the right people heard your covers and it kind of exploded," Tony said as he watched me sink a free throw. "Nice one."

"Yep. Things kind of went from zero to one hundred overnight." I shook my head. "Started getting approached by people who wanted to book me for shows. Everything from little rundown bars to big venues with thousands of people in the crowd. It's kind of weird, you know, having fans begging me to cover such and such song, give it my vibe. So I did. And it kinda snowballed from there."

Tony came up to the free-throw line and lined up to copy my last shot. "I can't believe Mike D from the Beastie Boys and Lizzo commented on your latest post."

"Never in a million years did I think anything like this would ever happen. Honestly, it's strange how quickly it happened."

"Ever get, you know, sick of it?"

I stepped to the side as he took his shot. The ball

bounced off the rim. "H! Yes!" I clapped. "I bet that's the only letter I'll get off you!"

He shoved me and darted after the ball, then shot a three-pointer and got nothing but net.

How he moved reminded me of Larry Bird. He had been my dad's favorite player. My heart pinged at the memory, but I shook it off and watched Tony shoot around for a second. His family had three generations of prosecution lawyers and they were expecting him to be the fourth. But they were way too snobby for him—those were his words.

He didn't come off entitled at all and I respected that.

"As for me getting sick of it?" I clapped for him to throw me the ball. "Yeah. I do a little."

I totally airballed the attempt and he stifled a laugh as he rebounded for me.

"Not. A. Word." I hung my head in shame.

"You play sports in high school when you went?" Tony asked.

"Track. Kinda miss it, too. The whole high school experience, I mean."

"And Victoria?" He threw up a three-pointer and got nothing but net. "Where's she fit in all this?"

I shook my head and slouched to his spot. "I have a feeling this game will be over pretty quickly."

"That's all right. I'm hungry. We'll go get some pizza after."

"Can't. I'm hanging with Tor." I shot the ball and at least I hit the rim this time. The ball ricocheted directly back to Tony as if he were a magnet.

"Hanging? As in…you're dating, right?"

Our whole idea was to keep people guessing, especially

Todd. But, more and more, I liked the idea of dating her for real. But we couldn't. "She's cool."

Tony started laughing so loud it bounced off the walls. "You are so full of shit."

"What?"

"You're totally into her."

"No...no. I mean, well—"

"Did you forget that I was sitting near you guys at the game last night? You've got it bad, dude."

I gulped. No I didn't.

No. I. Did. Not.

I was pretending. So was she. There were a few reasons she was totally off-limits, the main one being her dad was my agent. Plus, I had a pretty good chance of landing a spot on a new reality show *What's Your Note?* If I got the part, I'd be leaving in a few weeks. No way should I start anything with Victoria. It would crash and burn. Everyone knew long distance never worked.

"It's okay. I mean, Victoria is awesome. And Todd totally dissed her. I just—she's my friend." Tony propped the ball between his hip and the crook of his elbow as he stared at me. "I don't want to see her hurt again."

I shook out my hair and wiped my face. "I hear ya."

"Do you?" Tony dipped his head slightly. "You're cool, man. I don't wanna have to pound on you, you know?"

"Pound me, huh?"

He shrugged.

How *did* I feel about Victoria? My dating her was an agreement, nothing more. A role, a means to an end. But I also couldn't lie to myself—I was super excited about seeing her later. It would be just me and her this time, hanging at El

Ranchos before we went to the Ice Sculpture Gardens event at the Ice Festival tonight.

Ah, hell. Tony was right.

I was totally in *like* with her.

Chapter Seventeen

Victoria

"Orange is obviously superior to grape." I put my hands on my hips. "Everybody knows that."

Corey put the back of his hand to my forehead. "Are you ill? Coming down with a fever?"

I scrunched up my nose. "What?"

"Grape is superior to orange across the board. Gum, Fanta, fruit. Grape. All. The. Way. If you disagree, you've obviously come down with some kind of illness that requires medical attention."

I snatched his hand, but before I could remove it from my forehead, he circled his arm around my waist and pulled me to his chest.

The package of gum fell to the slick convenience store floor as our eyes met.

Everything but Corey faded into oblivion as his face

inched closer to mine. The swirl of his woodsy, melon-scented cologne wrapped around me and heat steamed my cheeks. Here we were, in Kwik Trip, seeking out a sugar rush, totally flirting and having a great time. And then this. Too bad Todd wasn't here to witness it. Then again, did I really care?

Dammit, I did.

But how much?

This fake relationship was starting to feel more and more real by the minute.

He pulled me close.

Heart racing, my mouth went dry in anticipation. His big brown eyes studied me as if he was memorizing my face. A bubble of heat erupted in my belly. It was like he was drinking me in, treasuring me. I'd never felt so noticed by anyone. Cherished.

Beneath the bright lights here in the store, I could see him clearer than I ever had. A subtle birthmark at the corner of his left eye that looked like a tear caught my attention. I'd never noticed it before. A slight variation of darkness in the form of a teardrop marred his smooth tanned skin.

Tendrils of warmth curled around my spine and I drew in a deep breath as he leaned in. I closed my eyes and waited for his lips to touch mine. What would they feel like? Hopefully my breath smelled okay. What if—

"Corey Chaos! Will you please sign this for me?"

My eyes flung open and I jerked away from Corey. Before us stood a girl who looked to be about thirteen years old. Her auburn hair was in two braids and she tugged on one while she held out what looked like a teen magazine toward Corey. Being in Corey's presence must have made her nervous, because the thing was practically vibrating.

"You are my absolute favorite YouTuber," she gushed. "When you covered 'Fight For Your Right,' by the Beastie Boys, I literally almost passed out!" Her smile stretched broadly across her face.

Corey's face turned a dark shade of crimson. "Thank you." He stole a quick glance at me, but I couldn't meet his gaze. My heart was still hammering against my ribs; I wasn't sure I could talk anyway. Plus, how embarrassing. Here we were in a convenience store and we got busted by a kid just as we were about to kiss.

I couldn't believe we almost kissed!

The fluorescent bulbs overhead buzzed. His cologne lingered in the space between us and heat fused in my cheeks. I had a winter coat on and I was starting to sweat standing this close to him.

Fake relationship or not, I was falling for him…hard and fast.

Did I even care anymore?

The reality of my feelings for him slammed into me like a wrecking ball. I *wanted* him to kiss me. Desperately. More than anything I'd ever wanted before.

Holy crap… I'm falling for Corey Chaos.

"That girl is soooo pretty," the little girl said. "She's like the luckiest person in the whole wide world!"

I turned toward her, a smile playing on my lips. I *was* the luckiest person in the world, wasn't I? Being with Corey had its perks, but the confidence boost was a side effect I hadn't counted on happening.

"Thank—" I started to say, but quickly snapped my mouth shut when I realized she wasn't talking about me.

The little girl had shoved an open tabloid magazine toward Corey. The two-page spread featured a picture of Corey and a stunning blonde who had blue eyes and perfectly puckered lips. The headline read, "Catching Chaos: The girl who has Corey's heart talks." I swallowed the lump in my throat as I zeroed in on the girl. She had her arms wrapped around Corey's neck and she was kissing him on the cheek.

The air whooshed out of my lungs with such force I took a step to the side to steady myself. Here I was thinking that girl was talking about me, but she wasn't. She was talking about the girl in the picture.

The one kissing Corey.

The one who has Corey's heart…

Crap.

Was I going to be seen as one of Corey's flings? I hadn't thought of that.

Was he still dating that girl? This had all happened so quickly I hadn't even thought to ask if he was seeing anyone.

Shit.

"I—um, I'm going to get some fresh air." Leaving the package of gum on the floor, I raced out of the little corner shop and didn't stop until I had crossed the street.

The frigid air stung my face and eyes as I clung to the light pole on the sidewalk. Across the street, Corey stood there, signing the magazine and talking to the young girl.

Bending over, I sucked in cool air and tried to ignore the tears stinging the corners of my eyes. My hands trembled as I placed them on my knees.

I had no right to be upset. We weren't in a real relationship. I had no claim on him.

Then why the *hell* did this hurt so much?

A sickening feeling settled in my stomach.

If that girl found that magazine article... So would everyone else. They'd think I was just another one of his flings. Nothing more than a way to pass the time in snowy Wisconsin.

The thought made me want to hurl.

I'd be the laughingstock of Twin River.

Again!

"Tor?" Corey yelled from across the street as he looked both ways, then hustled toward me. "What happened? Are you okay?"

I stood up and, like a deer in headlights, I froze. I wanted to run away from him and pretend we'd never started our fake relationship, but my feet refused to move. What had I done getting into this thing with Corey? I should have thought this through more. *Damn it.*

"Hey, what's wrong? You disappeared on me." He reached forward to put his arm around my shoulders, but I pulled back.

"Whoa," he said, surprised by my reaction.

"You do realize that as soon as everyone sees *that* article that I'm going to become the laughingstock of the school. For the second time in less than two weeks." I shook my head and stared at my feet. My fists clenched and unclenched several times.

"You mean that picture with Lauren?" He laughed, rubbing salt in the wound in the process.

"You think this is funny?" My voice skipped a few octaves. "You have a girlfriend in L.A. but you're dating me here in Twin River? I'll look like a fling. Or the other woman. Shit."

"I don't have a girlfriend in L.A." He showed me his palms as if trying to surrender to me. "I dated Lauren for a month. I broke up with her before I came out here." He shook his head. "She was more interested in posting pictures with me than actually dating me."

I kicked a small stone and sent it skidding across the sidewalk and into the short snowbank that lined the walkway. "You two look super happy in that picture and the magazine only came out yesterday…"

"That shit happens all the time. I promise. It's one hundred percent over with Lauren. Honestly, it never even really started; she was one of those girls who used me as arm candy; remember I told you about them?"

I nodded, my thudding heart slowing somewhat.

"And…despite what the rags report, I don't do *flings*." Corey reached for my hands. "Besides, you and Twin River are about the only things filling my stories these days."

I gulped.

My head swam and my knees felt like jelly. I'd jumped to conclusions. Been way too quick to make assumptions. It was like I was back in L.A., flying through life, not thinking things through… There absolutely, 110 percent, could not be another Grayson debacle.

"I'm sorry, Tor. I didn't mean for that to go down the way it did." He reached into his pocket and pulled something out. "I did get you something."

I looked down.

In his palm sat a pack of orange bubblegum.

"You said it was your favorite flavor…"

Without another word, I wrapped my arms around

his neck and hugged him with all my might. Even though we were both decked out in thick winter coats, I felt close to him. So close that the heat from his body radiated into mine. It might have been my overactive imagination, but I was going to go with it.

As he returned the embrace, I closed my eyes and hoped it would never end.

Chapter Eighteen

Corey

The orange gum peace offering didn't seem to be working.

Victoria's smile didn't brighten her face like it normally did and she slouched a little more than she had before.

Lauren was still wreaking havoc on my life. I'd dated her all but five minutes after meeting her during one of my magazine interviews last month and I thought we'd hit it off.

We so didn't. She was more into my social media status than me.

I shook my head and nudged Victoria as we strolled down the sidewalk. It'd started snowing again, but nothing impressive. Subtle, tiny flakes more floating around the air in the breeze than actually snowing.

It kind of felt like I was in a movie.

"You gonna share that orange goodness?" I nudged her with my elbow.

"Thought you didn't like this flavor."

"Oh no. I like it. It's just not superior to grape." I grinned and she smiled.

It dawned on me that I didn't like seeing her sad. Happy and smiling were way better and I kinda wanted to be the source of those happy times. For more than the few weeks I had left here.

Damn the time was going way too fast. I held out my hand and she set a piece of gum into it. I pulled off my gloves to unwrap the sugary goodness and popped it into my mouth.

"We good about what just happened?"

"Yes," she said. "Your life is so different than mine."

It was and it wasn't. Sure, we had the social media notoriety going on, but other than that, we actually had a lot in common. I still wondered if she liked me more than our agreement. If she wanted to kiss me. What it would be like to date her. And I was still stressing over that sociology paper I turned in to Rita earlier today on the effects of social media on mental health issues. I was praying to the writing gods that I get something better than a C.

"Do you miss it?"

"No," I said through the big wad of gum in my mouth.

"You sound pretty sure with that fast answer."

"Don't get me wrong, it has its perks. I mean, what guy wouldn't like being asked for his autograph? But…"

She glanced up from beside me, then looked ahead. The sidewalk was fairly empty. A row of hedges outlined the property of some historical house on our left, the street on our right. The lights were dim, so it was actually kind of romantic.

Up ahead there was a corner and I heard a faint whispering of music along the air. That had to be where the Ice Sculpture Gardens had been set up for the Ice Festival.

"But..." Victoria said, her hand brushing against mine. "Go on."

I wanted to tell her everything. My fears about going back to the L.A. chaos. My fears about not getting picked for this role on *What's Your Note?* My fears that if I did get the role, things with Victoria would get even more complicated. My fears that my mom wasn't ever going to get over the grief of losing Dad. My fears that I'd get cancer like he did.

I hated that I had so many fears. But even though it felt like Victoria could be someone I trusted with them, I didn't dare. I was leaving in a few weeks, right? This was a fake relationship. What if she used them against me? Exposed me for the fraud I was?

I blew a bubble and she smiled.

"But..." She elbowed me this time and not so gently. She really did look interested and not the kind of interested reporters seemed when they were trying to scoop something about me. This felt genuine.

She felt genuine.

Maybe I could trust her with a little. "But...I kind of like it here."

She spread a full-faced smile. "Really?"

If she only knew she was a majority of the reason I liked it so much.

"You have nice friends. And well, it's slower paced here."

"Those are good reasons." She nodded. "It was weird at first when we moved here from L.A., but I like the slower pace of it, too. The people here, they're more real. You know?"

"Yep."

"But L.A. is where you need to be for your music, right?"

"I guess. It's just that...well, I got into music and stuff because..." My heart picked up the pace in my chest as I toyed with telling her about my dad. Would she understand? Think I was being dramatic?

"Because of your dad," she said.

Whoa. How did she know that?

"You don't talk much about it, though, do you? You mentioned it once, I think. It was in an interview a couple of years ago."

Holy crap. I remembered that interview. It was one of the first Jethro had landed for me. I'd thought I'd do this whole music venture based on my dad, to honor him. But the interviewer turned it into an hour and a half of talking about herself, her goals, and which of my covers were my favorite.

And talking about him had hurt too much. Thinking about him. Missing him. So I'd backed off, not really mentioning it a lot in my interviews after that. He and I had played guitar together a lot when I was a kid. He taught me most of what I knew about music.

Whenever I played, I thought of him. Felt him close.

"I can't believe you remember that interview," I said.

"Walk light's on."

The music started up again and I reached for her hand. "How's a little hand-holding sound?"

"In case someone's watching?" She let out a nervous

laugh.

"How 'bout 'cause I *want* to hold your hand?" And I did. Way more than I should. My life was complicated and over two thousand miles away from hers. But still, I wanted to be close to her. "And because I know my holding the hand of the prettiest girl in Twin River will drive that Todd guy nuts."

"The prettiest girl in Twin River?" She scrunched up her nose.

"And in L.A."

A small smile formed on her lips. "Let's do it."

She offered me her hand, and in that instant, I wished we weren't wearing mittens and gloves. I'd love to twine my fingers with hers and feel the heat of her skin against mine.

I was playing with fire, entertaining thoughts like that, but I went with it. For once, I was with someone who was real, genuine. Deep in my gut I knew I could trust her. Todd was an asshat for sure for dropping Victoria. But I was getting the benefits.

"Okay?" I asked, coming closer to her and holding up our clasped hands.

"More than okay," she whispered.

We walked in silence for several minutes. After we crossed the street and our feet met the frozen grass, she turned toward me and asked, "Will you tell me about your dad?"

I gulped, but the instrumental music I heard gave me strength. Music always did. It was how I dealt with stress. The public didn't know I had tons of my own written music. Mostly about the hurt and pain of losing Dad, but also about life in general. In case I ever got taken seriously with my music other than covers and marketing angles.

What's Your Note? was supposed to be an avenue to getting my own music produced. Sure, I'd have to do a duet with one of the girls, but it'd be a song *I'd* written. My own lyrics and music playing on the airwaves.

It was my dream. One I'd shared with Dad before he'd died. He'd been nothing but encouraging.

"Bile duct cancer," I said, my chest tightening a little. He'd died five years ago, but some days, it felt like just yesterday. "It's rare. Not many people survive more than about ten to twelve months."

"I'm sorry, Corey. I can't imagine losing a parent." She squeezed our connected hands and leaned against me slightly as we walked. With those slight gestures, I felt heard. Listened to. Understood.

She had a way of making me feel important. Special.

"He made it almost twelve months before he…" The words pushed through my thickening throat. "Strong guy."

"I bet," she said. "Did you get to say goodbye? I mean… like, before he passed?"

"Mom and I were with him as he took his last breath." My eyes stung at the memory. "Got to say our goodbyes, but not everyone is so lucky."

"You've been through so much," Victoria whispered. She clutched my arm and rested her head on my shoulder as we meandered. It almost felt like she and I were in our own little bubble as my surroundings faded away.

"Thanks, for, well, letting me talk about it. I don't really have anyone who will just listen. My mom's still a wreck about it and well, all of my regular friends aren't really my friends anymore. Once things started getting big, I didn't have the time to hang out and talk anymore."

"I'll always be here for you, Corey."

The way her brown eyes stared up at me sent warmth fizzing through my chest.

The music piped in a little bit louder as we rounded some more hedges. They were at least twelve feet tall and worked as a nice—and pretty—fence around a structure.

"Thank you." I placed a kiss on her forehead.

We took another few steps before hopping a curb and walking down a freshly plowed street.

"So, what is this place? I didn't get a chance to read much up on it other than to find out this is where the Ice Sculpture Gardens are."

"Old Town Twin River. It was one of the first areas developed here, I guess. It's where the town hosts this Music in the Park thing and they play movies on the side of the old Woolworth's building every Saturday night. They do all kinds of activities here."

"And now, in the freezing cold middle of winter, it's an ice sculpture garden for the Ice Festival. That's pretty rad." We finished turning the corner and it opened into a small park.

Paths of plowed sidewalk split the ocean of white snow in several directions. Several feet off the path sat huge, glistening ice sculptures.

"Wow," I said.

"Yeah. They go all out. Some of these are pretty intricate."

We strolled, holding hands, along the main sidewalk. There were little pockets of people gathered together, some standing, some sitting on random benches placed near the sculptures.

Most were holding cups of steaming liquid. "We might have to score some of that hot cocoa," I said.

"Is the Californian getting *chilly*?"

"It's twenty degrees! I was cold fifty degrees ago," I teased.

Victoria laughed as we approached the next sculpture.

Small string lights hung from tree to tree and around the bases, giving a subtle glow over everything that gave it a nice and calm feeling. Up ahead and to the left was a small stage.

Nothing huge like a concert venue, but just enough to get the string quartet a tad above people so the music could travel. Heaters surrounded the musicians, but they didn't seem to mind the cold.

The sweet sounds of the cello and the violin flowed through the air like a whisper. "This is awesome," I said.

That stage would be perfect for me to sit smack dab in the middle, just me and my guitar, and belt out a few songs. A few of *my* songs. Damn, this place was fueling my creative vibes.

She wiggled our joined hands and steered us to a sculpture on the left. It was an extravagant image of Elsa from *Frozen*, her arms up in the air, snow streaming from them.

"Hey guys," Landon said, strolling by, holding Hope's hand.

I dipped my head at him. "Hey Landon. You all totally kicked ass at the snowshoe race the other day."

"Thanks," Landon said. "Those things are hard to run in!"

"Did you know that more than five million people go snowshoeing every year?" Hope asked.

"Wow!" Victoria said. "Must be a good workout."

Hope's cheeks reddened.

"Tell them your good news." Landon nudged Hope's side.

Hope bit her lower lip. "I got into MIT."

"What? That's amazing! Congrats!" Victoria let go of my hand and wrapped her arms around Hope.

"Thank you. I was super nervous about applying for early acceptance, but thanks to this guy, I totally rocked my essay and interview." Hope stood on her tiptoes and kissed Landon on the cheek.

Victoria stepped back and claimed my hand. "Seriously, Hope. Congrats."

Landon threw his arm around Hope's shoulders.

"We'll see you guys in a bit. We're going to go meet up with Eve and Alice," Landon said.

"See you all a little later." I smiled and fist-bumped Landon.

Weaving around some people on the sidewalk, looking at the sculptures, Victoria led us to a swing set a few beats away from the crowds. It was a shade darker here and totally perfect for still hearing the music.

She sat down on a swing and I gave her a little push. She kicked her legs out and smiled. It was a nice bit of calm while the music swirled through the soothing night air. Actually, pretty freaking awesome air. Sure, it was cold and practically froze my nose hairs, but it was clean. Fresh.

"Come on, please. Let's swing. Just for a few minutes. It's so romantic," someone said from behind where I was standing.

Victoria stiffened in the swing as it came back to me. Todd and his new girlfriend strutted into our area. They all but skidded to a stop when they saw us.

"Hey there, *Todd*," I said.

He glared at me, then shifted his focus to Victoria as she swung back to me. I caught the swing, holding her close to me. I brushed my cheek to hers and smiled.

"Yeah, it *is* romantic to swing in the dark," I said.

The girl's shiny, gloss-covered lips pressed into a thin line, and she stomped her foot. I had to bite back a laugh at the little tantrum I saw building in those big green eyes. Now might be a perfect time to kiss Victoria, but that didn't feel right. I wanted our first kiss to mean something more than making her ex-boyfriend jealous.

I pulled off my glove, then grabbed my cell phone for a selfie and hugged Victoria even closer. "Smile!"

She leaned in to me and let a full-wattage smile loose. It was about as bright as the moon hanging over us. I brushed my cheek to hers again, inhaling her sweet lilac scent, then dropped my phone into my pocket.

Todd's girlfriend started to drag him away, muttering something I couldn't make out.

"Thank you," Victoria whispered.

"That was pretty awesome." I held her close, not quite ready to let her go.

She leaned in to me even more, tucking her head into my neck. Our body heat mingled, warming me from the inside out. I wasn't going to need any hot cocoa if she kept doing that. But that was fine by me. Too bad we had this bulky winter stuff on.

"Wait, what is Todd doing?" Victoria asked, her body stiffening.

I looked up to see what she was talking about. Todd and his girlfriend were talking to someone with a camera. As in legit TV cameras. They must be a local news crew or something getting shots of the ice sculptures. Then Todd pointed in our direction, a smirk filling his face.

"Ah, shit…"

And just like that, a team of five people, two girls and three guys charged us, their phones and camera poised to capture every second.

Score one for the asshat.

Chapter Nineteen

Victoria

"Little houses on a frozen lake?" Corey tentatively stepped out of his Jeep. "I'm still not buying this."

I couldn't help but laugh, because I pretty much felt the same way my first time ice fishing. Shutting the car door, I stopped and drew in a long, deep breath. The arctic air seized up my lungs, so I had to cough. But it was refreshing.

The noon sun was bright against the backdrop of a robin's-egg blue sky. Not a cloud in sight. No wonder it was so cold.

"Is that a truck out there, too?" He pointed toward the lake.

"It's been cold enough for one or two to be on there. But we'll stick to parking here and walking to our fish house."

We made our way onto the lake and started a trek toward our spot.

"Aside from the fact that we're standing on frozen water that could probably crack open and kill us, this place is incredible," Corey whispered.

"It's not going to crack."

Fifty feet ahead was my dad's ice house. He and I came fishing here a lot during the winter. It was kind of our thing. Having Corey here with me, though, was pretty freaking awesome, too.

In one hand, Corey held a picnic basket. With his other, he grasped mine. We were both wearing thick gloves, but that didn't stop the heat from coursing through my palm and up my arm. Ever since last night in the Ice Sculpture Gardens when we'd gotten mobbed by the TV crew and we had to bolt, he'd held my hand a lot. Even when we weren't trying to make anyone jealous.

And I was totally okay with that.

"So, this is how you do picnics in the winter here in Wisconsin, huh?" Corey said as we started strolling toward our fish house.

"Got to break up the monotony of the ice-cold winters, otherwise you sit inside all the time and get cabin fever."

The lake was huge and lined with pine and aspen trees. In the fall, the colors were impressive. Corey would have loved them.

"So this part of the lake isn't where we were on the Ice Festival opener, right?"

"Right. We're about an hour north of Twin River. My parents bought this cabin our first winter here." I liked to come up here to clear my mind. It wasn't too far from the city, but far enough to feel like you were actually getting away. When we'd first moved here from L.A., I was up here a lot, writing, journaling, processing everything that'd happened with Grayson.

The wooden ice house wasn't more than six feet wide and ten feet long, but the tiny structure brought a smile to my face. With my free hand, I eased the door open.

Corey followed me as I stepped over the threshold.

I stepped in farther. "Hold the door open a second."

He stood there, holding the basket, propping the door open so I could use the outside light to find a lantern. There were two chairs in here, a cot and a small table with a folded stack of blankets on top. I snatched the lantern off a hook on the side of the wall and clicked it on.

"Okay, good to go."

Corey let the door slam shut behind him. "Oh, sorry, wind whipped through there a second."

He stepped in, eyes wide with wonder as he turned a slow circle. "Cozy," he said.

I went to work turning on the portable propane heater to get some warmth working in here while Corey set the picnic basket next to the door.

As the heat started to fill the small space, Corey took off his stocking cap and shook out his floppy brown hair.

"How does the heater not melt the ice?"

"It's way too thick. And it's not like we're going to make it a sauna in here."

He eased in beside me. His woodsy scent filled the small space and jump-started my heart. His presence triggered a flutter low in my belly that I hadn't felt in a long time. Not since my adrenaline-packed time with Grayson and Nomie out in L.A. Even Todd never stoked anything like this in me.

The rush of Corey's closeness both scared and enticed me.

Those lips... Would they be as soft as I'd imagined them to be?

"Need any help?" Corey's voice was quiet, lower, and his heated breath washed over me like warm bathwater.

"I'm good." I went to work grabbing the fishing poles and tackle box.

"Do you ever go swimming in this lake?" Corey asked as he sat in one of the two chairs near the fishing hole.

"Yeah. I spend most of my summer break up here with Mia, Sophia, Bailey, and a few other girls."

"And guys..." He quirked up an eyebrow.

"The boy who will not be named has come up here a few times with me, yes." I pulled off the ice hole cover and Corey leaned over it, looking down.

"Ever do a polar plunge?" Corey asked.

"Hard pass. I'm not that brave."

"Really?"

"Nope." I shook my head as a shiver sliced down my spine. "It's one of the Ice Festival events if you want to try it, though."

"Oh, if I'm going to try it, you are, too." Corey wrapped his arms around my waist and pulled me toward the fishing hole. "You might fit down this hole. Come on, let's try it."

I let out a shriek. He pulled me flush to him, my back to his chest. Warmth from the arms locked around my waist flushed my belly. His palm rested dangerously close to my abdomen, igniting what had been a simmer into a full-on roaring flame.

I wouldn't mind jumping into the lake, during the

summertime, with Corey. Wet clothes sticking to his toned body. Dunking each other. Hugging. Kissing...

I shook the thoughts from my head. It was dangerous hoping for things like that with a guy like Corey.

Still holding me, he drew in a deep breath, and I could feel his chest expanding against my back. His hold on me tightened briefly, then he slowly released me and stepped aside, to his chair.

He peeled off his jacket, then sat down. He was wearing a hoodie, jeans, and boots, and he looked like he fit right in here, sitting in our fish house.

I took off my jacket, too, and threw it on the cot. "Warms up fast, huh?"

"I'd say." His cheeks flushed and he shifted in his seat, then looked over the hole again. "You really catch fish and pull them up through this little hole?"

"You are in for a treat." I snagged two fishing poles and handed him one, then sat down.

It took a few tries, but I pulled a worm out of a Styrofoam cup as Corey's nose scrunched up. Holding it in the air, I said to him, "You're looking a little pale."

"I can't believe you know how to do all this." He shook his head. "This place is seriously cool."

"Small, but you're right. It's cool."

"I like how small it is. Quiet, too. I should have brought my guitar."

"Next time." I baited my hook, then dropped my line into the water and handed Corey the rod. "So, tell me about where you live."

"I live in an apartment. With Mom. It's not huge, but it's big enough, nice, modern, and close to everything. I like that. Mom works nearby so that helps, too."

"What's she do?"

"ER nurse."

"You don't talk much about her."

"She's—we're—working through some stuff." He let out a long breath and slumped in his chair, holding the fishing rod in front of him.

I baited my hook and dropped my line in, then asked, "Working through some stuff…"

Corey closed his eyes as he drew in a deep breath.

"I'm sorry. I was just curious. You don't have to—"

"Grief." He focused on the fishing rod as he spoke. "Mom's having trouble with Dad's death. Kind of… floundering."

That didn't sound good. I wasn't sure what to say, so I sat there in silence, hoping he'd tell me more. I wanted to know more. Stuff that wasn't online about him. I wanted to know the real him.

"She works all the time. You know? And the guys she sees. It's like…" He shook his head. "That first year after Dad died, she was pretty depressed. We both were. Then she started dating guys. But never the same one for very long."

"That must have been difficult."

"I was pissed off at first. But then, after a few years of it, I was just sad. She was trying to stay distracted or something. *Is* trying to." He raised his fishing pole slightly and looked into the hole again as if he had to do something, anything, rather than look at me.

I couldn't imagine the pain he felt when he lost his father.

"And you? I mean, the grief."

"It hits me like a freight train sometimes, but it's getting better," he said, his voice quieter than normal. "It's been five years, so I feel like I should be more over it sometimes, then other times, I just go with it. It's weird. Music helps."

"Writing your own songs?"

"Exactly. Not that anyone will ever hear them. All anyone wants are my covers." His jaw muscle ticked and he shifted in his seat again.

He'd mentioned it before, in passing, about how he had his own music and wished he could play it.

"I can't imagine everything you've gone through, Corey." I rested my hand on his knee, then gave it a quick squeeze. "Your mom'll come around. She probably just needs more time."

He locked gazes with me. "I hope so."

My heart started beating faster the moment our eyes met. The arms of our little chairs touched, we were so close, and it was in that moment I saw him clearly. Truly. He wasn't like anyone I'd ever met before, in L.A. or Twin River. Guys in L.A. Ugh, that was a loaded thought. Guys like Grayson. I tried to push the thought out of my mind as my stomach sank. No, this was nothing like that...nothing at all.

Corey was deep. He felt things. And from the emotions emanating from him in tangible waves right now, he felt things intensely.

"How do you do it?" I asked.

"What?"

"Deal with the media and fans always taking your picture? That was intense when they found us last night."

"After Asshat tipped them off." He shook his head,

then stiffened and squeezed the fishing rod with both hands. "Whoa! Something's happening here."

"You get a bite?" I squealed. "That was fast."

He pulled the pole back. "There was a tug, but now…" He slouched. "I think it got away. The line is slack."

"It's all good. The fish always bite in this spot."

"I think you're good luck."

"Damn straight I am." I grinned.

Corey shivered. "Okay, maybe I shouldn't have taken my jacket off."

"Never had bubblegum ice cream. Never ice fished." I clicked my tongue against the roof of my mouth. "It's a good thing you came here. Maybe the experience will end up in a song or something."

"Most definitely." He winked at me. "I know you will for sure."

That was unexpected. I sat up straighter and eyed him. Had he really meant *I'd* end up in a song? What kind of song would he write about me?

"Oh, and about last night. I'm sorry you got dragged into that press-fest."

Evidently he wanted to change the subject, and despite how much I wanted to ask if he meant he'd write a song about me, I didn't.

"It's fine. Kinda fun trying to ditch them." I giggled at the memory of us ducking down the alley between the UPS store and Kat's Bakery.

A growl rivaling a lion's echoed through the small fish house.

Corey gave me a coy look. "Might be time to unpack the epic picnic I prepared."

I secured our rods, so if we happened to get a bite we could reel it in, while Corey got up and snagged the picnic basket from beside the door. Hopefully we got a bite and landed a big fish. I'd love to see Corey's reaction.

He set the basket on his side of the chair so I couldn't see it, then leaned over. He was so secretive with what he'd packed, but what I liked most was the joy flickering to life in his eyes.

"To start, caprese kabobs. As you can see, they've been drizzled with a balsamic reduction."

Corey handed me a plate and carefully set the kabobs in the middle.

"Wow. You made those?" I asked.

"You better believe it. All in the pool house kitchenette, too."

Corey reached back into the basket. "Lemonade or sparkling water?"

"Sparkling, please."

I took a bite of the caprese kabob as Corey poured me a glass of carbonated water. The tangy balsamic reduction sent my taste buds into overdrive. Perfectly ripened tomatoes, fresh-picked basil, and mozzarella followed. "Oh my gosh. These are incredible."

"Definitely one of my favorite go-to snacks." He took a bite from his kabob. "Back in L.A. there's this little deli like three blocks from my place and I swear, they have the freshest mozzarella balls of all time. The owner and I are on a first-name basis."

We ate in a comfortable silence for a bit, then he pulled out his phone. "Little music okay?"

"Definitely. What's your favorite right now?"

"I'm in an alternative 1990's mood lately." He clicked play, then tossed his phone onto the cot behind us. "You?"

"I'm not a one-genre kind of girl. I like a little bit of everything."

"Nice." He leaned to the side and peered into the basket again. "Next up, we have goat cheese and cranberry tarts. Now, I didn't make this, but I did order it special from the Corner Kitchen."

"Wow. This is amazing." I accepted the food from him and bit right in. "Mmmm!"

He was so sweet. Todd never did anything like this for me. No one had. How had he even had the time to plan all of this? The thought of him making and picking out all of these special dishes sent a sensation of warmth cascading through my chest.

"I can't believe you did all this. And it's not even one of our non-contract dates."

"It's on me."

We both dug in, and I couldn't help the flicker of hope coming to life in my chest that he might actually want to spend time with me because he *wanted* to and not because of our agreement.

The mere thought scared the crap out of me but also made me smile.

It didn't take long to finish up the fruity treat and just in time, because my rod vibrated a little and Corey flinched. "Did you see that?"

I hopped up and snatched my pole. He stood beside me, hunched over the ice hole. And at that moment, it went still.

"Crap." I tugged at the pole a few times, but nothing took.

"These fish are teasing us," Corey said. "Mocking us, I think."

I laughed and secured the rod again. "It usually takes a while."

Swiveling around to sit back down in my chair, Corey reached out to me. "Got some...cranberry..." His thumb brushed over the corner of my mouth, igniting a firestorm in my chest. Tingles shot through my body as I stood there, frozen.

Corey brought his thumb to his mouth and licked off the bit of cranberry. My heart leaped into my throat and the air whooshed out of my lungs. His nostrils flared and his chest heaved in a deep breath as his eyes scanned my face ever so slowly.

He looked at me like I was the fresh drink of water he needed after running a marathon. Like I was the only thing in the world right now. This moment.

I gulped through the emotion choking me.

Lips parting, he leaned forward. "Victoria, I—"

I grabbed his shoulders and pulled him toward me. Our lips met with a burst of energy. He grunted but then smiled against my mouth. I curled my arms around his neck, hugging him tight. His hand combed through my hair and cupped the back of my head as he stepped in to me. I hugged him closer, nipping at his soft lips.

He tilted my head and I fell into bliss. Fireworks exploded in my chest as our connection intensified. He tasted tart from the cranberries and it made my mouth water. I needed more of it. I needed him closer.

I needed *him*.

Chapter Twenty

Corey

"Yo, Chaos, catch!" someone yelled from behind me and I whipped around in time to see a sweet spiral roll off Jace's fingertips.

"Eek!" Victoria ducked and I raised my gloved hand and palmed the ball. It would have totally been the most epic thing had I actually caught it. Instead, it flopped to the side and bounced off the pile of snow I was walking by.

"Dude!" Jace jogged toward me, plumes of white streaming from his mouth. The temperature hadn't even hit double digits today and here he was without gloves and wearing only a jacket and stocking cap for winter gear?

I had a scarf, double-layer gloves, the thickest stocking cap I could find, and hand and feet warmers. I was ready to get to the inside-the-convention-center portion of tonight's festivities with my girl.

My girl?

Holy shit, I just called her my girl.

Then again, that wicked-hot kiss in the ice house earlier today... I didn't kiss just anyone like that. But *my girl*? Would she even be interested in that title? Was I? It was moving pretty fast.

Sure, we'd known each other for a couple of years prior to this but still. I wasn't going to be here much longer. And if everything went as planned, I'd land the spot on *What's Your Note?*, get a record deal, and be able to start showcasing my own music.

But that kiss... I hadn't been able to stop thinking about it. About Victoria.

"Stick to the guitar playing, Chaos," Jace teased as he bent over and picked up the ball I so gracefully didn't catch. "Come on, let's see how you do throwing snowballs at targets."

Victoria grinned. "Oh yeah, this is a fun one."

"Another snowball fight?"

She nabbed my hand and tugged me into a jog, following Jace. Up ahead, Landon and Hope were strolling hand-in-hand, carrying steaming cups of something I might need stat.

Tony and Mia were ahead of them and turned in our direction.

"Hey!" Tony said to me, but they kept going.

"Snow Bowl!" Jace yelled as he trudged along. "Yeah, Chaos, see if you can win your girl a prize."

Your girl. *My girl.*

I started thinking about that kiss again.

It kind of made me want to get out my phone, call Jethro,

and tell him to pull me out of the running for the show. That I was moving here to live a normal life in Twin River.

I couldn't do that, though. This show was my chance to get a music deal. It was what I'd always wanted. It was way too soon to be thinking thoughts like this. But there was something about Victoria. I couldn't explain it, but I felt it.

"Should I be worried about something called *Snow Bowl*?" I asked Victoria as we hustled along. The little jog actually started warming me up.

"Just like the carnival game where you have bowling pins stacked and you whip baseballs at them to knock 'em down."

"Oh, yeah. I know that one." I'd actually been okay at that game.

"Well, instead of baseballs, it's snowballs!" Jace clapped his hands. "Outta the way."

The people milling around parted like the Red Sea for the big football player. At the end stood a row of booths, like a normal carnival in the summer. Except it was outside in the freezing cold and the games were slightly modified for snow.

"Please tell me the prizes are ridiculously huge teddy bears," I said as a Snow Bowl booth came into sight up ahead.

"That'd be a yes." Victoria smiled as she grabbed my hand.

I held up our joined hands and smiled. "This okay?"

"More than okay. This'll eat Todd up."

My heart sank a little at the idea that she wanted to hold my hand only to make him jealous. I mean, it was the whole reason we were doing this, what I'd agreed to do, but that kiss we'd shared earlier felt like way more than trying to make someone jealous. Plus, we'd been alone. It hadn't even counted as one of our seven public dates.

I was starting to hate that non-contract. *If any of this got out...*

"I had fun at the ice house today."

"You make a mean picnic," Victoria said.

"Thanks. I'm just sorry we didn't catch anything."

She smiled. "But you had fun...right?"

I nodded, thinking about that kiss *yet again*. My heart rate spiked as an image of her kissing me flashed before my mind's eye. How soft her lips were. Her scent. Soft little nips as she took control of the kiss.

"Can I ask you something?" she said.

"Anything."

"That kiss..."

My heart rate picked up as her bright brown eyes flickered. "Yeah?"

"I'm sorry... I—"

"Don't be sorry." I nudged her with my elbow while still keeping my hold on her hand. I'd become thoroughly addicted to holding her hand. And the fact that she let me... that made me feel even better. Then again, we were at one of our seven *public* dates, so...

Ugh.

"I just...well, it was nice. I liked it."

"Me too," I said, leaning toward her.

"You did?"

"If you couldn't tell, then I was doing something wrong." *Yikes.* Maybe she didn't like it? Thought it was a mistake.

"Oh, no. Um...you weren't. It was perfect." She tugged

at the scarf around her neck as if nervous. "But. It's—we agreed we wouldn't, but—"

"Don't worry. I won't sue you," I said, totally joking.

"Well, *that's* a relief." She giggled and leaned in to me. I let go of her hand and draped my arm around her shoulders.

"Come on, let me win you a prize."

Her cheeks reddened.

"Hey there! Ready to give this a try?" the booth attendant asked. He was about five feet tall and probably weighed barely a buck twenty—even with all his winter gear on.

"Yeah, well, let's do this." I handed him a fifty. "How many tries will this get me?"

"As many as you like." He offered up a huge silver-filled smile. He wore those braces loud and proud. "You have to knock all the pins off the stand with a snowball."

I accepted the snowball he gave me. "Thanks."

Victoria turned and cupped my hands. She inhaled and then blew on the snow.

"Did you just breathe on snow?"

"Yeah, for good luck!"

She winked at me, sending an instant shiver down my spine. And it wasn't because of the nearly sub-zero temps, either.

"That's in craps!"

"What can I say? I'm good luck."

I nudged her, then laughed as a couple people huddled in around us, watching.

"Ahhh, that's so cute," someone said.

Damn straight it was. Victoria was good luck. Scratch that, she was my good luck charm. I was gonna win my girl this stuffed bear if it was the last thing I did.

I wound up and tossed the snowball. All but one pin fell off the stand. Dang that thing was wide. This might be harder than I thought.

I threw another ball and it bounced off to the side again.

The small crowd around us sighed.

"Come on, Chaos," Jace yelled.

"Told you I'd need all the chances I can get," I said to the attendant as he handed me more snowballs.

I faced Victoria. "Okay, one more blow."

She licked her lips. As she leaned in, I ducked slightly and smiled. "On second thought... A kiss might bring me more luck."

I pressed my lips to hers for the briefest of seconds and she smiled. That look of happiness and trust thrilled me right down my spine.

"Okay." I cleared my throat, searching for some composure, and I focused on the pins. They were twenty feet away on a circular stand that was huge. How was I going to knock them all off?

I took in a deep breath and then tossed that damn snowball as hard as I could.

It was like everything else faded away. Only the snowball remained. Hovering in the air like an actual baseball. Time stood still. It felt like hours and the last pin wobbled, nearing the edge.

The crowd around me gasped.

"Yes!" Tony yelled.

And then the pin stopped wobbling, remaining on the stand.

"Dang it!" I yelled. "So close!"

Victoria clapped. "You got this! Come on!"

The scrawny kid behind the counter handed me another two snowballs. "You got this, man. Get your girl that prize!"

"You got this," she whispered, leaning in to me.

"Get a room." Todd came in beside her and rolled his eyes.

His date wasn't far behind, and she was carrying a brown teddy bear, about the size of a sack of cotton candy I'd seen hanging from the booth earlier.

Weak.

Victoria sagged, staying focused on me, and said again, "You got this."

Oh hell yes, I'd get this. I'd show this asshat a thing or two.

I threw another snowball and it didn't clear the pins. I almost let a cuss rip, but I held it in. I would stay classy and not let on how much I needed to cream Todd at this game. The jerk came up beside me, holding five snowballs.

"Booo," someone shouted from behind us. It kind of sounded like Tony, and I had to work pretty hard to not laugh.

Victoria moved to the other side of me while Todd's girl was on his opposite side. So I was shoulder to shoulder with the guy who busted up Victoria's heart.

I'd show him.

He tossed three balls and they all tanked.

"Okay, this is the one," I whispered to Victoria, leaning toward her. I held it up to her.

She blew on it, then leaned in and pressed a quick kiss to my lips. Oh yeah, this was it. I knew it. Focusing on the pins, I sent up a prayer to the baseball gods and pitched that snowball.

Boom. All the pins blasted in every direction.

Not a single one left on the stand.

"Yes!" a bunch of people shouted behind me.

I whipped around, then wrapped my arms around Victoria's waist and hoisted her up. "Boom!"

"Bada bing!" She wove her arms around my neck and planted a kiss on my lips. I let her slide down the front of me, staying connected, and buried my fingers in her hair, holding her lips to mine for a beat.

There was nothing more that I wanted to do than stay connected to her for days, but this definitely wasn't the place. I liked showing Todd up and all, but I wanted her to kiss me for real. As in, kiss me because she liked me and wanted to. Not to show anyone up, which was exactly what was happening right now.

I eased back and she looked up at me with wide, dilated eyes.

Okay, maybe not. Maybe she didn't do it for that.

"Thank you," she whispered.

I kissed the tip of her nose then looked at the attendant, holding a big pink teddy bear almost the size of Victoria.

"You did it!" she said, her big eyes bright.

"Corey Chaos: the Snow Bowl champion," the attendant said.

Oh wow, he'd known who I was but hadn't let on. That was cool.

A few people came in around us, but I distinctly noticed that Todd wasn't one of them.

Awesome. Score another one for team Victoria.

Chapter Twenty-One

Victoria

"This guy is pretty cute, huh?" Corey asked, motioning to the bear he was holding. It was pink with a white stomach and there was a big pink bow wrapped around its neck.

"Not as cute as you," I said. "But pretty close."

He winked at me.

Flirting came so natural with Corey. It was never like that with Todd.

Ugh, Todd.

I can't believe he tried to show Corey up at the Snow Bowl.

What a jerk.

That girl he's with is so pretty, though...

My shoulders drooped. She was model-level pretty, like most of the dates Corey had had over the last year or so. What was I compared to them? Was that why Todd dumped me? I wasn't pretty enough?

No. Todd was an ass. *I'm strong. I'm pretty.* And if the way Corey kissed me was any indication, he liked me for me. Sure. It started out as a contract...which I really needed to talk to him about. Confirm if all this was only because of the deal we'd made.

But I was scared of the answer.

"I'm glad we're at the indoors part of this event," Corey said, shivering. "But I think I still need a gallon of steaming hot cocoa to warm up. After the cotton candy sugar rush, though."

We'd dropped our winter gear at the coat check and were strolling around the indoor carnival. It was like Twin River's famous Ice Festival but *inside* the huge convention center.

Warm fingers threaded with mine and I looked down. His sun-kissed skin was several shades darker than my pale winter complexion. It surprised me how comfortable I felt with him holding my hand. In just a couple days it had gotten to the point where it felt natural.

I was so okay with that.

"One extra, extra, extra-large cotton candy, please," Corey said to the cashier as we approached the booth. He released his hold on me, so I wrapped my now-free arm around my teddy bear. Resting my face against the soft fabric, I drew in a deep, contented breath. Corey was absolutely the sweetest guy I knew. The joy flashing in his eyes when he gave me the teddy bear, my heart swelled.

I'd already had more fun in four days at this Ice Festival than I did last year with Todd.

Before I could waste another thought on Todd, Corey

handed me the biggest cotton candy I'd ever seen in my life.

"It's almost the size of the bear," I joked.

Corey's floppy brown hair was pushed off to the side. His chestnut eyes sparkled. It was easy to see why people were obsessed with him.

I led Corey over to an empty picnic table near the area that had been fashioned after a park in the summer. They even had heaters placed around the tables. It was a good spot for people watching and thanks to a big fake tree stooped over us, it felt like we were in a private little nook.

He propped the bear up next to me, but it promptly fell over.

Laying the bear on top of the table, we sat on the bench together, shoulder to shoulder. The big fuzzy thing kind of hid us, too, so I slouched down a little and he must have gotten the hint, because he did, too.

I tore a piece of cotton candy off and popped it into my mouth. "Mmmmmm."

Corey laughed.

"What?" I asked, my mouth full of the dissolving sugar.

He kissed me on the cheek. "You're adorable, you know that?"

"Are compliments in the non-contract?" I asked.

Corey's brows pulled together. "No. I mean it."

Heat crept up the back of my neck. "Really?"

He tipped up my chin and placed a sugary kiss on my lips. "Really."

Sticky fingers and all, I grabbed his face and pulled him closer.

Our lips crushed together and what started out sweet morphed into hunger. And I could feast on his mouth for hours. I knew I should talk to him about how we were blurring the lines of our deal, but I couldn't get enough of his kisses. His touch. His scent.

"Corey! Corey! Corey!"

I yanked back and there was a group of at least ten girls standing around us. Their cell phones were all out and one of them appeared to have just snapped a picture of us.

Seriously?

"Will you take a picture with me?" a beautiful girl with perfectly curled brunette hair asked. She had on tight jeans and a shirt with the shoulders cut out.

Corey flashed a killer smile as if he wasn't bothered by the interruption at all. "I'll make a deal with all of you."

The girls nodded, as if they'd agree to anything he proposed.

"If you delete the pictures you just took of me and my girl, I'll take one with each of you. Kiss on the cheek and all."

"Yes!" one girl screamed.

"Done," another said, flashing her screen to Corey.

"Cool, show me it's gone and we'll get our selfie on!" Corey winked at me as the girls lined up.

I wished the girls hadn't interrupted us. My lips burned. I desperately wanted to go back to kissing Corey, but the moment had passed.

"Be sure you're following me on Insta," Corey told the girls. "I'm going to post a story on there tomorrow with details about a meetup."

"Epic," one of the girls said.

Corey gave them a killer smile. "Now, if it's cool, I'm going to go spend some time with my girl."

"Totally cool," the apparent leader of the group said. She linked arms with two of the girls and motioned her head at the rest. "Come on, let's give them some privacy."

Giggles erupted as well as hushed voices as the girls walked away.

"Sorry about that," he said as he sat back down on the bench next to me.

"You handle these situations so well," I said. "If my dad would have seen a picture of us kissing…"

Corey shrugged. "No worries. All evidence has been erased."

"You manage to stay so calm."

"Taking charge of the situation helps a lot." Corey took a bite of the cotton candy. "And I am planning something. Maybe at Annie's Coffee Shop…haven't figured it out yet."

"Hey," I said with a big smile. "I've got an idea. Come with me!"

Keeping our heads down, we hugged the shadows and sped to the coat check.

"Hey, what's up?" Tony came up behind us.

"Perfect timing!" I yelled and shoved my bear toward him. "Can you hold this for me?"

Eli, one of Tony's basketball teammates, came up beside him, his eyes wide as he watched me.

"We're…disappearing." I reached over and pulled down the stocking cap Corey had thrown on until it almost covered his eyes. I zipped up his big jacket to his neck and said, "Hide that cute face of yours."

Tony checked our surroundings. "I think I get what's going on here."

"Glad someone does," Corey said.

"I'm hiding your identity and stealing you away!" I threw my stuff on, disguising myself as best I could in my thick winter clothing, then grinned at Tony. "Cover for us if anyone asks where we are, okay?"

He shielded us with his big body as we bolted out the front doors into the frigid cold.

"What's gotten into you?" Corey asked.

I tugged him along. Two horse-drawn carriages that gave rides through town and the Ice Sculpture Gardens were lined up near the curb.

"Ahhh, now I get it." Corey kept his head down and we jumped into one.

"Evening," the portly driver said. He was decked out in winter gear and I'd seen a mini heater near his feet as I settled in beside Corey.

I gathered up the blanket that was on the side of our seat and tossed it over us. Corey reached up and pulled the little canopy thing over us a bit more, creating our own semi private space.

"Great idea," Corey said as he leaned forward and snagged the thermos from his side of the seat. "We're gonna need this."

He poured us steaming hot drinks and handed me mine. Together we pulled the blanket up. Sitting so close, our legs brushed against each other's, I snuggled even farther beneath the cover. He draped his free arm over my shoulder and I basked in his warmth.

The cool air whipped through the carriage, but it was like we had our own protective bubble around us, because I didn't feel anything but Corey.

The carriage jerked into motion and some gentle music

floated from where the driver sat.

"They thought of everything."

I kissed Corey's cheek, then worked out my camera with my free hand. "Say Victoria is a genius!" And I snapped a picture.

Snuggling back to him, he kissed my forehead and held me close.

Electricity zipped from my head to my toes.

I took a sip of my cocoa.

"This is pretty freaking awesome, Tor."

"I didn't have it planned, it just kind of hit me." I'd acted impulsively, but this time, it was for the good.

"Well, I like the way your mind works," Corey said.

Cold wind whipped through the carriage.

Corey snuggled closer and quietly said, "My dad would have loved this Ice Festival."

"Yeah?"

"He always took me to the California State Fair."

Sadness tugged at my heart.

I kissed him on the cheek, encouraging him to continue. I wanted to know more about this awesome guy.

"I miss him," Corey said softly.

"What's one of your favorite memories?"

Corey stared ahead as he drew in a long, slow breath. "We used to make model rockets. Once they were done, he'd take me out into the desert and set them off. We'd pack a lunch and make a day of it. He was into nature, too, so he'd make this bingo board for us. We'd have to find all of these animals, different species of cacti, and stuff like that. It was so fun."

"That sounds special."

"And, of course, he'd bring his guitar. We'd sing, he'd show me more tips about playing the instrument, and we'd hang out. Me and him."

"How long have you played guitar?"

"For as long as I can remember. Maybe when I was, like, six he got me my first one."

"Wow. That's young."

Grinning, he tightened his grip on me.

"You're really sweet, you know that?"

He didn't say anything.

"I mean it," I said, resting my head on his shoulder. "You're not like most guys."

"I try not to be," he whispered.

"In a good way. Really, really good way." Beneath the blanket, my mittened hand found his and I held it tight. "Thanks for telling me that stuff about your dad."

Even though it was freezing cold outside, I felt warm and content sitting next to Corey.

He nodded, not saying much more, so we sat in a comfortable silence until I felt the carriage jostle again. I lifted my head and looked skyward to the black void dotted with bright stars. "It's really beautiful out there, huh?"

"Just like you." Corey tipped my chin up. "Can I kiss you again, even though no one is around to witness it?"

Nodding, I pulled him and claimed his lips.

And we didn't stop kissing until the carriage ride was over.

Chapter Twenty-Two

COREY

That chord sounded like I was scratching my nails down a chalkboard. I leaned over my guitar and scribbled it out.

I tossed the pencil to the side and settled back into the couch cushion, taking in a deep breath. Closing my eyes, I slid my fingers over the cool, smooth strings, finding the right position. Everything was calm and quiet in the pool house. Lights were dim. I'd had nearly two solid hours alone, working on this new piece.

Best. Two. Hours. Ever.

Well, besides the time I spent with Victoria last night. The carnival, winning her that prize, but mostly, the kissing on the carriage ride. We were so far outside the lines of our non-contract it wasn't even funny. But I didn't care. I freaking loved it.

And the inspiration was triggering lyrics and notes

streaming into my mind. I'd had a hard time keeping up with my thoughts today, they were coming so fast and furious.

I strummed the strings and finally found a combination that worked, then sang it, "Lost in the crowd. Adrift in the sea. I'd been hurting for so long, until you found me..."

Okay. That was better. Not perfect, but better.

I hunched over and scribbled out a few more bars, the melody floating through my mind. This was the first time in months that I'd had time to throw down some fresh lyrics and it felt amazing, like a weight off my chest. I closed my eyes again and let out a long, slow breath. Victoria's image slid along my mind's eye. Her sweet brown eyes. Her skin, so smooth and soft.

"Your pure heart, healed me to the core. All I wanted was to help this time."

I ran my fingers down the strings, then tapped them silent. "No, that doesn't work."

"Sounded good to me," Victoria's voice filtered into the room from behind me.

I glanced over my shoulder, surprised to see her standing in the pool house doorway, leaning against the frame with her arms crossed over her chest. Damn, she looked amazing, and she wasn't wearing a skintight designer dress, five-inch high heels, or ten pounds of makeup.

She was...Victoria. *Tor.* She was stunning in a Twin River High sweatshirt and dark-wash jeans. She had green and gray ribbons pinned throughout her hair and she had a Fighting Pike temporary tattoo on her cheek.

"You're home from school?" I checked my phone lying on the coffee table in front of me.

Damn, it was already three p.m.

"Oh shit. I'm sorry. I didn't come get you." I went to set my guitar on the couch beside me and go to her, but she put up her hand and smiled.

"No big deal. Mia gave me a ride."

I gave her a smile of relief. "You didn't have those ribbons and face tattoos when I dropped you off this morning."

"Ice Ball spirit week. Mia, Sophia, Bailey and I did ourselves up at the school."

"Looks awesome."

She grinned and her eyes crinkled and shimmered like I loved. "I just kind of let myself in. The door was open and... well, I heard you."

I grabbed the glass of water I had beside my sheets of music.

"Sorry if I—maybe I should have knocked. I can go. I—"

"No!" I set the glass down and waved her over. "It's totally fine."

She crossed the small room toward me, holding out a sweatshirt. "I got you something."

"Oh yeah?" I accepted the Fighting Pike sweatshirt from her.

"It's for the Ice Ball pep rally, so you have something spirit-like."

I held up the gray hoodie. "Love it. Thanks. So tonight's event isn't Ice Festival related?"

"Kind of. It's a rally to get everyone excited about the upcoming Annual Food Pantry Drive. The Twin River High student who gets the most food wins an awesome prize. Last year, I won second place. It was pretty cool."

"Hmm... Maybe I can help you win this year?"

She smiled. "You're sweet. Thanks, Corey."

"I'll do some brainstorming," I said, tapping my temple.

"Okay." She pointed to the mess of papers on the coffee table before me, then nodded toward the guitar in my hands. "The melody of that song you were playing sounded really nice. It's not a cover, is it?"

I shook my head.

"Can I hear some?"

"I'm stuck. Can't quite find the right words for this part." I tapped the second verse on the sheet of music before me. "It's a mess."

"Mind if I look?" She eased onto the couch beside me and a swirl of her lilac scent settled in around me. I loved that smell. It would forever remind me of Victoria.

I curled a strand of her hair behind her ear as she read the lyrics I'd jotted down so far. I never let anyone look at my stuff, especially when it was mid-project, not even my mom. But with Victoria, it felt natural. I was starting to trust her. That scared the shit out of me but also felt nice.

I'd only ever had that with my dad, since he was a musician, too. And then when all this Chaos thing started I wasn't sure who to trust.

"Hey, if you switch out this part it might flow better," she said, pointing to the sentence I'd just scribbled. "Something like...all I wanted was more and more?"

"Yes. That's perfect!" I scribbled out my words and jotted hers down, then picked up my guitar again. I strummed the melody from the top, humming through that first verse and the chorus. This song was about her and she added the perfect lyrics. Tor really was my lucky charm.

"All I wanted was more and more," I sang out and the change was perfect.

"That sounds great," she said. "Can I hear the whole thing?"

"Nope." I set the guitar down. "No can do."

"What?" She sat up, feigning sadness with a pouty lip.

I leaned in and kissed her cheek. I wasn't sure I was ready to tell her that she was the inspiration for the song. That I was starting to fall for her, pretty hard. Things were complicated with me and my world. I wasn't sure she'd want to try anything with me, either, so I changed the subject. "How was your day?"

"School's school."

"I'd better text Rita. I totally spaced my meeting with her during independent study." I snatched my phone from the tabletop and turned over my lyrics. "No peeking."

She showed her hands in surrender.

My phone vibrated in my hand before I could text Rita.

MOM: Hi honey. How are you??

ME: Great.

ME: Nice and rested, even writing a new song!

MOM: That's wonderful, honey.

MOM: Miss you and see you soon!

ME: Love you.

MOM: Love you too!

The thought of seeing my mom again brought mixed emotions. Of course I'd be happy to see her, but at the same time, it'd mean I was over two thousand miles away from

Victoria.

Pushing the conflicting thoughts out of my mind, I jetted a text to Rita, explaining how I got lost in some music and would get with my tutor ASAP, then I slid the phone in my back pocket and shuffled over to the fridge. I needed sugar. Water wasn't doing it for me right now. Mom hadn't texted me in four days. She was still working way too hard. I wished she'd slow down and actually start the grieving process. I didn't get why she always had to be doing something, going somewhere, or dating someone.

"Everything okay?" Victoria asked from the couch. She'd lain down on her back and propped her feet on the arm.

"Yeah." I snagged a grape Fanta from the fridge and held it up. "You want?"

"Naw. I'm good."

My phone vibrated again so I pulled it out as I cracked open my soda.

JETHRO: I think you're getting the part, kid!

ME: Oh wow!

JETHRO: Should hear the final decision this week.

Oh wow? That's the best I could come up with?

I should be way more excited than I felt. A music contract, for my own songs, not covers, looked like it was close to being real. This was the chance of a lifetime, but—

"Doesn't seem like everything's okay," Victoria said, still lying on the couch. "Missing school, forgetting to pick me up."

"I'm sorry, I got caught up in this new song and... Well, I haven't been able to create anything new in a while and I totally lost track of everything." I made my way toward the couch again.

"Oh, right." She gave a small nod and a pang of guilt cramped my stomach. First for forgetting to pick her up from school; it was always a great time to flaunt in front of Todd. But mostly for blurring the lines of the deal we'd made. This week I might find out I got the part in the show and I'd leave Twin River shortly after that.

The heaviness I'd gotten rid of during that music writing session settled right back on my shoulders. Heavier, too. I'd leave Victoria. And I wasn't so sure I wanted to do that anymore. I should say something. Tell her what Jethro had texted so she was in the know about it.

I wimped out instead and said, "Epic fail on my part. I know that's in the non-contract to come pick you up and drop you off." I lifted her feet, then plopped onto the couch and set them on my lap. "When I start writing music it's like I'm on a different planet."

"Yeah. Me too."

I raised my eyebrow at her.

She grinned. "I wrote a new poem last night."

"That's awesome. I want to read it."

She wiggled her finger back and forth. "Nope. No can do. As you would say."

I leaned over and tickled her stomach. She squealed and shoved my hands away and then started laughing. I got it, though. I usually didn't like people seeing my stuff until it was done. It was really personal.

"That's cool, Tor. I'm glad you're writing again. And

don't worry, I totally get the not-letting-me-read-it part. But I hope one day you'll let me check out something you've written."

"Maybe," she said, flirting.

"I'll make you a deal. When we're both ready, you let me read one of your poems and I'll play my new song for you."

"Deal." Her brown eyes sparkled. It was like she was magnetic. I was so drawn to her, it was almost scary.

I set my can of soda on the table, then crawled toward her. Her eyes shot wide and she drew in a quick breath. "Can I kiss you?"

She nodded and I crashed my lips against hers. A burst of her strawberry lip gloss danced across my taste buds. Her fingers combed through my hair until they cupped the back of my head. She pulled me onto her and her body formed to mine. Warmth from her seeped through her sweatshirt and into my chest. She kissed me with a sense of urgency and passion that tripped a jolt of heat straight down my spine.

I eased my hand down and slid it beneath her thigh, opening her more to me. Curling her leg around mine, Victoria arched into me, letting out a sigh that rocked my world. There was no better feeling than her beneath me.

I got lost in her kisses. Her touch. Nothing else mattered right now. No deals, no acting or singing, no Instagram. Nothing. Just me and her. Here. Together.

I wasn't sure how much time passed, but she eased away a fraction, her chest heaving. "We should probably get going... We don't want to be late for the pep rally."

"Absolutely not," I said, leaning in to her. "This is way more fun than anything else you have planned. Well, unless you're planning to take me to the bedroom."

"Corey!" She playfully slapped my shoulder.

"I'm kidding," I said, sort of not kidding, as I propped myself up beside her. Thoughts of her and I rolling around on the mattress in my pool house bedroom raced through my head.

Her cheeks were flushed and her lips shiny and swollen. Watching me with her cottonwood bark eyes, she grinned and brushed her thumb across my bottom lip. She cupped my face and drew in a deep breath all the while her gaze scanning my face. Looking almost pensive, she traced her thumb along the skin beneath my eye and smiled.

"I can't believe we're here, together, like this," she whispered.

Still on top of her, my elbows on either side of her head, propping me up, I touched a kiss to her nose. "Me neither."

My phone buzzed again and Victoria said, "Shoot... We really should get going."

"Right... The pep rally." I nipped at her bottom lip. "Yay. Rah. Rah." I touched a kiss to her lips. She chuckled and I pushed up off her, the last thing I wanted to do. Things were a little hot right now and I needed to be careful. I didn't want to hurt her.

"Okay." I stood up and reached for her. "Let's head out."

She slid her hand into mine and I pulled her to her feet. She pushed up onto her toes and brushed her lips to mine. "For the record... I'd rather stay here instead, too."

Chapter Twenty-Three

Victoria

MIA: I thought we were going to the pep rally together.

MIA: Your parents said you left five minutes ago with Corey.

ME: Sorry!

ME: I totally forgot.

ME: Corey and I are going to be there in ten minutes.

ME: Want us to save you a seat?

She sent an eye roll emoji.

ME: What's that supposed to mean?

ME: It was an accident.

MIA: You're always with him.

ME: You didn't care when I hung out with Todd…

MIA: Whatever, I'll see you later.

I chewed on my fingernail. A bad habit that I hadn't given in to in years. But Mia's attitude was anything but subtle. I'd let her down. Sure, Corey was here for only a month, but that didn't mean I should ditch my best friend.

"What's up?" Corey asked.

"I screwed up." I clicked the button on the side of my phone. After the screen went black, I tossed it into one of the cup holders in the console.

"How?" Corey took the familiar route to school.

"I told Mia that we'd ride to the pep rally together."

"Oh shoot," Corey said. "Should we go pick her up?"

"No, she's already on her way." I chewed on my nail. "And she thinks that you and I are spending too much time together."

Corey frowned. "I'm sorry."

"What are you apologizing for?" I asked. "It's not your fault."

"I'm the reason you haven't been hanging out with her." He put on his blinker and steered into the school parking lot.

"I'm the one who screwed up," I admitted. "But, honestly, the last time she had a boyfriend, she hung out with him like twenty-four seven." I knew it wasn't right to use that as an excuse, but it made me feel better saying it out loud.

"Boyfriend, huh?" Corey wiggled his eyebrows. "Are you saying I'm your boyfriend?"

I froze right there in my seat. I had just called him that, hadn't I? I mean, not exactly, but kind of implied it. Crap. What should I say now?

"It's okay, Tor," he whispered as he scanned the parking lot for an empty spot. We were totally running late.

"Oh, um, yeah, because of the contract. I mean the non-contract. My fake boyfriend," I said, my stomach churning. *Shit*. I wanted him for my *real* boyfriend. But he was leaving soon.

I took a deep breath and exhaled slowly. This whole thing had started out fake, him doing me a favor to shove it to Todd, but now…it'd turned into so much more.

"Yeah, for the non-contract," Corey said, turning away. "Maybe Mia can hang out with us tonight?"

"I don't know if she will. She sounded pretty mad." I twisted the end of my ponytail around my pointer finger.

"What's her favorite thing to do? Like, something that the two of you like doing together?"

"She loves Shane Redman," I said. "She makes me watch his videos on YouTube, like constantly."

"Ah, Shane," Corey said with a smile as he pulled into an open parking spot near the middle of the lot. "He's a good guy."

"You know him?" I asked.

"Yup," he said. "When's her birthday?"

"Next month." I arched an eyebrow. "Why?"

"We should throw her a surprise birthday party," he said

and we both got out of the Jeep. "Maybe I can get Shane to make her a video or something?"

"She'd love you forever." I could picture her face now. Lighting up as all of our friends jumped out and shouted, "Surprise!" and then Shane's video playing. I chuckled.

"I'll text Shane after the pep rally."

"You are the *best*, you know that?"

"Anything for my girl." Corey gave me a lopsided grin that made my knees nearly give out. Hearing him call me his girl again…even better the second time. The wind was whipping freezing cold snow around me and I didn't feel a thing. The warmth of hearing him call me his girl chased away any kind of chill in the air.

So did the memory of our time on the couch before coming here.

"She's going to be so pumped," I said as we walked through the main doors of Twin River High. It was the least I could do for my best friend. I had been spending all my free time with Corey lately and I hadn't told her about the fake relationship thing. Hopefully she wouldn't be too upset when I did. *If* I did. This might be a secret that I have to keep…forever.

"Ooh, there she is," I said to Corey. "I'm going to go talk to her."

"Take your time."

"Mia!" I exclaimed.

My best friend spun around. She had a sour look on her face.

"Sit with us?" I asked. "Please?"

She bit her lower lip, debating the offer.

"I'm sorry I've been MIA," I added. "But I'm going to

make it up to you *big-time*."

She gave me a wry smile. "Oh yeah?"

"Yes." I gave her a bear hug.

"I've got an apology to make, too." Mia shrugged. "I'm sorry I questioned your relationship with Corey the other day at the ice cream place. You guys really are perfect for each other."

"We totally are," I said, beaming.

Oh crap! I'd been acting like my relationship with Corey had been real this entire time, but I just admitted out loud that we're perfect for each other. But we're not. Our relationship is fake. Everything about us is fake!

Our kisses weren't fake...

Ugh! This is so freaking complicated.

Worst of all... He was leaving and probably starring in *What's Your Note?* The thought of him going out on dates and kissing someone made me want to hurl. Especially since it'd be on camera, for millions of viewers.

But what did I expect? That he'd stay here in Twin River? Give up his chance at making his own music and a record deal? No way. It was unfair to him to even think about it, let alone wish for it. I couldn't stand in the way of his amazing opportunity.

But I really did want him to stay.

Lost in my thoughts, Mia waved down Corey, who joined us as we walked into the gymnasium. Students, parents, and little brothers and sisters of Twin River students filled the stands. Streamers, pom-poms, and rally towels were everywhere.

We snagged a spot on the bottom bleacher by the boy's locker room.

"I haven't been to a pep rally in a long time," Corey said. "This is bringing back all of the memories."

A cheerleader jogged over to us and handed us pom-poms.

Principal Navarro walked into the middle of the gym. "Welcome to the Annual Food Pantry Drive pep rally!"

The crowd went wild, stomping on the wooden bleachers.

"As you know, the Fighting Pike has won the Food Pantry Drive trophy the past two years," he said. "This year, we've got a huge challenge on our hands. We have to raise more food for the Twin River Pantry than any of the other schools in town to keep our streak alive."

Everyone stomped their feet on the bleachers again and ripped whistles. A few kids even chanted, "Hat trick! Hat trick! Hat trick!"

"I'm asking that every student set a personal goal of gathering at least fifty items," Principal Navarro said. "It's a great cause and if we all try our hardest, we're sure to win. Don't forget, there's an awesome prize for the individual who raises the most food for our school."

Everyone cheered and waved their pom-poms and rally towels in the air.

"The student who turns in the most food, as in, the number of items, not weight, will win a party for themselves and nineteen of their friends at Adventure Zone and unlimited pizza and soda afterward at Giuseppe's Pizzeria."

The cheers got so loud I almost had to cover my ears.

Principal Navarro said with a massive smile on his face, "Food can be dropped off at your grade principal's office. Be sure to give the item count to Miss Yang or Mr. Kurtis, so it can be properly recorded."

Excitement coursed through the bleachers.

"Now our band and cheerleaders have a special presentation for you." He held his arms out, welcoming the two groups onto the gym floor.

Two of the band members ran to the front and waved massive silver flags back and forth in perfect synchroneity. The cheerleaders dragged something covered in a large cloth to the center of the gymnasium. With a tug, they revealed an ice sculpture of our mascot, the Mighty Pike. A few seconds later, the band started playing, and the cheerleaders broke out into a well-choreographed routine that included tumbling and stunt display.

I glanced over at Corey, who appeared to be mesmerized by everything.

"Having fun?" I asked, nudging his leg.

He winked. "How bad do you want to win the food drive?"

"What do you have in mind?" I asked as trumpets blared in front of us.

He put his mouth right up against my ear and whispered, "I think I might have an idea that could help us both out."

Chapter Twenty-Four

Corey

"I promised you a meet and greet!" I said into the camera on my phone. "Are you ready for this, my friends?"

The number of viewers jumped to nearly ten thousand over the first few minutes since I'd hit live on Instagram.

"If you're in Wisconsin, specifically Twin River, and you want a signed picture, or to ask a question, or even request a song, then come see me! But here's the thing. First, you have to *find* me, and I'll show you a shot of where I am in a bit. Second, you have to bring a can of food to donate."

The numbers of viewers jumped by the thousands again, so I kept going. I had to get Victoria some food. It would be so great if she won. And it wasn't only because it'd show Todd up, either. I *wanted* her to win. Those prizes the principal had mentioned during Monday's pep rally were pretty cool.

I held the camera to the side slightly, showing the coffee shop I was hanging out in. I didn't reveal anything that had the name of the shop, so it was a little harder, but hopefully people would think it fun to figure out.

"Not sure this coffee shop can handle the foot traffic you're sending its way." Jethro came up beside me, holding a steaming cup of joe.

I gave him a little nod, being sure to keep him out of the picture, then said, "Okay, everyone. Come find me and bring some canned food." I clicked end and flipped the phone over on the tabletop.

"You look good!" Jethro sat across from me at the four-person table I'd commandeered.

Annie's Coffee Shop had about twenty tables spread about the small square space, but only three tables were occupied. I'd been in here a few times since I'd come to Twin River and it never seemed very full. I'd dreamed this up on Monday during the pep rally and ran it by Annie, the owner, yesterday. Thankfully she was on board.

Hopefully this little post of mine would bring in some money for her, as well as help Victoria take in some food for the competition.

Anything to help her beat Todd. That jerk had been bragging to everyone all over Twin River that he was going to raise the most food.

"You really look good," Jethro said as he stared over his cup of coffee at me. He leaned back into the wooden chair, his dark brown eyes studying me. He wore a suit, which was funny, because he didn't work outside the house. Now that I thought about it, he always wore a suit.

I shook the random thought out of my mind and sipped

my chai latte. "What's up?"

"Haven't seen you much this past week." He set his cup down. "You getting some rest?"

"Yep. And hanging with Victoria. She's pretty cool."

"I kind of like her, too." He winked at me. "You guys seem to be getting along well."

His gaze hardened a little bit, so I turned on the charm. "She's been great, letting me hang out with her and her friends. I almost feel like I'm in high school again."

He dipped his head, his smile broadening. I knew he'd talked to Victoria about a few of our pictures he'd seen online and she'd said she explained them away as misconstrued, but I wasn't so sure he was buying it. She was worried how it would affect her dad if he knew about the fake but quickly turning real relationship going on with us.

Then again, I didn't even know what was happening anymore, because I was having some intense, not so fake feelings for her. So I needed to just smooth things over with him.

What I *wanted* to do was tell him how much I liked his daughter and wanted to date her for real. But he was my agent. How would that work? What would people think? Would Jethro drop me as a client?

I hadn't manned up and openly asked Victoria what she wanted yet, either. Maybe once I knew if I'd gotten the part on the show things would work out.

"I heard from Roberts," Jethro said.

"Is he calmed down yet with the fact that I'm here?" My publicist, Jacob Roberts, wasn't the most accommodating person, especially when it came to losing money. And the fact that I wasn't in L.A., making appearances, meant he wasn't making as much money with me right now.

"I've got him taken care of." Jethro grinned. "He says the part on the show is between you and Damion Winthrop. But Roberts says the producers are leaning your direction."

A mix of excitement and sadness rushed through my stomach like someone had kicked me. It was between me and Damion. I knew him. He was a pretty amazing performer. He did covers, too, but mostly his own music. And he'd had some pretty solid duets with some high-ranking pop stars out there.

I probably wouldn't get it. Compared to him, I was a no-name. Why would the show pick me? That'd make my decision to stay here in Twin River easy, though. So that was good. But the music deal.

I really wanted that.

"So...when would I have to report to the show if I get it?"

"Shooting would start in a couple of weeks. So you've got time for some solid R and R until then."

Crap, that meant cutting my month here short. "Thought you said I had four weeks here?"

"Give or take a few days." He reached for his coffee but didn't take his focus off me. "What's going on? You okay?"

I nodded. I wanted to tell him to bag it all. Scrap my entire schedule for the next two years so I could do school like a normal teenager. Date my girl like a normal guy. Just...be *normal*.

But I wasn't normal. Was I? I had a gift. I should use it, right? Like now. Why couldn't I use my fame for this kind of stuff instead of going onto a dating show? Sure, it wasn't the typical dating reality show, since it was more about the music. But it still had me dating girls, getting to know them so I could pick one to sing one of my original songs with.

"The relaxation has done well for ya." Jethro smiled. "Rita said your grades are up, too."

"Helps having daily study sessions and time to get my assignments done at Twin River High." I leaned my elbows onto the tabletop. "Jethro, can I ask you something?"

"Sure."

What would he think if he knew Victoria and I were dating? Would he be okay with it? But in reality, we weren't dating, were we? This was fake.

Shit. No. I liked her. I thought she liked me. I needed to know what might happen with it. What her dad might think of us dating.

"Jethro. What would happen if me and—"

"Corey Chaos!" someone screeched so loud I thought maybe the window next to me might shatter.

Jethro flinched and looked over his shoulder.

I hadn't even heard the front door ding open.

"We figured it out!" Two girls, about fourteen, full-on braces on their teeth, rushed at me with wide eyes. Both carried two cans of food. The door opened again and another few girls came in, carrying bags, hopefully full of canned goods.

"That didn't take long," Jethro said as he pushed back from the table. "Let's finish this chat tonight at dinner?"

I gulped, my hands getting sweaty. Maybe I'd dodged a bullet by not being able to ask him if I could date his daughter. Maybe I should talk to Victoria about it some more first. Like, see if she even wanted something real with me.

Then again, what was real? Besides, if I got the gig, would the producers even let me have a girlfriend? I was supposed to date the girls on the show, sing with them, and get closer to them to find my inspiration... Whatever, they probably wouldn't care. But what about Victoria? How would she feel about seeing me serenade other girls on television?

Oh man, my head was spinning with thoughts. What the hell did I even want?

"Okay, girls, let's get in line. You can drop your donation over there." Annie directed the girls to the side where there was a big empty box waiting to be filled with donations. At least if this little ploy turned out right.

Jethro gave me a smile, then bugged out of here. I waved the first girl over.

"One at a time," Annie said, standing at the front of the forming line.

Within a few minutes, there were seven people, all holding canned goods, standing through the middle of the shop. A few of them branched off to order some coffee, which was perfect. Maybe I should have said something about buying some in my Instagram live.

Next time.

"I love your music," the girl said. She had curly black hair and a big smile. Her face lit up as she stood in front of the table between us. Her leg was twitching like she was almost vibrating out of her skin.

"What's your name?" I asked as I slid a photo from the stack I'd set on the table.

"Raquel." Her eyes brightened even more as I uncapped a black sharpie.

I pressed the marker to the picture and said, "Raquel,

you have a beautiful smile. Much love, Corey Chaos."

"Omigosh." She gasped reaching for the picture. "Can I ask a question?"

"Shoot."

"That girl. The one in your stories, like all the time, is she your girlfriend? Do you love her? Are you going—"

"One question..." Yikes, I wasn't sure how to answer it, and thankfully, Victoria's dad had stepped out to take a phone call and hadn't overheard that.

Do I love Victoria Knight?

Chapter Twenty-Five

Victoria

"They are going to freak out when they see all of this food," Mia said from the back of the moving truck.

"Totally," I said, looking over my shoulder.

She'd crammed into the small space behind the driver seat. It technically wasn't a seat, but she made it work.

"You kids have really gone above and beyond," Annie said from behind the steering wheel.

There wasn't much space in the rented van and I was basically sitting on Corey's lap in the front seat. Thankfully we didn't have to go very far. Then again, I didn't mind sitting on Corey's lap, either. The Instagram live he'd done from Annie's yesterday was epic. He'd sat there for hours as people poured in from Twin River and surrounding towns to meet him. And everyone had brought so much food.

"Thanks, Annie, for doing this," Corey said.

"Happy to. Thank you for bringing in all those coffee drinkers yesterday."

Her hair was so gray it was nearly white. It looked amazing, though. Some girls tried to dye their hair that color gray, but she'd had it naturally since the age of thirty according to what she'd said earlier. She was close to sixty years old now, but I never would have guessed it by how spunky she was.

Maybe it was all the caffeine she consumed each day.

When I'd called Miss Yang and told her about the size of the donation, she asked if we could bring it directly to the convention center instead of to the junior class principal's office.

Navigating the full parking lot in a big truck was difficult and I was glad I wasn't driving.

"Ouch," Mia yelped as we went over a big dirt bump.

"Sorry," Annie said, her hands gripping the huge steering wheel. "I should have called my grandson, Lincoln, over to help."

"Lincoln Johnson?" I asked.

"You know him?" Annie asked.

"Senior. Don't know him super well, but pretty good. He's good friends with Carlin. I know her."

"Oh yes, her older brother is Lincoln's best friend." Annie nodded as she backed the van up to an open loading dock that we'd gotten special permission to use. The back of the van met the lip of the dock.

Mia stood up, but the van gave a slight jolt as Annie put it in park.

"Next time, if you could get a little less food, that would be great," Mia said sarcastically as she rubbed her head.

Corey laughed. "That was an awesome turnout, huh?"

Hundreds of people had flooded the little coffee shop yesterday, many bringing several cans of food, just to meet Corey. My dad had gone to get the moving truck once the box and the backup box had started to overflow. Good thing he had, because Corey had gathered over three thousand cans of food and other nonperishable items by the end of the day. Too bad Dad had an appointment in Milwaukee tonight and couldn't drive the van over.

We got out and took a short staircase up to the back of the stage.

A team of volunteers from Twin River High stood ready to get to work with several empty palettes at their feet. Everyone split off into two assembly lines and began unloading and stacking the canned items.

"Wow," Mia said, "this is quite the setup."

"Right?" I responded.

"Principal Navarro's here," Corey said, pointing off to the right.

"Victoria?" Principal Navarro said as he rubbed his gloved hands together. "This is all for the food drive? Mrs. Rupert mentioned you had a substantial donation. I just didn't know it would be *this* much!" His jaw dropped.

"Yup," I said. "It was all Corey, though."

Flabbergasted, my principal walked past the two assembly lines and peered into the packed truck. "This is incredible."

"Think it will help us win the competition?"

"Unless someone comes by with a packed eighteen-wheeler, I think we've got this in the bag."

Corey punched his fist into the air. "Go Twin River

High!"

"Fighting Pike! Fighting Pike! Fighting Pike!" Mia and I cheered as we jumped up and down, clapping our mittened hands.

"You kids did an amazing job," Principal Navarro said. "Congratulations!"

"Thank you. Corey made all of this possible." I bumped him with my hip.

Corey's cheeks turned red. "Mr. Navarro, after we help unload all of this, do you think we'll have time to get something to eat before the winner is announced?"

Principal Navarro checked his watch. "You should have about a half an hour. Keep an ear open for the announcement."

"Yes sir," Corey said.

Ten minutes later, the food was loaded onto palettes and stacked behind a long black curtain leading to the front of the stage.

Corey, Mia, and I all headed toward the side of the convention center that had a wooden arch with the sign Food Court on it. Even though it was freezing outside and there were several inches of snow on the ground, Twin River did it up right with an outdoor carnival. No rides or anything, but food stands and booths filled with local art and jewelry dotted the expansive grounds.

"What do you ladies want to eat?" Corey asked.

"Chili cheese corn dogs," Mia and I both said at the same time.

"Three chili cheese corn dogs coming up," Corey said.

Mia and I found a picnic table beside the food stands area. To our left sat a group of kids huddled by a heat lamp near their table.

"That was really cool," my best friend said, "getting the food donations like he did. You're going to win the prize for most collected, you realize that."

"Corey's a great guy."

"I can tell you like him," she said quietly. "A lot."

I paused. Even though she was my best friend, I hadn't told her much about my relationship with Corey. How could I without admitting that we were faking it? Or at least some of it? Everything had gotten so freaking complicated. The kisses, specifically the ones that made my knees go weak, were definitely not part of our deal, not that we'd signed it.

Crap. Speaking of the contract, I needed to shred that thing. I made a mental note to do that tonight. A small smile played on my lips. The last time I'd seen it had been when Corey and I were having some quality time on his couch. It had fallen underneath the coffee table.

"What are you going to do when he leaves?" she asked.

I dropped my gaze to the tabletop, not really sure how to answer.

Mia scooted closer to me. "Are you two going to try long distance or something?"

Those exact thoughts had bombarded my mind lately. But every time I tried to figure things out, I came up empty.

We could try long distance, but I had a year and a half left of high school, then college, and maybe graduate school. Corey was on a completely different path. He would be getting music and TV deals. His days would be spent at studios and in recording sessions. How would we ever make it work?

And then there was my dad. What would it do to his

rep if I got involved with another one of his clients? Corey was nothing like Grayson, but still. I'd been keeping my relationship with Corey from Dad like I had with Grayson. Flat-out lying to my dad on a few occasions when he'd asked me about some of the pictures he was seeing on Corey's feed.

"I'm sorry I doubted you guys. It's totally obvious you two are into each other."

What would she think if she knew it was fake? It started as a setup to stick it to Todd.

It wasn't fake for me, not anymore. It'd started out that way, but—

"Three chili cheese dogs, a basket of fries, and three sodas," Corey announced as he joined us at the table, holding a tray full of food.

Mia shot me a look, silently telling me that this conversation was far from over.

"Yummy," I said, although I failed to smile. I had too many questions swirling through my mind. Corey and I were into each other. But he was leaving. Should I ask him about it? Ask if he wants something more with me? Or was I being selfish? He had his career to think about. It wasn't like he'd turn down a music contract to stay around here, right?

That show. *Ugh*. The thought of him going out on dates with those girls...

"Everything okay?" Corey asked, placing his hand on my back as he sat beside me on the bench.

"Yeah, everything is fine...absolutely fine."

Twenty minutes later, we'd polished off all of the food and were throwing our garbage away when an announcement came on over the speakers.

"The winner of the Annual Food Pantry Drive will be announced in ten minutes," a loud voice boomed. "Please make your way to the stage."

"Let's go," Corey said.

He held my hand as we made our way to the stage. He was on my right and Mia, my best friend, was on my left. If only Corey wasn't going away in a couple weeks and it could stay like this. It took me by surprise how important he'd become to me. I'd known him for a couple years, but it hadn't been anything intimate. Now, so much about our relationship was different.

The things he'd shared with me about his family, how generous he was, and the fact that I felt like the most important girl in the universe when I was around him... It just felt natural to be with him.

A large crowd had already gathered at the front of the stage, so we ended up with a spot near the back. But that was okay; Todd and his new girlfriend were close to the front.

The mayor stood up on a small stage, holding a microphone. He was a tall, thin guy who kind of reminded me of a used car salesman I'd seen in movies with the slicked-back hair and big rings on his fingers. I didn't get how he wasn't wearing a hat; it was only about eighteen degrees right now.

"The high school students of Twin River, you all have done an *amazing* job!" He tucked the microphone under his arm and clapped, looking out over the crowd.

Cheers roared through the dark night air.

"This year, our city's high school students have collected more than five thousand nonperishable food items. *Five thousand!"*

Hoots and hollers rang out all around us and I couldn't help but smile at the sense of satisfaction thrumming through my chest. We'd been able to help an awesome cause. Well, Corey was able to. But he'd done this for me. When I'd seen his Instagram story, announcing his meet and greet and how he required a canned good donation to participate, I almost started crying.

"The race appeared to be fairly close until this evening, when one student managed to bring in three thousand and forty-seven items with a little help from a special friend."

People in the crowd started whispering.

"Thanks to that student's donation, the winner of this year's Food Pantry Drive is TWIN RIVER HIGH!"

Everyone erupted into a deafening round of applause.

"Now, we would like the student who raised more than half of the food collected to come up and receive the trophy for the school. Victoria Knight, please come up to the stage."

Heart thumping wildly, I reached for Corey's hand. "Come with me?"

He shook his head.

"Please? I'm freaking out. There's no way I can talk in front of all of these people!"

"But this is *your* moment."

My mouth went dry. "*Our* moment."

He smiled and accepted my hand, then we made our way through the crowd. My hands started sweating in my mittens and my throat tightened as we approached the stage. *Just breathe, Victoria.*

He guided me up the three steps. "You got this," he whispered, holding my hand up and turning me toward the crowd who went wild.

Flashes lit up the night and ignited a flurry of blue lights in my vision. I knew they were for Corey, but I was still nervous and my cheeks ached because I was smiling so broadly.

The mayor presented me with the two-foot-high golden trophy. "Thank you very much for your hard work. Not only have you helped Twin River High win the Annual Food Pantry Drive, but you also gathered the most food out of anyone in Twin River. Would you like to say anything to the crowd?"

"Ah, um, I, ah, um—"

Desperate to get the attention off of me, I shoved the microphone at Corey.

Flashing everyone a smile that would melt the coldest of hearts, Corey took the microphone and tapped it twice. "Hello, hello, is this thing working?"

The audience laughed.

"Listen, I'm only going to be up here a moment, but I'm really proud of everyone, at all of the schools, who participated in this event. When I was little, we weren't always sure where our next meal would come from. Thanks to generous donations like these"—he motioned over his shoulder—"we were able to have three meals a day."

Wow. I'd forgotten all about his upbringing being tough like that. He'd mentioned it on some talk shows before, how his parents had it rough for several years when he was barely in kindergarten.

Someone in the audience whistled, while a girl in the first row screamed, "I LOVE YOU, COREY!"

"Aw, thank you," he said.

"Victoria and I are proud to be able to make this donation. Thank you again to everyone who made it possible. Also, I have an important announcement. There is now a permanent food collection bin in Annie's Coffee Shop. Every time you donate ten cans of food, you'll get a free cup of coffee and a cookie. Annie is going to send me pictures when you donate so I can share them online. Thanks, Annie! Your dedication to helping those in need in Twin River is very commendable." He motioned to Annie, who was standing off to the right of the stage.

The crowd clapped and cheered. Damn, he was amazing. To be able to come up onstage like that and totally own it blew my mind. And then, to work with Annie and set that up. He was so genuine. Sweet. Thoughtful.

"Thanks again, Mayor Turnberry," Corey said as he handed the microphone back.

Crap... Corey does stuff like this all the time.

How will we ever work out if I can't even handle two seconds of fame in Twin River?

Shaking my head, I fought the tears that stung the corners of my eyes.

I'd fallen for Corey. I wanted to be with him. I'd figure out how to deal with his fans and the press. He was worth it. I just hoped he felt the same way about me.

Screw it, I'm going to talk to Corey—tonight.

Chapter Twenty-Six

COREY

"Dang, this trophy is heavy," I said, handing the metal monster back to Principal Navarro.

Clapping and whistling ripped through the air as he held it up. Victoria and I made our way down the three steps off the stage. Annie from the coffee shop came up to me and smiled. She opened her arms and wrapped me in a huge hug.

"You're a good kid, Corey Chaos." She held me by the shoulders and tilted her head at me like my mother did when she wanted me to know she was being serious. "You did well with your fame. You should be proud."

I *had* done something good, huh! It'd felt awesome, too. And a secondary bonus was that we'd absolutely crushed Todd and his measly contribution of two hundred cans. It was like he hadn't even tried.

Victoria won awesome prizes for how much she'd raised, but it was too bad I wouldn't be around to enjoy them with her. I hated how that always came back to bite me in the ass. How it clouded over my time with her.

Annie smiled at Victoria. "You are very lucky, young lady. And this surfer boy must really like you to be out here in this cold for you." She winked, then strode off, disappearing into the crowd.

I glanced down at my massive winter coat, boots, and thick mittens. Victoria was worth it.

"I didn't know she volunteered at the pantry we raised all this food for," Victoria said.

"I hadn't either. She told me while I was at the shop for my meet and greet."

From behind her a blonde strode by, her shoulder bumping Victoria's. She spun slightly, but I snagged her elbow, keeping her upright.

That was Todd's new girlfriend.

She whipped around and glared at us. "I see right through you guys."

"Excuse me?" Victoria said.

"As if *he'd* ever date *you* unless you bribed him." She flipped her long hair over her shoulder. "Loser."

Victoria's jaw dropped in shock. My response wasn't so passive. My blood actually felt like it caught on fire. My heart hammered. How dare she come rain on this success just because her boyfriend sucked ass at fundraising?

Victoria tugged me toward her. She planted a kiss on me that would make anyone within eyeshot blush. I wrapped my arm around her waist, holding her to me and dipping her slightly.

"Get a room." Todd's snobby girlfriend narrowed her evil green eyes at me, then stomped off.

"Oh my gosh," Victoria said, her eyes wide as I eased her fully upright.

"I know, right? What the hell?" I pointed after Todd's girlfriend. "The nerve—"

"No. That kiss!" Victoria said, touching her lips with her fingertips.

I froze, not sure if her look of surprise was a good one or she was pissed. She'd grabbed me, so I thought she'd be okay with it. We'd kissed lots in private. Why wouldn't that have been okay? Crap, was her dad nearby?

The stage was behind us and a sea of people were milling around before us, but there wasn't any sign of her father.

"That was amazing." She patted her chest. "Damn, you can kiss. And did you see how ticked off she was?"

My heart sank like it'd morphed into a fifteen-pound weight in my chest. She'd done it because of Todd's new girlfriend. *Shit.* I wanted her to do that because it was me. Because she liked me. Because she wanted to be with me.

We hugged the shadows of the stage. Up above, the sky was dark; the sun had set a while ago, but some flurries were starting to fall again.

We cornered the back of the stage and up ahead, there were Todd and Blondie talking.

"What's her name, anyway?" I asked.

"Harper Olson," Victoria said. "She goes to Twin River Prep."

"She's a bitch," I said, shaking my head.

Harper shoved Todd, then pointed toward the stage. I pulled Victoria to the side, so we were hidden in a shadow.

"She's so pissed they didn't win," she said. "Oh my gosh, this couldn't have gone any better. And then that kiss. The timing was awesome! I got a little nervous when she called us out for faking it, though. But after that kiss. No way could she doubt it."

I looked down at her, since she was in front of me a little bit, and bent over to see around the corner. Another twinge of fear popped up that she truly was using me for my fame only to make her ex-boyfriend jealous. Then again, that's what she'd asked me to do. Never hid her motives. Ever. So why had what she said hurt so much?

I knew exactly why. I'd totally done exactly what the non-contract indicated I shouldn't. I'd fallen for her.

Absolutely fallen for her. The phone in my front pocket vibrated, so I stepped into the shadows more and checked it.

MOM: How are you?

ME: Good! Hanging with Victoria.

MOM: You two are spending a lot of time together.

She sent a smiling emoji.

Wow. This was new. I didn't even know she knew how to use emojis.

ME: Yeah, she's pretty great!

MOM: What day are you coming back? Have you heard anything about the role?

ME: I should find out within the next day or so.

ME: I'll be back in a few weeks. You okay?

MOM: Missing you.

ME: Miss you, too. What are you up to?

MOM: At home, fixing dinner.

ME: Where's Brock?

MOM: With his wife.

ME: What?

MOM: Yeah. Shithead.

MOM: He really pulled one over on me.

ME: I'm sorry. What a loser.

ME: Better off without him!

ME: I'll FaceTime you tomorrow, k? We'll catch up.

MOM: It's a date. Love you!

ME: Love you, too!

"Everything okay?" Victoria came up beside me.

"Mom." I held up the phone, then put it in my pocket. "Just texted me. Sounds like the boyfriend of the month didn't work out."

"Oh no. Is she okay?"

"Yeah. I'll call her tomorrow. So…what's next?"

She gave me a one-armed hug. "Celebrate!"

"I have a feeling that might involve gumball ice cream…"

"You might be right." She giggled. "I'm so happy right

now. And then the dance is this Saturday. We're going to have so much fun."

She led me out of the darkness by the hand, chatting about how she and Mia were going to get their hair and nails done on Saturday morning, and I just listened, her happiness making me smile.

I loved her energy. Her passion.

I'd miss that when I was gone.

I really needed to tell her it was likely I'd get the part. That I'd be leaving in a couple weeks. We'd already planned the "we're better off as friends" statement, but the more I thought about that, it made my stomach churn. Maybe we could take this thing to the next level? Long distance dating. I could come back here all the time to see her. Then again, would the producers be okay with that? Coming out here to see my girlfriend while on a dating show? Eh, it's Hollywood, everything was fake anyway.

The dating on the show was secondary to the music, but still.

Later. I'd talk to her later about it.

"What do you think?" Victoria said, wiggling our connected hands.

"I'm sorry. What'd you say?"

"You okay?" She urged me to the side, out of the flow of people heading toward the concessions area.

"Just...thinking."

"About our success? Because you so *nailed it*. You totally need a picture of you holding that big trophy above your head! You could hang it up in the pool house!"

My chest ached. The pool house. My temporary living quarters in her backyard. My days with her were numbered and it looked like that reality just hit her over the head like it kicked me in the chest.

I let out a long breath and she looked up at me with those sweet brown eyes. "That kiss..."

I pulled off my mitten and cupped the side of her face, then ducked so I could get in her line of sight. I brushed my thumb over her cheek, reveling in her soft skin. The curve of her cheek. She covered my hand with hers, then tilted her head and pressed a kiss to my palm.

"What's happening, Corey?" she said, her voice not much more than a whisper.

I stepped toward her until our bodies were almost touching.

"That kiss," she whispered. "Us. Our...fake relationship."

"Things changed a little, didn't they?" I rested my forehead to hers, soaking in her soft skin and her warmth.

"I'm sorry. I didn't mean to do that," she said. "I mean, I did. I wanted to. It's just—"

"Complicated." I closed my eyes and took in a breath to try to slow my mind down so I could find the words.

"What is?" she asked.

"Us—no—not us. This. I want to kiss you like that, Tor. As in, I *really* want to. All the time."

"You do?" A small smile curved the corner of her sweet mouth.

Those lips were begging for me to kiss her. But I needed to talk to her about the show. Remind her—us both—that my time here was limited. I was leaving. I'd have to leave.

"I want you, too—er—to kiss you." She grinned. "Things changed for me, too."

I was so happy to hear that. Maybe we should try something. I hated that I kept going back to thinking she meant all of this kissing to be part of the fake boyfriend ruse. Maybe if I hadn't been burned so many times this past year or so I'd trust more easily.

No. I did trust her. She was legit. I needed to iron this out because Jethro said I might hear the decision about the show as early as tomorrow. And my day was slammed tomorrow with school and a few online appearances.

I kissed her temple, summoning the courage to spit this out. "Listen. I need to talk to you about something important. The show, well, your dad—er—Jethro. He said—"

"Hey, hey, hey! What up, fam?" Mia jumped beside us, holding up her phone. "Looks like you're Insta-Official!"

The screen was filled with a picture of the very kiss we were just talking about. I'd dipped her low, one hand around her waist, the other supporting her neck while I kissed her. It was so perfect, we looked like we were shooting a scene in a movie.

And it was a video.

Victoria looked at me with wide eyes. "Holy hell."

"What?" Mia said. "It's awesome."

"What if Dad sees this?" Victoria said.

"Are you guys hiding it from him that you're dating?" Mia asked. "Because he's your agent."

"Mia!" Victoria gasped, then looked at me. "I only told her. I swear. I didn't tell anyone else."

"It's okay, Tor. She's your best friend. I get it. Just know that if you tell anyone, I'll have to kill you," I said to Mia as I wiggled Victoria and my connected hands.

"Your secret is safe with me."

"Thanks. So, where's that posted?"

"All over Instagram." Her eyebrows crinkled as if she was confused by the question.

"Am I tagged?"

"Duh."

"Oh no," Victoria said. "Does Dad watch your tags and stuff? Wait. Is he even on IG?"

"Yes," I said with a nervous smile. "And no. He's not that much of a hands-on Insta watcher. Roberts, though, he is." He freaking watched my every move. "He's probably already texted me."

"Wait... Could this keep you from getting the part?" Victoria looked up at me, her eyes wide and filled with terror. "Corey. Be honest. Did I just screw up your career?"

"It's fine, Tor. I'll shoot Roberts a text."

I might send one more text, too. One to Jethro, telling him I wanted to date his daughter.

For real.

I pulled out my phone to text Roberts, but one from Jethro filled my screen.

JETHRO: You got the part.

Oh shit. How am I going to tell Victoria?

Chapter Twenty-Seven

Victoria

"Victoria Kate, get down here right now," my dad bellowed from the bottom of the stairs.

Frowning, I popped my head out of my bedroom door. "What's up?"

"Your mother and I need to speak to you."

He sounds angry!

Pulling my hair back into a ponytail, I made my way down the stairs. I didn't have much time left to get ready for school, so hopefully everything was okay.

Mom and Dad were sitting at the kitchen table, looking at me as I rounded the corner into the bright room.

"Sit, please," Mom said, gesturing to the chair across from them.

My dad shoved his phone in my direction. "Do you want to explain what's going on in this picture?"

Uh-oh...

The video of Corey dipping and kissing me last night filled his screen.

"Where did you get that?" I asked, reaching for Dad's phone.

His face turned a dark shade of red. "A gossip rag. I'm used to seeing Corey in these, doing stuff like this, but I certainly never expected to see my daughter in one! Especially not after what happened with Grayson."

"Um," I started to say, "well, it's actually, ah, I can explain."

He clicked the button on the side of the phone and the screen went black, then he set it down on the table and folded his hands while he let out a long, slow breath.

I was in some serious trouble right now. I had to salvage this. Somehow.

"Okay, you know how Todd broke up with me? In the cafeteria, in front of everyone? Totally embarrassing me, right?"

Mom nodded and her light brown eyes turned downward. She'd seen how upset I'd been when I'd come home from school that day. Hopefully I had that going for me.

"Well, when Corey showed up here the next day, he said he'd help me get back at Todd and restore my image."

My dad crossed his arms and his lips were pursed. But at least he wasn't doing his meditative breathing. I must be making progress here.

"And how did Corey do that?" my mom asked.

"Well, he pretended to like me. I mean, I asked him to. You know, to help me out." I left out the part where I'd actually started to fall for him and the fact that he'd all but admitted the same last night. "We've been going on pretend dates and hanging out a lot."

My dad uncrossed his arms, the flush returning to his cheeks. "Pretend dates?"

"It's not like we actually *like* each other. That kiss was just for the cameras," I lied.

I was going to have to find Corey stat after this conversation so I could let him know what was up. I didn't want him getting in trouble with Dad. This whole fake dating thing was my idea. I couldn't let him get hurt in all this. I was already freaked out that I might have affected his chance at getting on the TV show that would guarantee one of his original songs would be produced.

Selfish me wanted him to not get it so he could stay here and be with me. But that wasn't Corey's dream. He wanted to make music.

"Honey," my mom said, "being in a pretend relationship is dangerous."

"It's fine, I swear," I said. "It's not real. We're just helping each other out." I hated lying to them, but they were obviously disappointed to see my face all over gossip blogs again. "We even have a breakup protocol that we'll be following once he leaves."

"Victoria, you know the saying, when you play with fire, you risk getting burned," my dad said. "You barely know Corey. He lives a very different lifestyle from you. It's not one that your mother and I want you to be a part of, do you understand?"

"I'm seventeen years old. I understand what I've gotten myself into," I snapped.

"Watch your tone, young lady," my mom said.

"Sorry," I apologized, picking at my nails. "Mia will be here in ten minutes; we're driving to school together today. I need to go get changed. Am I in trouble?"

A line had formed across my mom's forehead. "Victoria, we don't want another Grayson situation."

"Corey's career is just getting started," my dad said.

"And you don't want me to ruin it."

"Getting involved with him—"

"Got it," I said in a clipped voice. "Also, please don't bring this up with Corey. We've got it handled."

I didn't wait for their answer before racing up the stairs to finish getting ready.

I threw on some ripped jeans and an off-the-shoulder sweatshirt, cursing the person who posted that video all over those stupid gossip blogs.

That's going to make the fake breakup even harder...

MIA: See you in 2 mins!

ME: K!

ME: Almost ready!

Crap!

I raked a comb through my hair and brushed my teeth.

This is not how I wanted this morning to start!

Instead of visiting Corey in the pool house to tell him what happened, I had to book it to school to maintain my perfect attendance record. I'd text him when I got in the car with Mia. She was going to freak when I told her this.

Snatching a small backpack purse off the back of my door, I slung it over my shoulders and headed back down the stairs. I paused at the landing halfway down and leaned over the rail.

"He got the part," I heard my dad whisper. "He found out last night and it doesn't sound like he's told her yet."

Last night? But we were together last night at the food drive event and then hanging out with Mia. And then it was curfew time so we didn't get to hang out alone at all.

But to not tell me? What the hell?

"When is he leaving?" my mom asked.

"Monday."

What? My stomach twisted. *That's only a few days away!*

My mom let out a sigh. "She's going to be crushed. The way they look at each other..."

I thought we had a couple of weeks left together, what the hell?

"This is a lesson she'll have to learn the hard way," my dad said.

MIA: I'm here!

MIA: Hurry up, we're late!

I needed to get moving, but it was like my feet were rooted to the floor. Everything felt heavy, weighted down, tugging at me. Corey got the part and didn't tell me?

Corey was leaving?

The room started to spin and my mouth went dry.

My phone buzzed again, kicking me back into the moment. Chest heaving from the shocking news, I made as much noise as possible coming down the second half of the stairs.

"Mia's here," I said, trying to quell the shaking in my voice. "Gotta go."

My mom popped her head around the corner of the family room. "We love you, Victoria. We just don't want you to get hurt."

Or for me to ruin Corey's career, like I did to Grayson...

"Love you, too." I threw on my boots and jacket, then headed out to the driveway.

"What up, fam?" Mia asked as I slid into the passenger's seat.

"Oh, not much. Just got accosted by my parents because they saw the video of Corey and me making out last night at the festival." I brought my finger to my lips to bite my nail but then stopped myself.

"Dang," she murmured.

"And," I added, not wanting to say the words out loud, "Corey got that spot in the dating show." And he didn't tell me.

Mia's shoulders slumped. "Oh, man."

"Yeah," I said quietly.

"How do you feel about that?" she asked.

"Honestly, really hurt. I knew he'd probably get it, but I overheard my dad tell my mom. Corey didn't tell me." I tugged the zipper on my backpack.

"Wait, when did he find out?"

"Apparently, yesterday."

"Before or after the fundraiser event?" Mia sucked in air through closed teeth.

"I don't know. Either way, he didn't say anything about it to me." How could he do that to me? To us? Maybe things weren't as real for him as they were for me?

"What are you going to do?" she asked.

"I don't know. We only have a few days left together."

"Few days?" Mia exclaimed.

"Yeah, sounds like he's leaving Monday." I let the backpack slide from my hands to my feet. "At least that's what I overheard my parents say."

"I'm sorry, Victoria." Mia reached over and gave my hand a squeeze.

Me too... Because if there's anything those gossip magazines got right, it was that I'd officially fallen for Corey Chaos...fake relationship and all.

Chapter Twenty-Eight

Corey

I kind of wanted to throw my laptop out the window. Staring at the finalized, signed contract, accepting the role on *What's Your Note?* should be the happiest moment of my life. Sure, I had to date ten strangers to find the girl to sing my original duet, but fuck it, Victoria had totally bailed on me.

Yesterday morning I'd wanted to catch her before heading to school to tell her I'd gotten the part, but I'd overheard her telling her folks everything was fake and she didn't even like me.

Talk about a kick to the balls. And here I thought that night at the festival we were on our way to taking our relationship to the next level, but I was wrong.

So very wrong.

And I might have dodged a bullet after hearing her parents talk about Grayson Stryker. I couldn't believe it was

Victoria who'd been involved in that. I'd heard whisperings of how Grayson got into some trouble but hadn't looked into it much.

I was just up-and-coming in the industry back then.

After hearing their discussion yesterday morning, I'd come right back to the pool house and Googled it. There wasn't much online about it and practically zero reference to Victoria. How was that even possible these days?

The fact that she never told me about it stung like a son of a bitch. I couldn't even talk to her about it, since she was at school all day. My virtual meetings had me booked up all night, too, which was why she'd gone to last night's game without me.

Now here I sat, in my tux, about to head to the main house to pick her up for the dance, when I just wanted to puke.

I leaned back into the leather couch and rested my hand atop my guitar sitting beside me. I should freaking write a country song about this messed-up situation. All that was missing was a freaking rusty pickup truck and a dog.

Instead, I pushed up from the couch and took in a deep breath. The walk from the pool house, around the side of the main house to that front door felt like sixteen miles uphill, with how heavy my legs felt.

And my heart.

I couldn't tell her today, right before the dance. Jethro had agreed to let me tell her, so I knew he wouldn't. The press release was scheduled for Monday, and from what I could tell, it hadn't been leaked to the press yet.

Then again, Victoria had pretty easily told her dad our relationship was completely fake anyway, so maybe she wouldn't be too upset.

My stomach cramped from the sandwich I'd just downed. I probably shouldn't have eaten. Damn it. Maybe I should leave now. I wasn't sure I could do tonight with her, not with everything going on.

I really liked her. Hell, before I'd overheard what I'd heard, I was tossing around the idea of turning down the offer. This town was cool. I could rent the apartment above Annie's Coffee Shop for Mom and me if she wanted to come here, too. Or just me. I was pretty sure I could have convinced Mom to let me.

But now it didn't matter. I'd do this dance for Victoria and then tell her first thing tomorrow.

The huge wooden door loomed before me. My arm felt like a fifty-pound weight as I raised it to knock. I held Victoria's corsage in my free hand. The limo was in the driveway. Stretched, shiny, and big enough to fit two families.

I let out a breath and knocked.

The door whooshed open and there stood Victoria, wearing a black dress that made her pale, smooth skin pop.

"Hey," she said. Her jaw was tense, but even with that, she was stunning.

My heart cracked a little more.

"Hey," I said.

"Ready?" She stepped through the doorway as she threw on a big jacket.

"Don't you want some pictures with—"

"No. I'm good." She pulled the door shut, then unceremoniously slid her corsage over her hand and adjusted it on her wrist. "We can do some selfies in the limo."

"Oh." I followed after her. It was like she was running a race or something. It was cold out, sure, but still.

And that tense jaw.

She was mad.

What the hell did she have to be mad about? I wasn't the one who'd proclaimed her "like" for me and then told her parents it was totally false. All of it fake to make Todd jealous.

But it was. I was the one who totally fell for her. But she'd said she had, too. This didn't freaking make sense.

The limo driver standing by the door let Victoria in.

"Hey," I said as I came up to him. "Thanks."

I crawled in and sat next to her.

"There are more seats here. You don't have to sit right next to me," she said.

"*This* is going to be a fun evening." I hopped over to the seat adjacent to her.

"What's it matter to you? You're leaving in two days." Her eyes locked onto mine.

I gulped. *Oh shit*.

"Yeah," she said. "I know all about it."

"How…?"

"Not how I should have." She crossed her arms over her chest. "Why didn't you tell me? You found out on Thursday night!"

I gulped. I'd been so shocked by the text from Jethro that I'd panicked. And she was so happy after winning the fundraising contest, I couldn't do it. I should have, but I just couldn't.

"I had to overhear it from my dad, Corey. *My dad*."

Guilt tore through my chest, but underneath it was a

layer of anger. I shook my head. "Yeah, well, you know what I overheard?"

"Oh please. You—"

"It's all fake. You told your parents I basically meant nothing to you. You used me. And why didn't you tell me about Grayson Stryker?"

"Grayson?" Her jaw twitched and she shook her head. "You're right, I should have told you. We got busted drinking in his car. He ended up with a DUI. Dad got me out of trouble. But it totally destroyed his squeaky-clean image."

"Yeah you should have told me about that. But what hurt most was what you said to your parents. So easily. That everything about us was fake."

"It was *supposed* to be fake." Tears lined her eyes. "But then I went and fell in love with you, Corey. And you're leaving. You're leaving me to go on a show and date other girls, become a huge music star and"—her breath hitched—"you'll forget all about me."

Her pained voice filled the limo and my heart cracked even more.

Victoria, *my Tor*, loved me?

She'd actually said it...

"You love me?" I asked.

She froze. Her eyes were wide and her jaw tensed again. The tear slipped out and she batted it away, looking every direction except mine.

"But I heard you—"

"I had to tell Dad *something*!" She slapped the seat beside her. "He totally caught us. It made some online gossip rag."

I'd been surprised it hadn't happened earlier.

"He was freaking out. So I lied. Said…it was all fake."

"You lied?"

She laughed, but her voice cracked, too, and she shifted in her seat. "Of course I lied. To protect you." She shook her head. "A lot of good it did me."

"You…love me? For real?"

"I don't kiss just anyone like that!"

"Not even Todd?"

"Oh please."

I wasn't sure what to do. I loved her, too. But it was true, I was leaving. As in leaving on Monday. I'd signed the contract for the show already. Dammit. So much had changed in the last five seconds.

But it was too late. There was nothing I could do to fix this.

Chapter Twenty-Nine

Victoria

"It's time to find that special one and head out to the dance floor," the DJ said into the microphone.

"May I have this dance?" Corey asked, taking a bow.

"Of course." I slid my hand into his.

Couples flooded the dance floor and began swaying to "Stay With Me," by Sam Smith.

Laying my head against his shoulder, I closed my eyes and wished this moment would last forever. But it couldn't. He was leaving town.

Leaving me.

Corey put his hands on the small of my back. The heat coming from his palms sent shivers up my spine.

The events of the day had left my head spinning. Corey was heading out on Monday to start shooting a musical dating reality show. A *dating* show. He'd be meeting girls.

Going out to dinner with them. Getting to know them. Probably going to the beach, teaching them how to surf. I wasn't naïve enough to think the producers wouldn't push him to kiss the girls. Probably even more, too.

A lump formed in my throat and tears wet the corners of my eyes.

Looked like we played out that breakup clause perfectly—it was just early.

I sniffled back the tears and focused on the moment. I was here with him now, hugging him, kissing him, dancing with him. I needed to focus on that, but I couldn't. It wasn't fair. I'd fallen for him, but now we were getting ripped apart.

The thought of him leaving literally felt like someone was stabbing me in the heart.

Maybe he won't go?

What would my dad do if he told him he wanted to stay in Twin River?

Would I be ruining yet another career of a promising star if he stayed?

I pictured us walking down the hallway together. Holding hands, sneaking kisses, and doing everything regular high school couples did.

The song ended and Corey threaded his fingers through mine as he guided me off to the side of the dance floor.

"Let's get a picture," Corey said, pulling out his phone.

I rested my forehead against his cheek, then turned slightly and smiled at the camera. We looked so cute together. Our smiles. The happiness. It made my heart soar, but also made my stomach clench. I didn't want him to go.

Should I tell him? No. I shouldn't. It was selfish of me to even think of asking him to give up his career to stay with me. We were seventeen.

He clicked the picture, then kissed my cheek as he took another.

A text rolled across the screen.

MOM: CALL ME! 911!

"Corey." I tapped his phone as he looked at it.

"Shit." Corey's face turned pale. "My phone has been buzzing nonstop. I figured it was just Roberts still bugging me about the pictures of us kissing. It's my mom. Nine one one. I better go call her. She never sends messages like this."

Disappointment seeped through my pores. "I totally understand. Do you want me to come with you?"

He shook his head. "No, I'll be right back. Save the next dance for me?"

"Sure," I said, forcing a smile, then he rushed toward the exit doors that would lead him out to the junior hallway.

Envious of the couples still dancing, I went to the refreshments table and grabbed a can of Sprite.

Is this what my future would be like if we kept dating while he was in L.A?

Sitting out the slow songs at every dance because he's in L.A. and I'm here?

The DJ tapped on the microphone as the song came to an end. "Ladies and gentlemen, it's what you've been waiting for! Time to announce the prince and princess of the Twin River High Ice Ball!"

Everyone cheered and headed toward the stage.

"Can everyone who's been elected to the court please head toward me?" the DJ asked.

Corey, where are you?

Looking over my shoulder for him, I let out a sigh. He wouldn't miss the crowning, would he? He'd told me plenty of times that his mom was struggling with a lot of stuff. But why did she need to get a hold of him so desperately all of a sudden? What if something was wrong? My stomach flip-flopped.

Screw this, I'm going to go check on Corey.

I turned to leave the gym, but Mrs. Rupert linked her arm in mine and directed me toward the stage. "This way, Miss Knight."

"No, I—"

"Shh! You're about to be called up on stage with Mr. Miller." Mrs. Rupert winked and let go of my arm as soon as we reached the front of the crowd.

My body stiffened and my stomach rolled. *Did that wink mean that Todd and I had won?* I felt like I was going to puke. Yeah, sure, I wanted to win, but not with Todd. I wanted Corey here by my side.

I hope he's okay.

Todd was already standing next to the stage when I got to the front. Rolling my eyes, I took my place next to him.

I looked over my shoulder, desperate to see Corey walk back through the doors with a smile on his face. A false alarm with his mom or something like that, but I came up empty. I needed him here. By my side. Especially if Todd and I won prince and princess and had to dance together in front of everyone.

"Where's your influencer boyfriend?" Todd's voice dripped with sarcasm.

I didn't dignify his comment with anything, not even

a look. Todd was a jerk, yeah, and what he'd done to me sucked big-time, but it had led me to Corey. So maybe I should thank him.

Hard pass.

One by one, the DJ announced the couples. The girls sat on black velvet chairs and the guys stood behind them. There was no way we'd win, right? I mean, who would vote for Todd after what he did to me? What'd that say about our class, even? I'd wanted this, big-time, in the beginning. It was a huge honor to be nominated, but now everything was different. *I* was different.

I needed to get this over with and find out how Corey was doing.

"Everyone, give your court a round of applause," the DJ said.

The students clapped and let out cheers. A girl named Kaja came onstage and handed the DJ an envelope.

I searched the crowd for Corey but he was nowhere to be seen. A sinking feeling flooded my stomach. There was no way he'd miss this. Something had to be really wrong. Being up here didn't matter, only Corey did, and something had to be seriously up right now if he wasn't here.

The audience burst out in cheers, ripping me from my worry.

Noelle, the girl next to me, tapped my shoulder. "Stand up, Victoria. You won!"

"Wait, what?"

"Go!" Noelle nudged my arm again.

Todd stood beside me, his arm extended for me to take. He looked like an emotionless robot. Directly in front of the stage stood his girlfriend. The scowl on her face said it all.

She hated my guts.

"You two have each won fifty dollar gift cards to the Vanilla Ice Cream Parlour. You will also have the honor of riding together in the Ice Festival's official float in the parade tomorrow morning."

No, no, no! Tomorrow was my last day with Corey. I guess this was my punishment for this whole fake relationship thing; now instead of spending the day with Corey I'd be with Todd!

Sophia, the chair of the Ice Ball, walked toward me with two crowns in her hand. Maybe I could ask her to sit next to Todd for me tomorrow?

She slipped one crown on me and the other on Todd. A month ago, I would have been ecstatic. Winning prince and princess with my boyfriend, the whole school watching as we took our first dance together… But so many things had changed. I thought about yanking off my crown and tossing it to the girl to my right, but before I could do that, the DJ turned toward us.

"Please stand to my left while I announce the king and queen of the Twin River High School Ice Ball." His voice boomed in my ears. I wanted to make a break for it. I couldn't be up here with my ex-boyfriend. The guy who stomped all over my heart during lunch. Plus, the guy I cared about was out in the hallway. Something must have happened, but what?

"Congratulations to our two senior winners, Rebecca Connor and Jeremiah Moss," the DJ announced. "You are our king and queen!"

Cheers and whistles cut through the air.

"Please clear the floor for Twin River High's Ice Ball

prince and princess as well as your king and queen's royal dance." The DJ motioned toward the stairs with his hand.

I nearly tripped over my feet as we were going down the stairs. Luckily, Jeremiah reached out and steadied me.

"Thank you," I whispered.

We made our way toward a spot in front of the stage. Our classmates encased us in a circle as a slow dance began to blare from the speakers. Begrudgingly, I placed one hand on Todd's shoulder. His hands found my waist. Instead of warm and secure like Corey's, they were icy cold.

Refusing to make eye contact, I stared past Todd and searched for Corey in the crowd.

Todd ducked his head slightly, getting in my line of sight. "I'm sorry," he whispered.

"Excuse me?" My response came out louder than I intended, but the music was so loud, there was no way anyone else heard it.

"I'm sorry, for the way things ended."

Is he serious right now?

"I never meant to hurt you," he added.

Could have fooled me by how he'd dumped me so epically in the lunchroom. I bit my lower lip, trying to hold back all the hateful things I wanted to spew at him. I refused to believe him and I refused to stoop to his level. So I ignored him, wishing the song would hurry up and be done. Better yet, I should just leave him standing here on the dance floor.

A little bit for revenge, but mostly because I needed to go find Corey.

Then he threw one last bombshell at me. "I wish I hadn't done it. I miss you."

What is even happening right now?

Todd's new girlfriend glared at Todd from a few feet away. She looked like a mountain lion, waiting for the perfect opportunity to pounce on its prey.

I bet she'd love to sever his jugular. I gulped. *Or mine?*

I didn't respond to Todd's confession or whatever that was. Instead, I went back to looking for Corey.

When he hadn't appeared by the time the song had ended, I pushed past my ex and made my way through the stunned crowd and down the hall where Corey had disappeared.

Slumped against a locker, Corey held his phone to his ear.

"Yes," he said. "I understand."

Is he still talking to his mom?

"Yes, as soon as possible." He paused. "Yes. I'll be on the first flight out of here. Thank you."

Corey's hands shook as he hung up his phone.

He turned toward me with tears in his eyes.

"I've gotta go home, Tor. Right now."

• • •

The first rays of the rising sun pierced my eyelids. I slowly opened one eye as the light filtered in through the pool house windows.

"Mmm," I said, half groaning from the crick in my neck.

"Oh shit!" I shot up off of the couch. "Corey! Corey, I fell asleep! Do you know what time it is? Did you miss your flight?"

My heart raced as I sprinted over to Corey's bedroom door. I didn't even knock, no time for that, instead I threw the door open. "Corey! We gotta—"

I froze. Ice radiated through my veins.

Corey wasn't in his room.

Neither was his suitcase.

Or his guitar.

Everything was perfectly still. The only thing that gave me any hint of him having been here was the faintest scent of his cologne clinging to the air.

"Corey?" I said his name one last time before sinking to my knees.

My stomach dropped. Tears stung my eyes.

He left.

He left me without waking me up and kissing me until my lips went numb.

Pain ripped through my heart. How could he leave me without even saying goodbye?

I stumbled to my feet, about to race back to the house to ask my dad what the hell had happened, but a note on the kitchenette counter caught my attention.

Victoria,

I'm so sorry for leaving without saying goodbye. An earlier flight opened up last minute and I had to take it. You looked way too perfect to disturb. I'll text you! ~Corey

"No. No. No!" I tossed the note aside. He wouldn't do that. How could he do that?

I bolted out the pool house door into the frigid air and ran smack into someone. Somehow I managed to stay upright by grabbing onto the offered arm.

"Corey?" I said, looking up.

Todd.

I blinked a few times, because I must be hallucinating,

then looked again. Todd Miller was standing in front of me, holding at least two dozen pink roses in his hand. The tip of his nose was red and his sky-blue eyes were wide as he watched me.

Normally that look would have melted my knees, but right now, it pissed me off.

Scrunching up my nose, I asked, "What are you doing?"

"I'm so sorry, Victoria. I meant what I said at the dance. I want you back."

Chapter Thirty

COREY

My head slipped to the side as I jerked awake. A pain shot down my neck.

"Sorry, didn't mean to wake you, man," a nurse with a shaved head said. The tip of a tattoo peeked out from the collar of his scrubs.

"It's okay." I stood up and reached toward the ceiling, stretching my back.

"You've been here for almost thirty hours straight, man. Maybe it's time to take a break?" The nurse checked the blood pressure sleeve around Mom's arm.

"I'm good," I said.

"Well, you might want a shower, then." He grinned.

He was by far my favorite nurse. I made my way to the window at the far side of the room that looked over the city. He was right, though. I should probably head to the apartment, get cleaned up, changed, and see what kind of shitstorm I'd fallen into while I ignored the world since I got here at the crack of dawn yesterday.

I hadn't even texted Victoria more than once or twice to let her know I'd arrived safely and that Mom was stable. I felt so bad for missing her crowning. But what really got me was that she had to dance with that dickhead Todd. I would have cut in within the first five seconds of that traditional royalty dance had I been there.

Nobody would have stopped me.

Instead, I'd spent that time on the phone with an ER nurse telling me my mom had gotten seriously injured when a car plowed into her.

The worst, though, was leaving without saying goodbye to Victoria. When that earlier flight opened up, I had to take it. I told myself that was the reason, but I was starting to think I took it so I wouldn't have to say goodbye.

It hurt so damn much.

"So, any change?" I asked, forcing myself back to the moment.

The nurse shook his head. "Doc will come in a few hours on rounds and give you an update."

I needed to get with the cops to find out the full story, but from what I'd heard so far, she was walking to the grocery store, which was about a block from our apartment, and she'd gotten hit crossing the street. Totally the driver's fault according to what I'd seen on the news. But he was doing thirty miles per hour, so lots of broken bones.

I'd even heard some of the doctors mentioning she might need a bit longer-term care for a couple weeks. They didn't think she could walk or take care of herself safely. Sure I'd be there, but it would probably be best if there was a female nurse there to help her go to the bathroom and shower.

Tears stung my eyes. I'd come close to losing her. My only living parent. I wasn't sure I could handle that.

No. I could *not* think about that. Right now, I was taking it one freaking minute at a time. It was about all I could handle.

I scrubbed my face with my hands. "You think it'd be okay if I left for an hour or so?"

"She'll be out for quite a while. Just gave her some pain medicine."

I tapped a text to the private car service I'd used to get here from the airport. "You sure?"

He nodded. "But, if she does wake up earlier than expected, I'll be here, and I can call you to let you know it's time to come back."

"Thanks, man. I'm going to head home and get cleaned up, maybe get some food, but only for a couple hours."

I grabbed a small pad of paper off the small table next to my mom's bed.

After scribbling down my number, I ripped off the piece of paper and handed it to him. "Here's my cell. Call, text, anything. I'll have it right next to me."

"Got it," he said. "And don't worry, I would never share this. Even if your scary publicist hadn't already had everyone here at the hospital sign NDAs."

I hadn't even thought of that. Then again, that was why I paid Roberts the big bucks, right? To think for me when it came to crap like that. "Thanks again. I really appreciate it," I said, gathering up my bag and guitar case.

The car was waiting for me when I hustled out of the

hospital entrance and I hopped right in.

I pulled out my phone to send a text to Victoria.

ME: You home?

I saw the three dots like she was texting me back, but then they vanished and my heart plunged.

Oh crap. It was the middle of the school day in Wisconsin. I was all mixed up what time of day it was. Hell, what *day* it was. Everything since the dance was a blur.

"Are you comfortable back there, sir? Can I offer you a bottle of water?"

"Oh I'm good. Except my wallet is jabbing me in the ass."

The driver laughed.

I leaned to the side and pulled it out. A slip of pink paper flew onto my lap. I unfolded and immediately recognized Victoria's handwriting.

From sand to snow.
I got to know,
This world can be rough.

Filled with mistakes and shame,
I barely knew your name.
But the idea of you was enough.

You crashed into my life.
Erasing the strife.
Calming my tortured soul.

We both planned on this being fake.
But those were words that were meant to break.
You made me whole.

Chaos brought us together,
then ripped us apart,
But that doesn't matter because you have my heart.

One of Victoria's poems. She must have slipped this in here at some point. It was beautiful, but right now, it ripped my guts out.

Man, I really loved Victoria. *I should have told her.* I skimmed it over one more time, then gently placed it back in my wallet. I couldn't wait to FaceTime her once she was done with classes.

The car stopped and I hopped out. The driver handed me my stuff and I thanked him, then bolted up the stairs to my place.

I tossed my keys onto the table beside the door. My phone vibrated again and I finally slid it out of my pocket to see what was so important.

Tapping it to life, I saw an email from *Randy's Rumors*. *Small-town Wisconsin girl dupes Instagram star Corey Chaos* was the subject line of the email.

"What the hell?" I said as I clicked it open.

My phone rang and it was Roberts.

Of course it was Roberts.

"Yeah?" I said after I hit answer.

"Are you seeing this?"

"Um...seeing wh—"

"Small-town Wisconsin girl dupes Instagram Star

Corey Chaos!" he shouted into the phone.

"Just saw the email. It's a gossip magazine, what do we—"

"Oh, so you *didn't* sign a contract with her to be her fake boyfriend?"

My stomach dropped and I almost puked right then and there. My world tilted and I staggered three steps to the back of the couch and grabbed hold.

"What?" I said, my mouth suddenly dry.

"There's a picture of a contract in this, Corey. Are you kidding me right now? What did you do in Podunk, Wisconsin?! Are you trying to ruin your career? *What's Your Note?* doesn't give a crap that you're a player, but this shit, this shit makes you look bad! Really bad!"

"What's it say?" I slouched on the leather couch, closing my eyes as I pressed the phone to my ear. My heart was hammering so loud I almost couldn't hear him.

"It says here that she got you to sign this to pose as her boyfriend to help her get crowned at some high school dance? There are pictures of you kissing her. Holding hands. What the—"

"I have to go." I pulled the phone away from my ear to the shouts of my publicist.

"Don't you dare hang up."

I brought the phone to my ear again. "In case you haven't heard, Roberts, my mother was hit by a car. She's in the hospital hooked up to monitors. So, you know what? This story, stupid Twin River, Wisconsin, and Victoria Knight can all suck it."

I pressed end and tossed my phone across the room. It smacked against the window overlooking the city. It was bright outside, but just dark enough that I could see the reflection of the apartment in the window.

There I was, flopped onto the couch, alone.

Alone-freaking-again.

How could Victoria do this?

She obviously didn't give a crap about me or her dad.

I rolled off the couch, some sick part of me needing to see that article, and crawled to my phone. A massive crack marred the face of it, but the screen still lit up. So much for this case that claimed I could drop my phone from an airplane without it breaking.

I swiped the screen. My hand shook as I held the phone.

Skimming over the text, it pretty much confirmed what Roberts said.

"Victoria Knight, daughter of esteemed talent agent, Jethro Knight, used young Instagram sensation, Corey Chaos, to get back at her ex-boyfriend and be crowned princess of her school's Ice Ball.

"She was quoted as saying she used Corey only to get her boyfriend back, and here they are pictured, just yesterday, holding hands while getting ice cream at a local shop."

"Holy shit," I said, tears welling, starting to blur out the words. Todd and Victoria were holding hands, smiling, right outside the Vanilla Ice Cream Parlour. The very ice cream place we'd gone to several times while I was there.

"Both were crowned in the school event, which led to a rekindling of their relationship, leaving Corey Chaos out to dry just before his debut on *What's Your Note?* But why would our superstar sign such a childish agreement? Look at item number four—"

I dropped the phone onto the floor and leaned against

the wall. "Son of a bitch!"

I jammed my fingers into my hair and closed my eyes as tears spilled out over my face.

"See if I ever trust anyone ever again."

Chapter Thirty-One

Victoria

The last bell of the day finally rang.

I couldn't wait to FaceTime Corey. I missed him so much I barely heard a word of Miss Alexander's lecture on George Washington.

Students flooded the hallways, bumping into one another on their way to their lockers and the bus line or the parking lot.

I pulled my phone from my backpack and leaned up against the wall next to the Twin River High trophy case.

Before I could call Corey, Sophia texted me.

SOPHIA: 911

SOPHIA: READ THIS!

SOPHIA: www.lagossip.com/CoreyChaosGetsDuped

"What the..." I muttered under my breath as I clicked the link.

My jaw fell open as a picture of me and Todd dancing at the Ice Ball popped up on the website.

The article was titled, "Corey Chaos Gets Duped by His Agent's Daughter."

"Victoria!" Sophia raced over to me, her phone in her hand. "Did you read this crap?"

"Just the headline. What the hell is going on?"

"The article says that you used Corey to get popular and that you duped him and are back with Todd." Sophia shook her head. "This is complete crap!"

"W-W-Why would someone write an article like this? None of that is true," I gasped.

"You better call Corey," Sophia said, her eyes wide. "He's probably going to freak out."

"You're right. Talk to you later." I didn't even wait for her to respond.

Pushing through the crowd, I ran all the way to my car.

As soon as I got in, I unlocked my phone and called Corey.

Instead of answering, it went straight to voicemail, so I texted him instead.

ME: I'm done with school.

ME: Call me?

ME: I miss you!

My phone buzzed. It wasn't Corey responding though, it was Nomie texting me.

NOMIE: Have you seen this?

NOMIE: This site is saying that you were in a fake relationship with Corey??

NOMIE: AND A REAL ONE WITH GRAYSON!

NOMIE: I didn't think anyone knew about that!?!

NOMIE: www.RandysFumors.com/ChaosTheFakeBoyfriendGetsDumped

Fake boyfriend?

I clicked on the article and let out a shriek. Right there, in front of my eyes, was a picture of the fake relationship agreement I'd made for me and Corey. Everything about it was correct, except the signature. Corey never signed it... for this exact reason. It'd been a verbal agreement so there wasn't a paper trail.

But there it was, his sloppy signature, staring back at me from the screen of my phone.

I suddenly felt hot, then cold.

I'm going to puke!

Holding my hand to my mouth, I closed my eyes and took several deep breaths. Once I felt the nausea subside, I opened them again.

How in the hell had a crappy online gossip magazine gotten their hands on a copy of that thing? And a picture of me and Todd? Looking like a happy couple— That was a picture from last year! They even found an old picture of me and Grayson cuddled up in the back of a limo. Ugh... This was a complete nightmare!

The rest of the article claimed that I'd used Corey to

win the crown at the Twin River High Ice Ball and get back with my ex-boyfriend.

I tried to call Corey again. It rang once and then went to voicemail.

ME: Corey, please call me back!

COREY: Was it worth it?

ME: What?

COREY: Screwing me over?

COREY: Leaking the contract you were supposed to shred?

COREY: So you could win the crown and get back with Todd?

ME: I swear I didn't give it to anyone!

ME: I don't give two craps about being the Ice Ball Princess.

ME: And I hate Todd!

ME: I'd never get back with him.

COREY: Apparently you would and you did.

My hands shook and my head started pounding. *How could he believe these sites?*

ME: I would never do that to you!

ME: I love you!

A message popped up on my phone.

"This message cannot be delivered."

I tried sending it again, but the same message flashed across my screen.

"He blocked me," I whispered to myself.

Tears in my eyes, I started the car and peeled out of my parking spot.

The drive back to my house was a blur. I barely remembered pulling into the garage and racing up to my room.

Head pounding, I tried to call Corey over and over again.

"This call cannot be completed," a computerized voice said on repeat.

How did this happen?

My laptop was in my backpack and with me practically twenty-four seven; there was no way someone got into it and I didn't realize it.

Did someone find out Corey was staying here and break into our house?

I raced downstairs and to the pool house. The contract was gone. Nowhere to be found. I double-checked Corey's room, the wastebaskets. I even looked in the refrigerator and only found it full of Fanta.

My mind raced so fast I could barely think straight. The only person who'd come over since Corey had temporarily moved in with us was Mia. She'd never do anything like that to me.

MIA: I'm coming over.

ME: Please don't.

MIA: Too late.

MIA: I'm in your driveway.

"Victoria, honey. Mia's here," my mom shouted from the back door. "She's coming around the side."

A moment later, she appeared with her phone in her hand.

"What the heck happened?" Mia asked, pulling me into a hug.

I pushed back and began pacing back and forth in front of the fireplace in the pool house. "That's what I'm trying to figure out."

"Have you talked to Corey?" she asked, sitting on the couch. The very couch Corey and I had sat on together just a few days ago.

Tears streamed down my face. "He blocked me."

Mia waved me to her and I joined her on the couch. My stomach lurched, grumbling. I hadn't eaten since lunch, but I wasn't sure I'd be able to eat ever again. This had to be a nightmare. Had to be.

"What happened?" she asked softly. "Between you and Corey? Everywhere is reporting that you two were in a fake relationship and that you were doing it to get back with Todd and to win the princess title for the Ice Ball."

Bringing my trembling finger to my mouth, I chewed on my manicured nail. They were still so pretty from when we were at the dance. Together. Kissing. And now...he'd blocked me. Freaking blocked me because of these lies. How could he believe them? I wouldn't ever do that to him.

"Victoria? Talk to me."

"I love him, Mia," I whispered. "And he's never going to talk to me again."

"Was the contract real?" she asked.

I let my head fall into my hands. "Yes."

"Wait, *what*?" Her eyes went wide and she leaned forward.

I wiped my cheeks with the sleeves of my sweater. "When Corey got here, Todd had just dumped me. I was humiliated. I told Corey about it and asked him to help. We decided to pretend to like each other. Go out on a set number of dates, follow strict PDA guidelines, the whole nine yards..."

Mia rubbed her face. "So what happened?"

"I fell in love with him." Tears started streaming from my eyes again, but even harder. "But then he got the part and was leaving. And then his mom got in a bad accident the night of the dance and he had to go back. He left Sunday morning before I was even awake." Wiping my cheeks with the backs of my hands, I shook my head. "Todd showed up with a bunch of flowers. He apologized, like, fifty bazillion times, begged me to take him back, but I sent his ass packing."

"Where is the contract?"

"It's gone." I pointed to the side. "I don't know how anyone got their hands on it. There's only one copy. Corey would never leak it and it sure as hell wasn't me."

"Wait... Where did you and Todd talk?" Mia asked as she sat up.

Ice shot through my veins. "Out here, by the pool."

"Were you with him the whole time?" The suspicion in

her voice was palpable.

Heart racing, I shook my head. "He had to use the bathroom, but it was like six in the morning. Everyone was still sleeping, so I told him to use the one in the pool house..."

"Shit," Mia said.

"Mia," I said with a lump in my throat, "Todd had to have taken it!" I raked my hands through my unbrushed hair.

"Call Corey! You need to tell him what happened," she insisted.

My chest ached. *Shit*. I'd done it again. I'd ruined another career. And my dad. *Shit. Shit.* What was this going to do to his reputation as an agent?

"It's too late, Mia. He's blocked my number. Plus, it doesn't matter who did it, the information is out there now. I can't undo it. Corey will never forgive me for this and I don't blame him."

"That's bullshit. You didn't do this. This isn't your fault."

"I know it's not," I said, pushing up from the couch. "But the damage is done. His mom is hurt. He's starting that new show. He doesn't need this crap right now."

"Vict—"

I held my hand up and stopped her. "It's too late, Mia. I've lost him for good."

Chapter Thirty-Two

Corey

"Strumming away at my six-string, passing the hours…" I strummed my guitar hard, then snatched the pencil beside my music.

"This sucks!" I scribbled over the lyrics and the chords I'd written, then crumpled the paper.

I threw the wadded-up paper to the floor and it joined the fifty others I'd tossed there over the past four hours. The sudden movement of my tantrum shifted the sheet music and revealed the music I'd started back in Twin River.

Victoria.

A sharp stab of pain sliced through my heart at the thought of her name. I'd been away from her for not even four full days, but it felt like years. Like my time in Twin River was a dream. Those had been the best weeks of my life, right up until this past Monday, when Victoria leaked our non-contract to the bloggers whose sole job was to talk crap about people like me.

I shook my head, refusing to look at the sheets of music. It hurt too much.

Betrayed once again.

I never thought it would have been her, though, who would do something like this. But I must like to torture myself or something, because I picked up the papers.

There were the scribbles I'd made when Victoria suggested a few word changes. I couldn't help but smile. Even though I was so hurt by her and really pissed at myself for opening up to someone, I still smiled.

Damn, that girl got inside my heart.

Yeah, and left a piece of jagged glass wedged in the middle.

I set the sheet music on the little table I was sitting at beside Mom's hospital bed and glanced at her. She was still sleeping peacefully.

There was one window in this rehab room and the early afternoon sun spilled in, lighting up Mom's dark hair. The bruises on her forehead, cheek, and lips were turning purple now, being almost five days old. She was looking rough still, but better than that Sunday I'd arrived. But she still had a broken femur, ankle, and arm to deal with.

She'd be in this rehab hospital for a week or two, at least.

Brushing my fingers over the strings, the gentle sound of my guitar filled the small room.

I let out a long breath and went through the melody of Victoria's song. Within seconds, I got lost in the tune. It was soft, flowing, and spot-on, so I shut my eyes and kept playing. My heartbeat picked up a few notches and I felt a smile come over my face as Victoria's sweet eyes came into mind. Her lips. Our ice cream dates. Her kisses. Her tender touch.

And then, the tears of betrayal started flowing again.

I let out a breath and slowly opened my eyes. Maybe this was what my life would be. Me and Mom. Me not trusting anyone and—

"I love when you strum the chords like that," Mom whispered.

"Hey," I said, leaning forward.

"Don't stop." She smiled—at least half of her mouth did. The other was still too swollen and injured.

I kept playing some chords as I asked, "How are you feeling?"

"Better. This morning's physical therapy took a bit out of me." She pushed herself up in the bed and let out a smile. "I'm hungry."

I was so happy she'd said that. It sounded like her. She was always hungry even though her five-foot-two, barely one-hundred-pound body would not indicate such.

"I'll call the kitchen—"

"Don't stop playing. That's a new melody, right?"

"Something I did while on vacation."

"You liked it there, didn't you?"

"I did," I said.

She shifted the pillow behind her so she could sit up more, then pulled her dark brown hair up into a messy bun the best she could with a casted wrist. Despite the bruises and cuts littering her face, she was still beautiful.

It'd been ages since we'd sat together in the same room for more than an hour these past five years. Since Dad had died. I hated that it was because she'd been struck by a car and admitted into the hospital that we were spending so much time together.

Yet I was thankful to be here with her. To be there for her.

"I'm so sick of this place," she said, resting back as if that little movement of doing her hair exhausted her.

"A week or so here in rehab, to get you strong enough, then we'll have in-home care for a bit."

"I just can't wait to get home." Mom grinned. "So, new melody, huh?"

I nodded and kept playing. "Just working through some...stuff with it."

"Some stuff, huh?" She shifted in the bed to face me.

I focused on my fingers caressing the strings so I wouldn't tear up and sob like a little kid. I had to be strong for Mom. She was hurt. I had to keep my shit together for her.

"And then your show. When's that start?" Mom asked.

My phone chose that very second to go off. It was Roberts's ringtone, too. My publicist had been on me nonstop, dealing with the Victoria fallout. I'd blocked every unknown number and a few chosen ones, like Victoria's, because my phone was going off every fourteen seconds. It was the worst it had ever been.

"You get that. I'll call for food," she said, reaching for the phone beside her bed. "I have to start doing it for myself again anyway."

I grinned, so relieved she was feeling better, and answered my phone.

"Hey, Roberts."

"Where are you?"

"I'm surprised you haven't done a Find my iPhone yet."

"I did, it's not loading."

"Okay. I'm so disconnecting you from that." I shook my head. "I'm with Mom. What's up?"

"Running lines. Today. Don't be late."

"I can't. I—"

"You will be there. And not a minute past four p.m." Roberts's voice always went militant when he was stressed. And I'd stressed him out beyond measure lately. But how did he expect me to focus on a TV show with everything going on in my life?

"It's a reality show, why would I have to run lines with the girl if it was supposed to be real time?"

"You know they use the term 'reality' loosely," he said. "I'll send a car for you."

"Fine." I rolled my eyes at Mom as she hung up her phone.

"And this deal with Victoria—you should consider firing Jethro. That was absolutely—"

"I'm hanging up now," I said, then clicked end.

He'd been ragging on me about that for two days straight. I was not going to fire Jethro over this. Victoria and I got this trouble started; it wasn't Jethro. Though he'd not called as much as normal anymore.

I checked the last text he'd sent.

JETHRO: Hang in there, kid.

He was a great guy. Really sorry how everything had turned out, but he didn't once bring up Victoria or offer anything on the situation other than to just hang in there.

It'd blow over.

I didn't want to fire him, but maybe it was what was best?

Knock, knock.

"Food already?" I said, standing up.

"No way," Mom said.

The door clicked open and a girl's head peeked through the opening. She had long blond hair. Her makeup was done up to stage-worthy caliber. Her skin was flawless and she stepped into the room with toned, sexy legs. She wore a tiny miniskirt and tank top with a little cover-up over her shoulder.

"Hey, Corey. I'm—"

"Shannon Sage." The girl I would *date* first on *What's Your Note?*

Shit.

She was pretty.

"I—figured I'd find you here. You know, with your mom. So I thought we could run lines here."

Wow. That was thoughtful.

She stepped fully into the room and a subtle scent of coconut and vanilla followed her in. "Hello," she said to my mom. "I'm Shannon. I'll be in the show with your son."

"Oh, that's nice," Mom said.

"I'm sorry to hear what happened to you. Do you need anything?" she asked with a smile.

I stood there, staring at this stranger talking with my mom like they were friends. She was sweet. Thoughtful. And seemed genuinely interested in my mom. It was weird. But cool.

"So you came *here* to run lines?"

"Jethro, your agent, sent me a text. Said you'd be here, so I figured you'd prefer that. You know, so you could be close to your mom. I'm sure there's an empty room somewhere we could hang out in."

I'd actually planned on *not* going to the line run, but now that she was here, I wouldn't be able to get out of it. Even worse, the scene they had us going through was a kissing scene. Sure, the producers said it was optional, but everyone knew they wanted kissing to up the ratings…

I didn't want to kiss anyone.

Not anymore.

Actually, I didn't want to be on this show, acting, pretending like everything was fine. I just wanted to play music—

My phone chimed again and I checked the screen.

Mia?

How the heck did she get through? I didn't even think I had her number in here. *Oh, right.* She'd texted me once asking about picking her and Victoria up from school. I'd forgotten she'd ever had my number so I hadn't blocked her.

I thought the only number I'd kept on my approved list was Tony's. We'd talked a couple times since I'd left. He was awesome the way he asked about my mom and not at all about the media shitstorm raging right now.

"Do you need to get that?" Shannon asked.

I'd actually been thinking of clicking ignore and block, but a twinge of fear about Victoria crept in at the fact that Mia was calling. Maybe something had happened to Victoria.

"Um…yeah." I held up the phone.

"You go on outside," Mom said with a smile and a quick

wave of her hand, shooing me out of the room. "I'll get to know Shannon a little better, since you two will be working closely together for a bit."

I frowned as I slid my finger across the screen to answer. "Thanks, Mom. Hey Mia. What's up?"

"Todd did it," she said, her voice almost a shriek. No hello. No nothing other than Todd did it. Did what? What the hell was she talking about?

"Excuse me?" I stepped into the hallway and shut the door.

Her room was across from the chapel, so I peeked in to see if it was empty. It was, so I jumped in.

"Todd stole the fake dating contract and leaked it to the press."

My heart stalled and I leaned against the wall directly inside the chapel. Todd stole it? But how? The only copy was in the pool house. We kept forgetting to shred it.

Had he been in there with Victoria?

"Hello?" Mia yelled.

"I'm here." I shook my head, sure I'd heard wrong. "Can you…say that again?"

"Oh, and you're a jerk for blocking my girl. Let me get that in there. But Todd, you know Todd the everlasting asshole of Twin River High? He leaked the contract to *Randy's Rumors*."

"How'd he even find it? I—"

"Let me talk, Chaos. Just let me talk."

I switched the phone to my other ear and slid down the wall so I sat on the floor. Resting my elbows on my knees, I listened.

"Todd showed up at Victoria's Sunday morning. You

know, after you bailed in the middle of the night? Anyway, he said he wanted to get back together."

"Um...what?" She'd never said anything. We'd texted briefly a couple times on that Sunday once I got here and got to Mom's. Talked that night. "She never said—"

"Remember. You're supposed to be listening to me."

"Sorry." My heart rate picked back up at the thought of her not doing this to me. Not having leaked the contract.

"Some gossip writer asshole must have picked up on Todd's assholery and got him to help him," Mia said, her voice faltering a little bit. "He started telling her that he missed her, at the dance, after they were crowned prince and princess. She brushed him off, but then he freaking showed up, faking that he wanted to get back with her to get in her house. Jerk lied, said he had to go to the bathroom, then searched through the pool house and took the contract."

I was *soooo* going to sue somebody. Hope flared to life in my chest along with a whole load of anger. Todd would *not* get away with this.

"She's an absolute mess trying to reach you, but no, you go and block her? Really, Corey, you thought she did this to you? I mean, she's all *wanting* to talk to you, but I'm kind of pissed at you that you'd think she'd do this to you."

I wanted to say something, but I bit my tongue. Mia had no clue how many times something like this had happened to me. Not as bad as what happened with Victoria, but close. I'd been used several times, but she was right. I should have talked to her. I was freaked out with everything that'd happened with Mom and then that awful article. Everything was out of control and a mess when this happened.

I was hurt. Pissed. Confused.

And I might have completely ruined my chances with Victoria.

"Okay. You can talk now," Mia said.

"Mia, I need your help."

"Duh," she huffed. "What'd you have in mind?"

"It was actually meant as a surprise for you, but I think with a few changes, I might be able to win Victoria back."

Chapter Thirty-Three

Victoria

"Please make your way to the auditorium in an orderly fashion," Principal Navarro announced over the loudspeakers.

"Ugh," I muttered. "I think I'm going to skip this month's in-service. I'm not ready to learn about college interviewing. I haven't even figured out where I want to go."

"Come on," Mia said, linking her arm through mine. "You'd rather sit by yourself in the library?"

"No. I was actually thinking of leaving. There's about a pound of chocolate at home I want to get started on."

"You are not leaving me alone in this." She tugged at me. "Come on!"

She led me through the busy hallways and I just kept my head down.

Even though a handful of days had passed since the

contract had been leaked, people were still pointing, whispering, and laughing at me. The humiliation had reached a new level of epic that I didn't even think was possible.

At least Todd had stayed out of my path. I couldn't believe that asshole.

The doors to the auditorium came into view and I slowed us down. "Mia, seriously. I think I'm going to bail. Can't you sit with McKenna or someone else?"

"Victoria, it's time to put your big girl panties on and face everyone. You've been a hermit for five days." She clasped my hand and smiled. "And I mean that in the nicest yet firmest way possible."

This girl was the absolute best person on the planet. She didn't let me get away with shit and that was what I needed right now. I needed her strength. I would not let this embarrassment chase me into hiding anymore.

"Fine." We kept moving onward, hand in hand, as I focused on my breathing. *In and out. Just get through the next hour.*

"Has your dad said anything about *you know who* lately?" Mia asked.

"Nope. He's refusing to get involved." My shoulders slumped, both happy and sad that Dad was staying out of it. After I'd told him the entire story, he'd been so upset. Mostly disappointed, which hurt like a knife to the chest.

If only he'd get one message to Corey for me. I wanted to talk to him one last time to make sure he knew I didn't do this to him.

"I'm sorry," Mia responded.

Weaving our way through a group of girls, we walked

through the open auditorium doors. The lights on the stage shone brightly. Principal Navarro and Mrs. Chesterfield, the school guidance counselor, stood on the stage.

I motioned to two empty seats. "Let's sit near the back."

Settling in, I unlocked my phone. I opened Instagram and typed in Corey's username.

Whoa!

It worked. His pictures loaded. No more dreaded, "No results found."

"He unblocked me from Instagram," I whispered to Mia as I showed her my phone. "Look!"

Eyebrows shooting up, she looked as surprised as I felt.

He hadn't posted anything since the night of the Ice Ball. No stories, either.

A knot formed in my stomach as I scrolled through his pictures from his time in Twin River. All of the posts with me and him were gone, but pictures of him and Tony and a few others remained.

How had things gone from perfect to disastrous in a matter of days?

Todd is what happened.

My shoulders stiffened and I balled up my fists. I still couldn't believe he'd done that to me.

"Have a seat, everyone," Principal Navarro announced into a microphone. "The assembly will begin in two minutes."

"Why do you think he unblocked me?" I asked Mia.

She shrugged. "I dunno, but it seems like it could be a good sign, right?"

"I guess." I wanted to try to text him. To see if he'd unblocked my phone number as well, but Mrs. Dixon, the librarian, walked by and she was notorious for taking phones during junior assemblies.

These were held monthly for juniors and seniors, and they brought in pretty high-end speakers for us to learn from. Today's was about college interviews. I just wasn't into it.

Maybe I should do a post, telling the world what really happened with Corey and what Todd had done. My Instagram wasn't as huge as his, so it probably would go unnoticed. I had to do something, though.

"Ladies and gentlemen," Principal Navarro said. "Before we begin the assembly we've arranged for you on college interviewing, we want to start out with some Ice Festival news. As you know, last week Twin River High absolutely crushed the Annual Food Pantry Drive this year."

My classmates cheered in response.

"We managed to bring in a record number of nonperishable food."

The students all around us clapped and a few even whistled.

"For the first time in a decade, the Twin River Pantry is completely full." Principal Navarro smiled broadly. "You all did your part to make this happen, but there's one student who went above and beyond."

I sank into my chair. It wasn't me, it was all Corey.

"Victoria Knight gathered over three thousand items to donate," he said.

"With Corey Chaos's help," someone from the crowd yelled.

My cheeks burned as I sank even lower into the seat.

I can't do this. I need to get out of here!

"Victoria Knight, we have a special certificate for you. Please come to the stage."

"No. No. No..." I whispered to Mia. "What is he doing?" My heart catapulted into my throat and I suddenly felt dizzy.

"Go up there," she whispered.

"No. I went onstage at the festival. What..." I spoke around the lump in my throat. My hands went sweaty.

"Come on. Get up," she said, helping me to my feet. "Because you're taking me zip-lining at Adventure Zone, followed by all we can eat pizza at Giuseppe's!"

Taking a deep breath and exhaling slowly, I made my way toward the stage.

"Hey Vic," Kyle Walker said to me as I walked by. "Will you *fake* go out with me?" He burst out in an exaggerated laugh. Hailey Johnston snickered alongside him.

This is so humiliating. I thought they were just going to call me down to the office to collect my prize when it was ready. What was with this calling me to the stage crap at our college prep assembly?

Nearly missing the first step, I wobbled as I made my way to the stage.

Mrs. Chesterfield held a certificate in one hand and a microphone in the other. "Victoria Knight, we would like to present you with this certificate of achievement on behalf of Twin River High School and Twin River Pantry."

As I accepted it, several kids in the audience started jeering.

Principal Navarro glared and slashed his hand through the air to silence them.

"Thanks to your hard work, more than four hundred

families will have access to food for the rest of the year." Mrs. Chesterfield smiled and gave me a nod of encouragement. "We'd also like to present you with the Adventure Zone & Giuseppe's prize that you've won." She handed me an envelope.

"Please give Victoria a round of applause," she said into the microphone.

Most kids clapped, but a few continued to heckle. One or two even booed.

"Thank you," she said again.

"Ah, yeah. Welcome," I said before making a beeline to the steps.

I practically ran up the aisle. My eyes stung with fresh tears. This was even more embarrassing than the cafeteria debacle with Todd. I ducked my head and didn't stop until I pushed through the auditorium doors.

No way was I going to stay in there. It was like me losing Corey all over again. He'd helped me win that prize. He'd used his fame for a great cause. He was generous and selfless.

I hated that he might still think I betrayed him.

As soon as I was in the clear from the auditorium doors, I crumbled to the floor. My chest heaved, my stomach twisted into a knot, and it took everything in me not to puke.

The certificate fell from my fingers and slid across the linoleum tile. Corey had helped get all that food. He should be here with me accepting this prize. It was him I wanted to share them with. I missed him with every particle of my soul.

Tears streamed down my cheeks as I opened up my phone and clicked on Corey's Instagram profile.

I miss you so much.

Just then, a notification popped up. Corey was going live?

Fingers shaking, I tapped on it.

"Hey, everyone! Corey Chaos here! Sorry it's been a while."

I couldn't make out where he was. It was dark behind him, not the light and airy apartment he usually went live from. I was sitting on the floor directly outside the auditorium so I crossed my legs and propped my elbows on my knees as I watched.

It was so good to see him again. He was smiling and his cheeks were flushed. He looked good.

My heart cracked a little.

"Things have been a bit hectic around here lately, but I wanted to hop on here to clear the air. First and foremost, *Randy's Rumors*, answer your phone. It's my lawyer and he's coming for you. Paying Todd Miller to steal that contract from my agent's house is going to bite you in the ass."

Holy crap! He knows it wasn't me...

My heart was pounding so intensely, I could feel it in my ears. I sat up straighter, holding the phone out in front of me, and leaned against the cold wall to watch.

"Secondly, an update on my mom. She's doing much better. Thank you so much for all of your love, thoughts, and prayers."

Thank goodness.

"Third and lastly, I have some new *original* music for you."

The students in the auditorium started cheering. Crap, hopefully the assembly wasn't ending. I really wanted to finish watching this in peace. Wait a minute, the in-service couldn't be over already...

"But before I play it on here, I'm giving the students at Twin River High a sneak peek."

"Wait, what?" I said, my voice echoing off the walls of the empty hallway I was sitting in.

More cheers poured out from beneath the closed auditorium doors...and I heard the same thing on Corey's live.

Heart nearly exploding out of my chest, I hopped to my feet. I reached for the auditorium doors as another round of cheers blasted through the air. I flung them open and there stood Corey Freaking Chaos, the boy I loved, on the stage. Guitar in hand.

"Tor, this one's for you."

Chapter Thirty-Four

Corey

"Lost in the crowd. Adrift in the sea.
I'd been hurting for so long, until you found me.
Your pure heart, healed me to the core.
All I wanted was more and more.
It ended way too soon.
It was my fault for not believing in you.
My heart is broken, like shards of glass.
All I want is you back in my life, for you to give this fool a pass.
I promise to treat you right, never make the same mistakes.
Fight for you and love you until my heart feels like it might break.
Because you're the only one for me.

And, until I make this up to you,
I'll be lost in the crowd.
Adrift in the sea."

I strummed the last chord and there was a beat of silence. Then nothing. Not a sound. Just silence. They hated it. They hated my song. *What have I—*

A loud whistle interrupted my negative thoughts. The kind that someone did with two fingers. The kind that was so loud it could make your eardrums hurt.

The audience broke out into cheers.

Some kids even started screaming.

The sounds echoed off the auditorium walls, bounced off the ceilings, and landed straight in my soul. My first original song *ever* and I was playing for a high school assembly.

Not exactly what I thought the venue would be, but it was exactly where I wanted to be.

Jethro stood in the wings, his thumb up and a smile filling his face. He'd picked me up this morning at the airport, along with Mia's birthday surprise. Jethro was more than supportive of me coming back to make things right with Victoria.

He'd objected at first, pissed that we'd lied to him, but after we talked, he understood.

I loved her and he knew it.

He hadn't even brought up the fact that I'd gotten out of my *What's Your Note?* contract.

And somehow, during all this mess, he'd managed to secure me a record deal with a legit record company.

Scanning the crowd, I ducked under my guitar strap and

handed the instrument to Principal Navarro, who'd come up alongside me once I'd finished.

"Thanks for letting me do this," I said to him.

He nodded and then I shaded my eyes from the spotlight to see the crowd. Where was she? Where was my girl?

Hopefully Mia was right in telling me Victoria would take me back. But what if she was wrong? What if Victoria bolted at the sight of me? I'd totally blocked her out of my life.

My heart hammered. My mouth went dry. I couldn't find her.

I reached for the microphone and yanked it out of the stand. "Tor. Where are you, girl?"

A whistle so loud it nearly busted out my eardrum ripped through the air. Straight ahead. Tony, the six-foot-four spectacle stood, waving his massive arms.

"Chaos. Over here!" he yelled.

And there she was. Right beside my new friend. Her hands covered her cheeks. Mia stood beside her, crying her eyes out. She'd known what I was going to do. What the heck was she crying for?

"Okay, guys," I said into the microphone. "You're going to have to give me some room. Because what may have started out as a fake relationship, is now 110 percent real and I need to get to my girl!"

My girl.

Tor was my girl and it was out in the open. Finally!

Screams ensued.

I hopped down the first few steps of the stage.

"You're awesome, man."

"You're so sweet," a girl said, then yelled. "Back up.

Give him room!"

"Great song, man." A pat on the back followed.

"You're awesome."

"Corey, I'm sorry I..." Todd stepped toward me.

I shoved by the asshat without a word.

"Tor!" I yelled. "I'm coming."

"Get out of the way!" Jace Rovers, the wide receiver from the football team, stepped in front of me.

I grabbed the back of his shirt as he plowed the path for me, shoving people out of the way. "He's gotta get to his girl, can't you see that?"

"Us hopeless romantics gotta stick together!" I slapped his back. "I'm coming, Tor!"

I peered over his shoulder and, through the last few layers of people, I saw her. Tears streamed down her face. Tony stood on her left and Mia on her right. They were holding off people, not that they were totally crowding in, but they wanted to see.

Finally Jace peeled off, shoving the last of the people out of our way, and there I stood, in front of Victoria.

I dipped my head slightly, to get a clearer view of her, and she grinned. That was all I needed. I hoisted her into my arms and spun. She buried her face in my neck and squeezed me hard.

"Corey," she whispered against my neck. "I can't believe you're here."

"I don't want to be anywhere else."

She kissed my neck and I leaned back to see her face. She pushed my hair from my face. I brushed my lips against hers. "I'm sorry, Tor."

She came in for a whopper of a kiss and I didn't mind

at all.

All of a sudden, gasps and shrieks broke out from the students surrounding us. Their attention snapped back toward the stage.

"Is there a Mia Reynolds out there?" Shane Redman, my YouTube friend, asked.

I glanced over my shoulder to find my buddy standing in the middle of the stage, a guitar strapped over his shoulder. He was shading his eyes from the spotlight, too.

He wore his blond hair spiked up and his traditional flannel shirt flapped around his black jeans.

Mia shrieked and looked at me. "Is...that...Shane Redman?"

"It is."

"As in...Shane Redman and he's asking for *me*?" She pointed at herself, big blue eyes wide and filled with excitement.

"Happy birthday." She'd taken a risk for her best friend by calling me and then calling me out for blocking Victoria. Getting my friend Shane to come sing a few songs for her for a little birthday surprise...totally worth it. "Get up there!"

More tears streamed down her face and then she darted ahead. I didn't bother to watch; I had someone to kiss and make up with.

I eased Victoria to her feet. "Can we get out of here?"

"Yes!" She led me through the auditorium doors.

Once away from the hysterics, I pulled her into my arms again. "I'm so sorry, Victoria. I jumped to conclusions. I—"

"It's okay, Corey. It's okay."

"No. Let me say this. I—at the first test I bailed. I didn't even give you a chance to explain. Jerk move. I'm so sorry."

I leaned back, looking down at her. I kissed her cheek. "Can you ever forgive me?"

She pressed her mouth to mine, then said, "How could I refuse after that song?"

I laughed and hugged her tight.

"Seriously. I forgive you. I love you. I'm so glad you're here."

"I love you, too, Tor. And…I'm here to stay."

"What?" Victoria asked, pushing away from me enough to see my face.

I nodded, working pretty dang hard to keep my burning eyes from spilling tears of joy. Then again, who cared if I did? I was holding Victoria. I was able to stay here for good and be a normal teen.

Well, somewhat normal.

I eased Victoria down but kept her close by holding her hands. "I bailed on *What's Your Note?*"

"Oh, Corey!" Tears spilled out from her eyes. "No! You can't. I can't. I mean, I can't be the reason your music career—"

"No, it's fine. I got a record deal anyway!" I brushed her tears away with my thumb and kissed her nose.

"What?"

I was still a little in disbelief myself. "Your dad, the fabulous agent he is, brokered a deal with *a different* record label while working on getting me out of *What's Your Note?* It was amazing. I can't even believe it. I swore him to secrecy so I could tell you today."

"I'm so sorry, Corey. This whole fake relationship thing was my idea. None of this bad press for you would have ever happened if I hadn't come up with the idea to get back at

Todd."

"I forgive you." I kissed the tip of her nose. "Do you forgive me?"

"Yes. So much, yes!" She hugged me tight. "Corey. Here? Twin River? Really?"

"I like it here. I like high school. I want to take AP U.S. history with you, have fun study dates where we don't study very much..." I winked and she giggled.

"What about your mom? And your place in L.A? And—"

"She's going to be at the rehab facility for another week, building up her strength, then I'll drive her out here." I grinned, getting to the best part. "She said she's ready for a slower pace of life. No more boyfriend of the month. Just focusing on her recovery and hanging with me."

"Wow. That's awesome."

When Mom had told me that yesterday, I'd known for sure I'd chosen the right thing to do. She and I would be more of a family now. Finally.

"You're never going to guess where we're going to live," I said.

"Where?" She wiped away more tears.

"The apartment above Annie's Coffee Shop!"

"What?" She leaped at me and wrapped her arms around my neck. "That's absolutely perfect."

"And close to gumball ice cream," I said into her hair, drinking in her scent.

I'd missed her so much. I didn't realize how much until this very moment, holding her like this, kissing her, breathing her in.

"You got Shane Redman here," Victoria whispered.

"You really are incredible, you know that?"

"Yeah, well, Mia deserved it. It's her birthday soon and she was a huge part in helping me pull my head out of my ass about everything that had happened."

"I am so sorry!" She stepped back, but I moved with her until her back was against the wall directly outside of the auditorium doors. "I can't believe I didn't shred the contract the moment you told me it could turn into a PR nightmare."

"Don't worry. It's done. It's over. We're together." I stepped in to her and her body softened against mine. "Maybe we can skip the rest of the day and just do this."

"I have a better idea," she said, then grabbed my hand and tugged me down the hallway.

I wasn't sure there could be anything better than kissing the rest of the day away with her. But I went with it, happy to be here with her. She ducked into a classroom, then hustled to the desk at the front of the room.

"What are you doing?" I caught up to her as she pulled out some paper and snagged a pen from the top of the desk.

"I think we need a *new* contract." She leaned over and started writing. "Rule One: we tell EVERYONE we're in a relationship. Rule Two: both parties agree on regular public outings commonly referred to as dates."

"I've got one." I had to jump in with one of my own. "Rule Three: both parties agree to be each other's dates for all future school dances."

"Yes!" Victoria said. "Rule Four: both parties agree to hand-holding and kissing…like all the time. Rule Five: both parties agree to not keep things professional, to totally fall for each other."

"I think you forgot something," I said, looking over her

shoulder. "Remember that questionnaire you wanted me to fill out? What if someone asks me what your favorite flavor of Fanta is and I say grape? Because it's obviously superior to orange."

She let out a loud laugh, then slapped her hand over her mouth and looked around. "Oh my gosh, that questionnaire. I can't believe I—"

"It was cute." I couldn't help but smile. "I'll sign *this* contract. Because I couldn't care less if it gets published online!"

She scribbled her name at the bottom, then handed me the pen. I scrawled my name beneath hers, then tossed the pen onto the desk.

"Come here." I planted a whopper of a kiss on her, right there in the classroom, and I didn't care who saw. I was back together with Victoria. She loved me. I loved her. Everything was perfect.

And best of all, there was nothing *fake* about our relationship.

Acknowledgments

From Kelly Anne Blount:

To my sweetest hubby, Lee Roy, thank you for helping me achieve my dreams.

Bella Rose, you are my whole heart. Thank you for making every day special.

To my mom and dad, thank you for instilling a love of reading in my soul. I hope to be doing the same thing for Bells! She literally sleeps with her favorite books, so I think we're on the right track! Ha ha!

To Mike and Lynn, thank you for being the best mother-in-law and father-in-law! You are both so kind, generous, and loving!

Nicole and Jen, thank you for your support and guidance. Grateful to have both of you by my side!

To the team at Entangled Publishing, thank you! Can you believe we've already worked on seven books together?

Wow!

I know Lynn gave a similar shout out below, but seriously, Katie Prouty, you are amazing! You are so sweet, hilarious, and your support of our work means the world to us! Thank you!

To everyone on my street team and to my friends who have helped along the way, thank you!

Lastly, to everyone who has read the Twin River High series, THANK YOU! When we started brainstorming this amazing series, Lynn and I knew there was something special in the works. We are over the moon with the results and are so thrilled you took the ride with us! :) Oh, and, we have a lot more in the works! So stay tuned!

Kelly Anne xoxo

From Lynn Rush:

My sweet hubby, Charlie: You are my soul mate! I'm blessed to do life with you!

To KELLY ANNE BLOUNT: This has been a wild ride. I love you! Nicole Resciniti: I don't have words that could possibly express my thanks enough.

The team at Entangled Publishing: Thanks for believing in the Twin River High series.

Kelsey and Chloe Evans: Thank you for all your help with the high school side of things. I appreciate you so much!!!

Katie Prouty: Thank you so much for your support. You make my heart smile.

To my dear friends and #SnotRockets: Michele, Beth, Tracy, Ann, Courtney, Corey, Marisa, Erika, Maya, Lisa,

Cyndi, Amanda Lynn, Jess. Thank you for living life with me. I treasure you.

To the Legionnaires over at Lynn's Legion: Thank you for your support and help sharing all my fun writing news. I appreciate you!

And finally, to the fans of Corey and Victoria, and the whole Twin River High crew: Thank you from the bottom of my heart for your support and enthusiasm. We hope you enjoyed reading *Chaos Theory* as much as we enjoyed writing it.

About the Authors

New York Times and *USA Today* bestselling author LYNN RUSH is a full-time writer, wife, and trail runner, living in the Sonoran Desert, despite her fear of rattlesnakes. Known as #TheRunningWriter, she can't resist posting epic sunrise pictures while running in the desert with her trail sisters, even if she has to occasionally hop over a scorpion. When she's not running, writing, or reading, she and her Ironman husband are watching movies that fuel her undying love of superheroes, vampires, and all things Supernatural.

Find her on social media: @LynnRushWrites. Sign-up for her newsletter: http://bit.ly/LRNewsletter

KELLY ANNE BLOUNT is a *USA Today* bestselling author of young adult novels. She loves to alternate writing sweet romances, gritty thrillers, and fantasy books. She's a firm believer in balancing light with dark.

When she's not writing, she's probably lost in a book,

watching *Coronation Street*, or having an adventure with her sweet family, which includes her handsome husband, their darling daughter, and their loving fur children.

After living in a palace in Scotland, across the beach from the Caribbean Sea, and in the snowy land of Wisconsin, Kelly and her family reside in beautiful Asheville, North Carolina. She draws inspiration from the places she's lived and the people she's met while worldbuilding in her books.

Kelly loves connecting with readers on social media! Stop by and say, "Hi!" or ask a question. You can find her everywhere @KellyAnneBlount. Sign up for her newsletter here: http://bit.ly/KellyAnneBlountNewsletter

Discover the Twin River High series

COVERUP CRUSH

PROJECT PERSONALITY

Also by Lynn Rush and Kelly Anne Blount...

IN THE PENALTY BOX

CROSSING THE LINE

Also by Kelly Anne Blount

I HATE YOU, FULLER JAMES

Discover more of Entangled Teen Crush's books…

THE CRUSH COLLISION
a Southern Charmed novel by Danielle Ellison

Haley's had a crush on her brother's best friend, Jake Lexington, for as long as she can remember. To bad to him, she'll forever be off-limits. But with senior year comes new confidence. Haley's read to get Jake to notice her—whatever it takes. Jake's looking for an escape; Haley's looking for a chance. Together, they'll find exactly what they need…if only they're willing to cross that line and risk it all.

HOW TO QUIT YOUR CRUSH
a novel by Amy Fellner Dominy

Mai knows Anthony is no good for her. She's valedictorian; he's a surf bum. But they can't seem to stay away from each other. Good thing Anthony's got the perfect plan: two weeks to prove they're not good together. Whoever comes up with the worst date—proving how incompatible they are—wins. But when the competition turns into something more, and Mai's future is at stake, will they be able to quit each other forever?

STUCK WITH YOU
a First Kiss Hypothesis novel by Christina Mandelski

Catie Dixon got over her hot childhood frenemy Caleb Gray ages ago. So when he unexpectedly shows up at their families' Texas beach house, as unsettled about his future as she is about hers, she's irritated by the draw to let him back in. A forced week of togetherness sparks more than an understanding, but what do you do when the person standing in the way of your future is the one person you suddenly don't want to live without?

Made in United States
Orlando, FL
14 March 2025